P9-CFM-928

"You want your life and your body back the way they were. Isn't that right?"

"You can guarantee you'll undo whatever was done to me?" she asked slowly.

"Guarantees are for suckers, Violet, and there aren't any here. But think about it. All the information about what was done to you is inside that facility. We're going in anyway. You come with us, we'll make sure you leave with that information in hand."

She shook her head. "Look, Jackson—"

"Sleep on it, and we'll talk in the morning."

"I've got nowhere to sleep."

"I can put you in a safe house," he said, "if you trust me."

She'd be a fool to trust him completely, but she didn't think he intended to hurt her. Use her, yes. Con her, certainly.

"No strings attached?"

He held his hands wide, his face innocent. "No strings attached."

She took a deep breath. "Then I guess I trust you just enough."

Dear Reader,

This all started with an innocent little exercise: write a ten-page story about a character in trouble. I closed my eyes, started dreaming and Violet Marsh was born. I had no idea what I was getting myself into.

The Vi I met that day was different from the one you're about to encounter—she was a little more savvy and a lot more skilled. But I realized that if I wanted to write a book about her, I would have to go back to a time when powerful, purposeful Vi was a little more unsure, a little more overwhelmed, a little more...like me. And maybe, like you.

I've been forever fascinated with the concepts of strength and fearlessness, and especially what those things can mean for women. That's why I'm excited to be writing for Bombshell, a line that celebrates powerful women.

I hope you like reading about Vi. I hope that watching her struggles and triumphs makes you feel strong. And I hope you'll feel free to drop me a line anytime. You can find me at my Web site, www.ellenhenderson.com.

Thanks for reading.

Ellen Henderson

ELLEN HENDERSON

ULTRA VIOLET

Silhouette®

BOMBSHELL™

Published by Silhouette Books

America's Publisher of Contemporary Romance

If you purchased this book without a cover you should be aware
that this book is stolen property. It was reported as "unsold and
destroyed" to the publisher, and neither the author nor the
publisher has received any payment for this "stripped book."

 SILHOUETTE BOOKS

ISBN 0-373-51378-X

ULTRA VIOLET

Copyright © 2005 by Ellen Henderson

All rights reserved. Except for use in any review, the reproduction
or utilization of this work in whole or in part in any form by any
electronic, mechanical or other means, now known or hereafter
invented, including xerography, photocopying and recording, or in
any information storage or retrieval system, is forbidden without
the written permission of the editorial office, Silhouette Books,
233 Broadway, New York, NY 10279 U.S.A.

All characters in this book have no existence outside the imagination of
the author and have no relation whatsoever to anyone bearing the same
name or names. They are not even distantly inspired by any individual
known or unknown to the author, and all incidents are pure invention.

This edition published by arrangement with Harlequin Books S.A.

® and TM are trademarks of Harlequin Books S.A., used under license.
Trademarks indicated with ® are registered in the United States Patent
and Trademark Office, the Canadian Trade Marks Office and in other
countries.

www.SilhouetteBombshell.com

Printed in U.S.A.

ELLEN HENDERSON

has gone scuba diving with sharks in Cozumel, taken a fast train through the Swiss Alps in the dead of night and been stranded with no money and no flight home from Italy. Surviving all that, she turned to writing novels, which may yet be the death of her. Still, she's having too much fun to quit. She lives in Dallas, Texas, with her much-loved husband and cats, and she is an online editor for a newspaper. When she's not writing, working, chatting with the husband, or petting the cats, Ellen enjoys reading, watching too much television, wasting time on the Internet and practicing yoga. Visit her Web site at www.ellenhenderson.com.

For Travis, who helped with absolutely everything,
and whom I love, absolutely.

Chapter 1

The cops were going to think she was nuts.

Violet Marsh gripped the steering wheel of her Honda sedan and stared at the no-nonsense police station building in front of her. Yep, they were going to think she was a whack job, and she had nothing to prove otherwise but five days missing from her life and a really bad feeling.

Her stomach roiled as she imagined the looks they would give her. She winced a little but made herself let go of the wheel and pop the fastener on her seat belt. No, it wasn't going to be pretty, but she couldn't think of a way around it.

She pushed open the driver's door and slid out slowly, rehearsing possible opening lines: *Hi, I seem to have lost five days, and I swear I wasn't drinking.* Too defensive. *Hello, what do you think the chances are that*

I was abducted by aliens? Ha. Definitely loopy. *Hi, there, I got home from work the other day and then I don't remember anything....*

A swell of panicky fear rose up in her chest, and she closed her eyes. Oh, hell. She just wasn't going to be able to joke her way out of this. She shut the car door and leaned against it for a minute, pressing her lips together hard and trying to breathe.

You're okay, it's okay. She said it loud and clear inside her mind in the way that had calmed her for most of her twenty-six years, and it helped. A little.

"Now, don't fall apart on me."

Vi jerked her head up and looked around for the owner of the voice—a rich, warm, assured voice coming from behind her.

A woman stood there, tall, black and striking, with sharp brown eyes and a stark, pixie-cut hairstyle. She had a concerned look on her angular face.

Pushing herself off the car, Vi straightened up and tried to pull the anxious expression off her own face. She always felt puzzled when strangers spoke to her; she never knew whether she was dealing with an outgoing normal person or a barrier-crossing crazy person.

"I'm fine," she said, giving the woman a quick, polite smile.

"Well, that's a good thing," the woman said, smiling back. "'Cause if you'll fall to pieces now, there's no way you're going to handle everything that's about to happen to you."

A skittering chill sheeted across Vi's back, and she felt her smile slip into a frown. "What's that supposed to mean?"

The woman shrugged one shoulder. "It means I see some rough times ahead for you, that's all."

Vi's anxiety slackened. "Oh, what are you, some kind of psychic?" she asked, recognizing that she was stalling. You had to know your life was messed up when you'd rather chitchat with a potential crazy than talk to the police.

The woman laughed, a low chuckle. "Don't I wish. But if I could tell the future, you think I'd be standing here talking to you instead of down at the 7-Eleven getting my lottery tickets? You've got to use your head, honey."

Vi nodded, eyebrows raised. "Ri-i-i-ight. Thanks for clearing that up. I have to go now." She turned away and stepped up onto the sidewalk, heading for the building's front doors.

"Wait a minute, Violet."

Vi stopped, a wash of cold pouring down into her stomach and clenching there. What the hell? She turned around again and peered at the woman.

"Do I know you?" Even as she said it, she knew it wasn't possible. She was good with faces and names; she didn't forget people. She'd never seen this woman before.

She ignored a little shiver of fear and thought of a better question. "How do you know my name?"

"Oh, I know a lot about you, Violet," the woman said, leaning back against the car parked next to her and crossing one long leg over the other. "Fact is, I probably know more about you right now than you know about yourself."

"What do you mean? What is this? Who are you?"

Vi's hands were starting to shake a little, and she was torn, unsure how to feel. A few days ago, she'd have assumed she was on some kind of hidden camera show and laughed this woman off. But since she'd recently woken up in her own bed and then discovered five days had apparently passed without her…well, she was more inclined to take weird things seriously.

"Now, calm down. I'm going to explain. I'm not here to mess with you—I'm here to help you."

"Why?"

"Someone's got to," the woman said, her face going serious. "You're in way over your head, and that's a fact."

Vi's stomach clenched again, and she forced herself to take hold of the situation. "What are you talking about? And is it possible for you to stop with the mysterioso act and just say whatever the hell you want to say?"

"Ohh, someone's cranky," the woman said. "Listen, I know you've had a bad couple days, but that's no reason to take it out on me." She shook her head. "I never thought you'd be so crabby. I think it's all that junk food you've been eating. Cheeseburgers and ice cream and French fries—you've got to lay off that stuff."

Vi stared. What…how did she…had this woman been *following* her?

Before she could get her mind around the concept, the woman dug into the pocket of her black denim jacket and pulled out a business card.

"Here, this'll help," she said.

Feeling slightly numb, Vi reached out and took the card. Gideon Enterprises, it read in bold letters. And down in the corner, a name—Natalie Warner—and a phone number. That was all.

"Oh, you're right," Vi said. "This explains everything."

"That's me," the woman said, pointing at the card. "I'm Natalie Warner. I work for a man named Mal Gideon, and he owns Gideon Enterprises."

"Congratulations. What does that have to do with me?"

"Well now, that's complicated. It's kind of a long story."

"What about the part of the story where you've been following me?" Vi asked. Her breath was coming faster. "Can you explain that?"

"I could," Natalie said, nodding. "But I can see you're starting to get upset, and I think that'd just make it worse."

"Try me," Vi said, forcing the words out through her clenched teeth. Be mad, she told herself. It was better than any alternative.

Natalie was shaking her head. "No, I think I better let Gideon do that part. I'll just mess it up. You might've noticed I'm not a real people person. Now you just call that number—"

She reached out, and Vi flinched and stepped backward, stumbling a little. She saw now that Natalie had just been gesturing toward the card, but she kept backing up, heading for the police station doors.

"Stay away from me," Vi said, knowing it was irrational because Natalie wasn't moving at all. Her voice sounded high-pitched and thin in her own ears. "I'm going to tell the police all about this," she said. "There are stalking laws, you know."

Natalie just smiled gently. "You tell them, honey." She straightened up just as Vi reached the door and put her hand on the metal pull bar. "Watch that door, now," she added. "Careful not to break it."

Vi froze, her hand clamped on the cool metal. *She knows.* The thought raced through her mind, blocking out everything else, paralyzing her.

"Been happening a lot lately, huh?" Natalie said.

Vi stared at her, trying to steer her mind toward logic. Of course she knew. She knew because she'd been watching—she'd seen it happen. That was all.

"Put a hole in your dining room wall yesterday, didn't you?" Natalie said, taking a few slow steps forward. "Just knocked right through the sheetrock. And this morning you grabbed that big, thick coffee mug and shattered it."

"What do you know?" Vi said. Her voice was quavery now, but her mind had slipped to a place of some cool distance, as if she were watching herself in a movie.

"I know a little. There's other things, too. Right? You burned your hand on the coffee when that mug broke, but it's all right now, isn't it? It got all right quick. And you're hungry all the time."

"What do you *know?*" Vi asked again.

"Don't worry about what I know. Gideon knows. He can tell you. You just keep that card."

Vi looked down at the business card crumpled in her hand.

"And when you're ready to know the rest, you call me."

When Vi looked up again, Natalie was gone.

Vi clutched the card in her fist and turned back toward the door, swallowing hard. Well, at least now she had something to show the police.

Vi sat on the brown-and-orange-flowered couch in her living room, gnawing on the only remaining fingernail on her right hand that wasn't bitten to the quick. Her police station visit had been a bust and just as humiliating as she'd feared, and now she wasn't sure what to do. Between trying not to freak out and trying not to eat the rest of the jumbo bag of pretzels she'd torn open half an hour ago, she'd been too distracted to guard against her old nail-chewing habit.

Every few moments she tuned in to a sentence or phrase from the local news on TV, which she'd switched on for comforting noise. *Eight-car pileup on the Interstate… fire at Broadbrook Methodist… nine-year-old Ruby Mulligan still missing….* It was mostly bad news. Everyone had problems, not just her.

The doorbell woke her from her daze. Jerking her hand away from her mouth, she stood up and reached for the remote to turn off the TV.

She had her hand on the doorknob before she thought to be cautious. Fear tingled through her as she realized it could be Natalie again…or someone else. Someone worse.

The bell rang again, and she slid her hand off the doorknob and pressed her eye to the peephole.

Melissa.

Slumping against the door in relief, Vi drew a long breath and then pulled the door open.

Melissa Delgado, neat and stylish and gorgeous as

always in a short lilac business skirt and a white silk blouse, stood on the porch holding a plastic bag and frowning.

"Hey," she said, her sleek black eyebrows dipping down in concern. "You had me worried there for a minute."

Despite all the thoughts and anxieties cramming her brain full, Vi found she still had room to mentally compare Melissa's stylish, elegant clothes with her own faded jeans and blue T-shirt with a ketchup stain, Melissa's long, glossy black curls to her own stick-straight brown hair, and Melissa's tiny size-two figure to her own tall size ten.

Well, Mel could make anyone feel like Miss Average America, but you just couldn't hate her for it.

"Sorry," Vi said, shrugging off her momentary low-self-esteemfest. "I'm moving a little slow."

"That's okay—I've got the cure," Melissa said, holding up the bag in her hand. "My *abuela*'s world-famous chicken soup. This'll have you up to speed in no time."

Vi's stomach gurgled at the faint scent of the soup wafting from the bag, but her heart sank. She'd been so relieved to see a friendly face at the door, she hadn't stopped to realize that she was in no shape to deal with Melissa. She needed time to think, and Melissa only ever wanted to act.

"The place is a mess," she said weakly, but Melissa shook her head and pushed past her into the house.

"Of course it is. You've been sick. That's the only good thing about being sick—no one expects you to do anything but recover," she said over her shoulder as she headed for the kitchen.

Vi trailed after her, trying to prepare herself to deflect probing questions. She'd told Mel she'd spent her missing week in the hospital, back when she was still hoping that was true, and maybe it was best to leave it at that. If Mel found out about the time blank and the weird encounter with that Natalie person and all the rest, she'd have a fit and demand immediate action. Vi wasn't ready to do anything yet.

"Speaking of which," Natalie continued, "please tell me you did not go back to work yet."

"No, not yet," Vi said, leaning against the doorjamb as Melissa unloaded a large Tupperware container and set it on the avocado-green kitchen counter. "I think I'm going to use a couple more sick days." At least a couple. No way could she go back to work until she got this mess figured out.

Melissa snorted. "God knows you've got them saved up." She shot Vi an evil grin. "I bet Steve is freaking out, right?"

"Three guesses," Vi said, rolling her eyes and remembering the false, buck-up cheerfulness in her boss's voice when she'd talked to him that morning. *Gotta take one for the team, Vi-let,* he'd twanged. *Time to suck it up, show what you're made of,* he'd said, along with about a dozen other clichés that basically meant he didn't care if her head had fallen off, he wanted her back in the office and finishing the quarterly financials for Payton Furnishings.

She was surprised she didn't feel much of the anxious pull to obey, but she supposed her mind was a bit preoccupied for that.

"He actually told me there was no one to cover my

work," Vi said, realizing that bitching about work stuff was a surefire diversion for Melissa's attention. They'd been bonding over bad bosses and busywork since their college days.

"You're kidding me," Melissa said as she peeled the lid off the Tupperware container. "After you took all of Judy's work last month when she went on that stupid three-week golf vacation?"

"I know," Vi said, nodding. "Suddenly we have no 'slack in the system,' whatever that means."

A wave of the soup's salty, brothy scent rolled over Vi, and her stomach clenched crazily. She shouldn't have any of that soup. She'd already had cereal and a bagel with cream cheese, four boxes of raisins, a bag of corn chips, a blueberry muffin, a double cheese-burger, a large order of French fries, an ice cream sand-wich and, of course, half a jumbo bag of pretzels.

It was only five o'clock in the afternoon.

Melissa paused in the act of pulling a bowl down from a cabinet. "I'm sorry," she said. "I didn't even ask if you wanted this now. Are you hungry?"

Oh, what the hell.

"Starved," Vi said, reaching into the pantry for the rest of the pretzels to go with the soup. "Thanks, by the way."

"For the soup?" Melissa shook her head and put a brimming bowl on the kitchen table. "It's nothing. The least I could do. I've been racked with guilt ever since I talked to you yesterday. I can't believe the one time you get sick I'm out of the frickin' state."

Vi sat at the table and took the spoon Melissa handed her. "Don't feel bad. There was nothing you could've done."

"I could've gone to see you in the hospital. I could've cornered all the doctors and nurses and made sure they were taking care of you. I hate that you were there all by yourself."

Stiffening a little, Vi stared down at her soup. "I can take care of myself, Mel," she said, trying to keep her voice light. "I have been doing it most of my life."

There was a pause. "I know your mom was…" Melissa let the sentence trail off. "But your grandparents—"

"Weren't the same as parents," Vi finished. She looked up, noted Melissa's concerned expression and shook her head. "Hey, they tried. And they left me the house." She glanced around at the kitchen's green countertops, gold-leaf wallpaper and Spanish-mission-style light fixtures, then smiled at Melissa. "Such as it is."

Melissa smiled, too. "At least the rent's cheap."

Vi nodded, knowing it was more than that. She should've sold the place and gotten something normal, had considered it a hundred times, but she couldn't bear to part with the old, funky house. It held all the memories of the closest thing she'd had to a childhood, and just being surrounded by its ugly walls made her feel safe.

"Well, anyway," Melissa said, "since I missed everything while I was gone, you have to tell me all about it now. What exactly were you sick with?"

Vi felt her smile fade as her mind went to all the things she didn't want to get into with Melissa yet. But she hated to lie to her best friend. This was going to get tricky.

"I think it was a sort of flu," she said. She took a

quick sip of the soup. "Oh my God. This is delicious. What's the secret?"

"The avocado," Melissa said. "What do you mean, you think it was flu? You don't know for sure?"

Vi shook her head, looked at her soup again. "I was pretty out of it the whole time when I was…in the hospital. I forgot a lot of the specifics."

She could feel Melissa frowning at her, but she didn't look up.

"Well, what are you doing for follow-up? What does your paperwork say?"

A little trickle of the fear she'd been pushing down for the past two days slipped up to her throat and made it tighten. *You can handle this.* She sucked in a breath.

"I haven't really looked at it yet," she said. There. That wasn't a lie.

Melissa didn't answer, and when Vi glanced up, she saw her friend waiting with her eyebrows raised.

"Well…" Melissa said after a long beat. "Can I look at it?"

Vi looked around, tried to seem absentminded. "I'm not sure where it is." That wasn't a lie, either. She was disturbingly good at this. "Hey, how did your trip go, anyway? You think it's going to get you that promotion?"

But Melissa was regarding her with narrowed eyes. "What's going on? Why are you sidestepping me?"

Crap. Serious evasive action needed now. If Melissa really got her teeth into something, she'd never let up. "Nothing, I'm not. I just don't want everything to be all about me. I'm trying to be a g   friend, here. Speaking of which…" She hesitated, h mind churning as she scrolled through possible distractions. "Oh, did I tell you that Tracy Peterson from college is a lawyer now? Can you picture that? Ten-watt Tracy?"

"Okay, now I know something's up," Melissa said, folding her arms and sitting back. "You never start the gossip—I start the gossip. You're trying to throw me off something. Spill it."

Vi sighed. It was over. Melissa had reached impossible-to-deflect stage. The fact that her best friend was pushy and warmly interfering was one of the reasons Vi loved her so much, but it was also damned inconvenient at times.

In any case, the only thing to be done now was to try to minimize the impact by caving immediately.

"Fine. It's just…I don't have any paperwork."

Melissa frowned. "What do you mean? From the hospital?"

Nodding, Vi took another sip of soup.

"Not even a bill?" Melissa asked. "Or a copy of whatever they sent your insurance?"

Vi shook her head. "I'm sure it's just some administrative screw-up. Some…massive administrative screw-up. It'll probably all show up in the mail in a day or two." She tried a little laugh. "Probably right when I'm feeling all the way better, and then the bill will give me a heart attack."

All right, it was a weak joke, but Melissa wasn't even smiling.

"Vi," she said. "That's weird."

It was. Vi tried not to let it show on her face.

"Did you call them?" Melissa asked. "What hospital was it, anyway?"

Oh, boy. Her throat tightened as she thought about

the truth, and she wondered how long she was going to be able to hide it from Melissa, the most persistent person she knew.

Melissa was leaning forward now, her brown eyes intent. "Vi, what's going on?"

Vi closed her eyes and put down her spoon. She was cornered. There was no way Melissa was dropping this now. Maybe it was for the best. Maybe talking it out— okay, arguing it out—with Melissa would help her decide what to do. God knows she wasn't getting anywhere by herself, chewing on her fingernails and thinking herself in circles.

"I don't know what hospital," she said. "In fact, I'm not even sure there was a hospital. I've called them all, and no one has any record of me, and my insurance didn't get anything, and I don't have any paperwork, and the truth is…I don't remember a thing."

She smiled ruefully at Melissa's wide eyes, then pushed herself away from the table and stood to pace around Nana Martha's ugly but comfortingly familiar kitchen.

"And wait," she said, looking back at Melissa. "There's more."

Chapter 2

Vi was back on Nana Martha's couch in the living room, watching Melissa, who was slumped in Grandpa Jack's big chair.

Melissa was having trouble taking it in. Vi didn't blame her. She'd had a day and a half to put it all together, and she was closer to losing her grip than she would ever let on. Poor Melissa had to absorb it all in minutes.

Squeezing her eyes closed, Melissa shook her head.

"Okay, let's see if I've got all this straight," she said, turning her worried eyes to Vi. "You remember driving home from work last Friday."

Vi nodded. "Right. And I stopped at Banderas to get tacos."

"Like you do every night, because you work too late and everything else is closed," Melissa put in.

"Right," Vi said again. "And I ate one on the way home, and then I started to feel sick."

"And you got home and got inside and then…"

"Nothing," Vi said.

"Until yesterday morning," Melissa said.

Nodding again, Vi suppressed a shudder as that slow, weird unfolding of reality came back to her. The way she'd woken up surprised that her alarm hadn't gone off, that her white noise machine wasn't on, not sure how long she'd slept. The way she'd stumbled into the kitchen and found her milk gone sour and a string of messages on her answering machine—her dentist's office, calling about an appointment she'd missed. Robert, mad because she'd stood him up.

She'd never, never felt so lost in her entire messed-up life as she had in those groundless moments. She shook her head. *Can't think about that now.*

"Then you called work," Melissa said, pulling Vi back from her thoughts.

"Yeah," Vi said, taking a breath. "Once I figured out it was Thursday and not Saturday, like I'd expected, I figured they'd be freaking out at the office, but they just asked how I was feeling. I was too—I don't know—embarrassed, I guess, to tell Marjorie in reception that I didn't know what was going on, so I called Lisa and made her give me the whole story."

"And she said—what? That someone called in for you?"

"Yeah. Some doctor, but no one wrote down the name. He said he couldn't give them any details about what was wrong or where I was—something about the new medical privacy laws—but that I'd be out for several days. Lisa said she'd been worried sick, but she didn't know what to do. And that was it."

"Until this morning, when some crazy lady told you she was stalking you," Melissa said.

Vi smiled ruefully. "Well, according to the cops, it's not stalking if certain conditions apply—no criminal intent, no continual intrusion, having a private investigator's license…"

Melissa's eyes went wide. "She's a private investigator? You didn't tell me that part."

Vi nodded. "Yeah. And apparently, I have no legal right to not be followed."

"Well, did you tell the police about the rest?" Melissa asked, frowning. "About the missing days and all that?"

"It sounded so crazy," Vi said, closing her eyes as she remembered. "They just looked at me, and I realized I didn't even know what I wanted them to do. I mean, I don't have anything to go on—no proof of anything, not a clue. For all they know, I've been holed up in my bedroom for five days, avoiding work. Hell, if I didn't know someone called me in sick, I'd be tempted to think I just slept the time away."

They sat in silence for a moment, Melissa biting her lip as she thought it over.

"But you don't feel sick, right?" she said at last.

Vi shook her head. "No, I feel fine. Except for…"

"The weird stuff," Melissa finished. She wrinkled her nose. "The hunger thing…that really worries me. I mean, the other stuff, maybe it was just accidents. Maybe your wall was already messed up, and the mug, too, and maybe the coffee didn't really burn you."

"That's what I thought," Vi said, sitting up. "It doesn't have to mean—"

"But the hunger thing," Melissa interrupted. "That's odd. Are you really eating all the time?"

Vi shrugged and glanced away, but she knew the answer. It was embarrassing to admit how much she'd been eating, especially around Melissa, who could get a little healthier-than-thou. "I guess."

She looked up after a silent moment to find Melissa scrutinizing her. "What?"

Melissa was shaking her head slowly. "You don't look like you've gained any weight. Have you?"

"Hell if I know. You know I avoid getting on scales."

"Well, you're getting on one today," Melissa said, standing up and smoothing her unwrinkled skirt. "Come on."

Vi groaned and sat back. "Oh, Mel, no. Let's not."

"Come on," Melissa said again. "This doesn't make sense to me. I want to know what we're dealing with. And you know I'm not dropping this, so let's just go get it over with."

Vi sighed. "Fine, let's go. The scale's in the bathroom. If it's still working."

She followed Melissa to the back bedroom, the only room she'd redecorated in the year and a half since she'd inherited the house. Most of the house was a horror show of decorating disasters from 1969, the year her grandparents had bought it and dressed it up for the first and last time. Still, she couldn't bear to change much about it. Ugly as it was, the place had been her only stable refuge as a child, and every painful wallpaper pattern and hideous macramé hanging brought back the most pleasant childhood memories she had.

But the bedroom had just been too much to bear—all brown shag and gold-veined mirrors and fake-colonial prints on the walls. She'd done it over to her own taste, and the peaceful sea-green walls and sleek natural woods soothed her now, as she followed Melissa to the master bathroom.

Melissa was wrinkling her nose at the scale.

"This is a piece of crap," she said. "It doesn't even have decimals, let alone body-fat analysis. You know, you can get a scale with that stuff."

"Not for ten bucks at Target, you can't." Vi hesitated. "Hey, shouldn't I take off all these clothes? It's going to skew the weight."

Melissa rolled her eyes. "Not that much. We'll subtract a pound for clothes. Come on."

Frowning, Vi stepped onto the scale. "This is a very heavy T-shirt. It's a dense weave. It's probably more than a pound all by itself."

"Shh...stop talking and stand still."

They both watched the digital numbers flick past and stop.

"Huh," Melissa said. "That's not bad. Have you gained any?"

Vi stared at the number, blinking. It wasn't possible.

"Vi, how much have you gained?"

Tearing her eyes away from the impossible number, Vi looked at Melissa. "It's wrong," she said. "It has to be."

"Why? It's not bad. How much more is it?"

"It's *less*," Vi said. "That's what I mean, it can't be right."

They stared at each other for a moment, and Vi felt her stomach tighten with anxiety.

Melissa waved her aside. "Let me try it. I weighed myself this morning at the gym."

Vi moved off and Melissa stepped on, and they waited again for the numbers to settle.

"Totally normal," Melissa said. "That's what I got this morning."

They exchanged another look, then Melissa stepped off the scale. Vi led the way back to the living room and sat down on the couch again, clasping her hands around her knees.

Melissa perched on the edge of the big chair. Neither said anything for a moment. At last Melissa spoke.

"Vi, there's something wrong with you."

"I know," Vi answered quietly.

"I think we need to get you to the hospital. You need to find out what's going on."

"I do," Vi said. This was the point she'd been stuck on all afternoon. Which way to go? Which decision to make? She felt that old familiar free-fall feeling, the ground shifting under her feet, and she violently rejected it. She could control this, she wasn't powerless.

"I do need answers," she said slowly. "But I don't think I'm going to find them at the hospital. And the cops aren't going to help me. And I think that leaves one person."

Melissa was already shaking her head. "Oh, no. Don't even tell me you're going to call that crazy lady."

Vi shrugged. "She knows something."

"So she says. For all you know it's some kind of scam. It could even be dangerous, Vi. You don't know anything about her, or this Gideon Enterprises."

When Melissa said it out loud, it sounded even more convincing than it had in Vi's head. But still…even though she trusted her friend, she trusted herself and her own gut instincts even more. For a whole chunk of her life, they'd been all she'd had to rely on. And her instincts were pushing her forward now.

"That's why I want to check it out."

"Vi," Melissa groaned, but Vi cut her off.

"I'm not going to do anything rash, but I think this is right, and I'm doing it. Now you can help me or not. But this is what I'm doing." There. It felt good to have the decision made. Squaring her shoulders, she looked at Melissa, who was sitting with her arms crossed.

There was a long, tense moment of silence. Then Melissa sighed and lifted both hands.

"Fine. Let's get started."

A day later Vi stared out the passenger-side window of Melissa's car at the thin crowd milling around the memorial statue at the center of a downtown park. She squinted at the faces but spotted no one who looked like a spy. Or, correction, a "private security specialist," according to www.GideonEnterprises.net.

"You can still back out, you know," Melissa said, her tone coaxing.

Vi shook her head. "I'm here. They're here—somewhere. I might as well talk to them." Swiveling her head around, she strained for a glimpse of Natalie. Nothing. She supposed she shouldn't be surprised the woman was good at hiding.

She looked over at Melissa, who had her face scrunched up into an anxious expression.

"Stop worrying," Vi said, ignoring the flutter in her own stomach. "I'll be fine. They're not going to hurt me. Remember, it's a real business."

"Yeah, 'protection, transportation and investigation,'" Melissa said, quoting the scant information they'd found on the Gideon Enterprises Web site. "You have to read between the lines to understand what that means. *Protection* means they beat people up for money, *transportation* probably has something to do with smuggling, and *investigation* just means they spy on people. Yeah, they sound like great folks."

Vi snorted. "That's not reading between the lines. That's reading from a different book. They do private security—it means they're bodyguards and couriers and private investigators. There's nothing illegal about it."

"Whatever. I still think this is all wrong. You should be at the hospital."

Rolling her eyes, Vi scooted toward the door. "Yeah, your feelings on the subject have been made clear, okay? I'm going now."

Melissa grabbed her shoulder. "Be careful."

"I will."

"You have your phone, right? You'll call me the minute you want me to pick you up?"

"I have it. I'll call." She smiled at her friend and pulled on the door handle.

"You're sure you don't want me to come with you?"

Vi stepped out of the car and turned, leaning down to look in at Melissa. "I told you, Mel, I don't want you any more involved with…whatever this is than you already are. This is my weird life, and I can handle it. It's going to be fine."

She held the words in her own mind, reassuring herself. She'd done what she could to protect herself; now she was going to get some answers. With a final wave, she shut the door and turned away from Melissa.

Her cell phone, tucked in a side pocket of her olive green cargo pants, banged comfortingly against her thigh as she walked across the park toward the statue. She'd left her purse with Melissa so she'd be light on her feet, unencumbered, ready for anything. And she *was* ready—ready to square off with these people and get the information she needed. She'd be cool, she'd be calm, she'd be—

"Ms. Marsh?"

With a gasp, she whirled around to face the man who'd spoken behind her.

Then she blinked. Even with her heart suddenly pounding in her throat, her brain still had time for a "Hello, handsome!"

Which he was. Spiky, dark hair, chiseled face, deep-green eyes, all attached to a long, lean, hard body in a black T-shirt and faded jeans. She swallowed.

Of course, the fact that he knew her name meant that he either worked for Gideon Enterprises, which made him a scary mercenary, or that he'd been spying on her independently, which made him just plain scary.

"Are you Violet?" he asked. His voice was low and terse, a little gruff.

Willing herself to stop noticing things about him, she drew in a breath.

"Are you Gideon?"

He smiled a little at that, the barest quirk, but he

turned his head to the side as he did, as if the smile wasn't for her because she didn't know the joke.

"No," he answered. "But he's here. I can take you to him."

He lifted an eyebrow. A beautiful, silky eyebrow. *Stop noticing.*

"You sure you want to go through with this?" he asked.

She frowned at him. He sounded like Melissa. But she didn't see any reason to lie.

"No," she answered.

He smiled again, and this time it was for her. For just a moment she felt like a normal twentysomething single girl, standing in a park getting fluttery over a hot guy's sly smile. Then—

"Well, honey, it's too late to turn back now."

Vi turned to see Natalie walking up to them, her hands tucked into the pockets of her denim jacket.

"Nice of you to show up," Vi said, scowling at her.

Natalie shrugged. "I could hardly get here first, since I had to follow you. Your friend drives like a granny, by the way."

"You followed me here?" Vi shook her head. "Boy, you never quit, do you? Even when you already know where I'm going."

"Had to make sure no one else was on your tail, now, didn't I?"

Vi frowned, not sure what to make of that. "As far as I know, you're the only one stalking me."

Natalie started walking again. "Uh-huh. Well, come on. Let's go see Gideon." She looked back over her shoulder. "Jackson, you want to take this side, and I'll go south?"

Mr. Hot and Scary—Jackson—gave a curt nod and half turned away, his eyes scanning the park. With a strange reluctance, Vi stepped away from him and followed Natalie toward a string of benches near the statue.

As they drew closer, she spotted a man sitting on one of the benches, looking completely at ease with his ankle crossed over his knee. He was in his late thirties, she decided as she stepped toward him, noting his slightly salt-and-pepper hair and the crinkly crows' feet around his blue eyes. His gray suit looked expensive, his manner exuded confidence, and while he wasn't as drop-dead gorgeous as Jackson, he was still pretty damn good-looking.

Vi thought about Jackson, flicked her eyes to Natalie, and looked back at the man who must be Gideon. So…what? Did you have to be hot to be a spy? Was it some kind of prerequisite? Did Gideon Enterprises double as a modeling agency?

Whatever it was about, it was damned annoying. She was dealing with a personal crisis here, and she didn't need to have her average looks thrown in her face on top of everything else.

Natalie stopped in front of Gideon.

"Here she is," she said, then she turned and winked at Vi and walked away, toward the end of the park that Jackson wasn't covering.

Vi stopped, feeling awkward and hoping it didn't show.

Gideon smiled at her—an interesting smile. Sort of sad and wise and kind and cold, all at the same time. It made her instantly suspicious.

"So," he said, "you're Violet Marsh."

She nodded. "And you must be Gideon."

"Mal Gideon. Malcolm," he added with a smile. "But you can see why I don't use that."

Uh-oh. Self-deprecating humor. He could be dangerous.

"I'm glad you're here," he said. "I've been wanting to talk to you."

That was better. Now she remembered exactly why she wasn't going to like this guy.

"Yeah, I kind of figured as much when I found out you'd set a spy on me. You know, when you want to talk to someone, it's customary to pick up the phone, maybe write a note."

He grinned at her. "True. But this situation is a little unusual, wouldn't you say?"

"You tell me. I don't have a clue what you're up to. And, honestly, I don't care. I just want to know whatever it is you know about me."

For the first time he stopped smiling. His eyebrows drew together in concern. "Yes," he said, then sighed. "Why don't you sit down?" He gestured to the opposite end of the long bench he sat on.

She hesitated, since she kind of liked the power position of standing over him, then decided she'd be wise not to start playing power games with this guy. She'd probably find out quickly that she was out of her league. Trying to move with assurance, she sat down on the edge of the bench, as far from him as possible.

Gideon dropped the foot that had been resting on his knee and leaned forward. "What I know, Violet—may I call you Violet?"

She shrugged, impatient. "Whatever."

"What I know…" He shook his head. "There isn't a good way to say this, so I'll just say it. Something has been done to you."

A prickling sensation rushed over her scalp. She didn't understand, but she didn't like the ominous sound of his words. "What do you mean?"

"You've lost some time, haven't you?"

She nodded, eyeing him warily. He must know already. "I was in the hospital. Apparently."

He shook his head again, slowly. "I'm afraid not, Violet. Where you were was no hospital."

Icy prickles poked at her stomach, and she suddenly felt light-headed. She wished she'd eaten more that morning. She'd been too nervous to eat as much as her body seemed to be demanding, but now she knew she could've used the fortification.

"Let's just say," she began, trying to keep her breathing under control. "Let's just say I believe you on that for the moment. Where was I, and how do you know about it?"

He looked slightly pained. "I can't tell you everything. There's…something else at stake. What I can tell you is that there's a…facility. We've been watching it for the past several days for another purpose. Three days ago, we saw you taken out of that facility under very suspicious circumstances. We thought there might be some connection to the case we're working on, so we tracked you down and watched you."

"And?" Her skin had gone clammy, cold, and her mind felt cold, too—almost numb.

"And what we've seen since has convinced us that…" He paused, watching her closely. "That some procedure was done to you at that facility that has changed you."

A beam of skepticism pierced the chilly fog in her brain. "What do you mean? What procedure?"

He drew in a breath. "We can't be sure at this point. But given what we've seen, it seems likely that you've undergone some kind of genetic enhancement."

The words seemed to ring in the silence of the open air. *Genetic enhancement.* Hanging there like something from a dream.

Vi burst out laughing. "Oh, man," she said, closing her eyes for a moment and shaking her head. "Wow. That was pretty good. You had me going there for a minute, but I think you just pushed it a bit too far."

Gideon narrowed his eyes at her. "I assure you this is not a joke."

"Oh, I believe that. I don't think it's a joke, I think it must be some kind of test to see how stupid I am. I would say it was a con, but I can't imagine what you'd hope to get out of me with that bullshit story."

"You know something's wrong. You know you're different. You can't ignore the symptoms."

She nodded, standing up and brushing off the seat of her pants. A strange kind of disappointment trickled through her. "Yeah, something's wrong with me, but it's not something anyone did to me. It's not this. You just made all this up, and I don't know why you did it, but I'm not interested."

"I know it sounds far-fetched."

"Far-fetched? Well, that's one way to put it. Ridiculous might be another. I mean, come on. You're asking me to believe that I was abducted or something by some—what? Mad scientists? Who used me for their evil experiment? Give me a break."

She turned to go, shaking her head in disgust.

"Violet, may I show you something?"

Sighing with exaggeration, she faced him again. "What?"

He reached into the pocket of his jacket and pulled out a small, flat electronic device about the width of his palm. He extended it toward her.

"What is it?" She eyed it warily.

"A digital video player. Press the play button, please."

What was this game? Was this supposed to hold her attention so someone—Jackson, maybe—could come running up and grab her before she could slip away? Her too-empty stomach clenched.

"No one's going to hurt you, Violet," Gideon said. "I just need you to see something. It'll only take a moment."

She thought hard about walking away—even running away. But she'd come here to find out what Gideon knew. She might as well see it through to the end.

She took the video player from him and hit the play button. A rather grainy black-and-white image filled the small screen—an exterior doorway into a building, a security light over it. As she watched, the door swung open and a man walked out. She couldn't make out his face, but he had some sort of rifle in his hands.

Glancing up and over her shoulder to make sure no one was coming after her, Vi refocused on the screen just in time to see a hospital gurney bump out of the doorway. Someone was on it, stretched out, first just the top of the head and then a face.

Her face.

Chapter 3

"Mr. Harriman, please listen."

Brian Bolsham, M.D., Ph.D., gripped the phone and swallowed hard as he tried to choose his words carefully.

"Well, what?" Harriman barked, and Brian winced a little and pulled the phone away from his ear. That rasping growl of a voice. It reminded him of every coach and phys ed teacher he'd ever disappointed in childhood.

For a cruel moment his mind flashed back to a time—not so long ago—when Oliver Harriman's gruff voice had been much kinder. And so much more persuasive.

You're too good for this nickel-and-dime business. A brilliant mind like yours shouldn't be hemmed in with rules and regulations. We can give you everything you've ever wanted—your own lab, plenty of money and no one to tell you what you can't do.

Brian had lapped up every word, fool that he'd been. His ego stroked and his mind alive with possibilities, he'd left the university behind so quickly their heads were probably still spinning.

"You got something to say, Bolsham?"

What a difference a few short years could make.

Snapped back to the present, Brian collected his thoughts. "Sir, please. I need you to…undo what you've done. You misunderstood. It wasn't what I wanted."

Over the still phone line, he heard the rumble of Harriman's throat clearing. "With the girl? We had this conversation already," Harriman said. "It's done. No going back."

"But if you'd reconsider, it's not too late—"

"There's no going back," Harriman repeated, his voice flat with finality. "What I did was remove a road-block you complained about. And yet, what do I hear now? More complaints."

Brian shook his head. "No, no. Sir, I'm not complaining, I'm just not comfortable with—"

"I don't give a good goddamn what you're comfortable with," Harriman cut in. "All I care about is the results you haven't provided yet, and they'd damn well better be dazzling. I'm running out of patience, Bolsham, and you're running out of excuses. Now get to work."

He hung up.

Brian placed the receiver carefully in its cradle on the desk in front of him and pinched his lips together. He ran his thumb and forefinger under the bridge of his glasses and squeezed his nose, sucking in a rasping breath.

Crumbling, it was all crumbling. What he was running out of, in fact, was options. He huffed a quiet, humorless laugh. That was apparent, given that he'd actually attempted to persuade Harriman to show a little human decency. Little chance of that happening.

What more could he do?

An idea—the worst idea—occurred to him, but he pushed it away. No, he wasn't ready yet to sacrifice his work, his hopes—possibly his very life—to be the hero. Perhaps he would. If it came to that. Certainly he could, if needs must. He had a soul, unlike Harriman and his director cronies.

Of course, he wouldn't even have to consider it if his last attempt hadn't fallen so flat. Damn it, it should've worked on her. She'd been a near perfect subject, a rarer-than-rare find, and he'd been so sure she was the answer to his problems. If not for her, if not for that failure...

Clutching his pathetically thinning hair—*he was only thirty, it wasn't fair*—he went through the test results again in his mind, obsessively looking for something he might have missed. But he hadn't missed anything, couldn't have. Five days he'd checked for the smallest change in her circulatory, metabolic, regenerative or immune systems—the smallest change in *anything*. There had been nothing there.

At least he'd let her go. A small thrill of defiant pride trickled up his spine. Harriman would never, never have done that. It was something to hang on to. A little something.

He shook his head. So tired. He hadn't managed an unbroken sleep cycle in days. Not surprising, he supposed, given his current circumstances. Abductions, prisoners, guards with guns…he wasn't cut out for this.

Enough. No time for self-pity. He hadn't started this—not really, not intentionally. It was Harriman who'd moved the situation into the cruel and criminal. And even before that, it was Harriman who'd pushed too hard, threatened too much, asked for more than was reasonable. Science took time—that's what Harriman didn't understand, wouldn't even try to explain to the directors.

And, damn it, it was that kind of pressure he'd intended to leave behind when he'd left the university. *Everything you want, no one looking over your shoulder,* Harriman had promised, but soon enough it was, *I stuck my neck out for you, and I expect results.*

Well, he *was* close, and that was the truth. No matter what had gone wrong with her, he knew the process was sound. And that was his only hope.

No, he hadn't started this, but he would have to finish it. He would check the list again, bring in another subject, somehow make it work in the time that was left. He'd have to.

The alternative was unthinkable.

Vi sat down blindly on the park bench, her eyes fastened on the small screen. She wanted to say something, or ask something, but when she opened her mouth, she found that all her brain power was going to her eyes.

It was her on that screen, on that gurney. Unconscious, helpless, utterly powerless. And Gideon was right—there was no way that building, with that armed guard, was a hospital. Where had she been?

"What is this?" she managed to ask. Her stomach clenched and rolled, and she couldn't tell if it was hunger or nausea or fear.

She felt Gideon lean toward her, almost as if he meant to be comforting. She drew back.

"It's from the facility's security monitoring system," he said. "We tapped into it looking for…something else, and we saw this. It's how we tracked you down— matching this image to a…well, a database of images we had access to."

The screen went black, and she pulled her eyes away from it. "What database? I'm in a database? What does that mean?" She heard the sliver of panic in her voice.

He sighed, shook his head. "It's nothing to…it's just a database of driver's license photos, nothing to worry about. We have a computer specialist who happens to be a genius at image matching, developed his own software…it's not important."

She closed her eyes. It was too much: her brain was overloading, and she could feel a full-on freak-out creeping up from her chest to her throat, threatening to reach her brain and take over. She had to clamp down. *You're okay, it's okay.* Sucking in a breath, she gathered her focus and opened her eyes.

"I don't know what this means," she said, holding out the video player and shaking it a little. "I know it's bad, but I don't know…what I'm supposed to do with it."

"Take it as proof that I'm telling you the truth, for one thing," Gideon said, slipping the player out of her hand and back into his pocket. "I'm not trying to con you or sell you anything or hurt you. We were only watching you to see if you had any connection to our case, and when Natalie saw that you were in trouble, she thought you should know the truth. I agreed. With SynCor involved, we knew you'd need some kind of help.

"Wait, what? SynCor?"

He shook his head. "That part's complicated."

"Well, explain it to me. All of it. If you know so much, and I'm supposed to trust you, tell me what you've got, and I'll listen."

Watching her closely, he was silent for a moment. "It's going to be hard to take and hard to believe. Try to hear me out with an open mind, and remember that I have nothing to gain by telling you this. In fact," he quirked an eyebrow at her in a way she found intensely annoying, "I'm doing you a favor."

Indignation rolled in to push back the edge of her calm. "Oh, well, you have my eternal gratitude for barging into my life and spying on me and invading my privacy. Thanks loads."

"You're welcome," he said. "Now, would you like to hear what I have to say, or would you like to continue your self-righteous huff?"

Man, he was pissing her off. Scowling at him, she crossed her arms over her chest and leaned back. "Fine, go ahead. I'm all grateful ears."

He sat back against the wooden planks of the bench. "What's the last thing you remember, before you lost the time?"

"Getting home from work last Friday," she said.

"And after you got home it's a blank?"

She nodded. "I remember feeling sort of sick. And then I woke up and it was Thursday."

"And did you feel sick at work that day? Any strangers approach you? Anything unusual happen at all?"

She strained to think, then shook her head. "No, nothing. I worked late, I stopped for tacos on the way home, totally my usual routine."

He looked at her intently. "You ate on the way home? Food from someplace you get dinner often?"

"Yeah, so?"

"That's probably how they got you."

"What? What do you mean?"

"If you go there often, anyone watching you over a few days would've noticed the pattern. If they wanted to grab you without much fuss, it wouldn't have been difficult to extrapolate what you'd eat and put some sort of drug into it."

She stared at him. "What are you saying? Someone *infiltrated* Banderas Taqueria to slip me a mickey?" Ridiculous. But, of course, now that he'd put the stupid idea into her head, she couldn't help remembering that things *had* seemed odd at Banderas that day. That guy working the counter had been so tight-lipped and stiff when he'd handed her the food.

"Possibly," Gideon said. "More likely, they just paid off one of the employees. It wouldn't be hard to do, and it makes for a very simple plan. You willingly ingest what they've given you, they wait for you to crash, then they slip in and take you away. If they kept you drugged the entire time they had you, it's no wonder you don't remember anything."

"And then what? They just decide enough's enough,

and they slip me quietly back into my own bed? Why? Why would they do that?"

He shook his head. "We don't know that. SynCor sometimes works in mysterious ways."

"What is this SynCor thing?" she asked, glad for a distraction. She didn't much like thinking about the details of how someone might have abducted her. All because of a taco.

Gideon blew out a breath. "All right, SynCor… How to explain SynCor," he said, his eyebrows drawing down. Then he nodded. "About seven years ago, I was working for an outfit that specialized in getting people out of the country. As a rule we didn't ask a lot of questions, but one particular assignment I had—he talked a lot. Crazy things, nothing I believed, about a supersecret organization he called SynCor. It was supposedly run by a bunch of CEOs and international power players, maybe even some military types, and set up to do whatever dirty work they wanted done. Corporate espionage, smuggling, illegal research—and all done with enough distance that nothing could be traced back to those in charge."

He paused, shook his head. "At first I just ignored him, but he had so much specific information, so much detail, that I started listening just for the hell of it. He said he'd been an operative, that's why he had to get away, said they'd never let him go."

He stopped again, and Vi frowned, interested in spite of herself. "So, what happened?"

"They didn't let him go. Somehow, they tracked us down at an outdoor market in Mexico City, shot him and everyone around him."

"They shot you?" Vi asked.

"Yes, not that they particularly cared about me—I was just right next to him. They did care enough to leave me for dead, but luckily I don't die that easily. They also let me see their faces, which has come in handy, and they certainly got me believing SynCor was real."

"Just because they shot him? They could've been anyone, drug dealers or—"

"I don't take much on faith," he said with a slight smile. "Once I got back on my feet I started tracking down every detail I remembered. Everything checked out. SynCor does a good job of hiding itself, but it does exist."

Vi studied him skeptically. He was a convincing storyteller, she'd give him that, but a supersecret-bad-guy organization? Doubtful. Still, she'd said she'd hear him out, so she suppressed the urge to roll her eyes.

"Okay," she said. "Let's just say for the moment—"

"That you believe me," he finished. "Now you're going to ask what this has to do with you."

"Right."

He nodded. "SynCor has many interests, from what I've uncovered, and one of them is experimental research. They tend to recruit the brightest minds with the most questionable ethics, then turn them loose, fully funded. And if anyone had developed a method for the genetic enhancement of humans…let's just say they wouldn't be applying for the usual research grants. They'd need underground funding."

Vi closed her eyes and gave her head a shake. "So, wait. You're saying that somebody—funded by this

SynCor thing—is doing experiments on humans, and I'm one of the guinea pigs?"

"That's the working theory."

"Okay, let's just say for the moment…" She waved a hand to stand in for the rest of the sentence. "Why me? Why would they pick me? I don't have any connection to this stuff. I'm normal. I'm boring. I'm an *accountant,* for chrissakes."

Gideon shook his head. "We're not sure. It may be because you're alone—no husband, no family nearby, your grandparents gone. But there may be something else, something physical about you."

She stared at him. "How do you know all that stuff?" she asked, then caught herself. "Oh, right. You weren't just watching me, you were digging up dirt, too. You probably know everything about me. You probably have my credit report, and my tax records, and my Internet password."

For the first time, he had the decency to look a little guilty. "We know a few things about you, yes."

She sighed. "This is crazy. I must be crazy. I can't believe I'm sitting here talking to a man who admits he's been spying on me."

He held up a hand. "You're free to go at any time."

"I think I'll take you up on that," she said. "Except…"

"There's still one big question, isn't there?"

She turned her head slowly to look at him. Why did she even want to hear it? He was just going to say some unbelievable thing. Still…

"All right," she said. "What have they supposedly done to me?"

"I'm not completely sure. I can only go on what Natalie's observed—"

"Spare me the disclaimer," she said, waving a hand. "Just tell me what you think. You said…" She paused, shaking her head at the insanity of it. "You said 'genetic enhancement.' What's that supposed to mean?"

He looked thoughtful. "In a nutshell, it means that certain processes in your body have been improved."

"Like what processes?"

"Look at the symptoms. You've been hungry all the time for the past few days. That may mean that your metabolism was boosted, so you're actually burning through your energy sources more quickly."

On cue, her stomach growled loudly, and she felt a new type of emptiness there—a bit more intense, a bit more painful. Trying to ignore it, she thought about his words. A faster metabolism didn't sound incredibly farfetched. And it would explain why she hadn't gained any weight even with all the power eating. Still, if someone had really figured out how to fix you up so you could eat anything and not gain weight, wouldn't it be on the front page of every newspaper?

"What else?" she asked.

He studied her for a moment, then took a slow, careful look around, apparently making sure no one was near them. "I want you to try something," he said. "It might sound strange, but bear with me."

"Oh, *now* you're worried about sounding strange? Jeez, how bad could it be?"

His lips quirked. "Grab on to the bench there," he said, pointing to the slat of wood at the edge of the bench's seat. "And press down on it."

She felt her forehead wrinkle. "You want me to press on the bench?"

He nodded, so she shrugged and placed the palm of her hand on the bench slat. It was thick and sturdy wood, lacquered with a clear sheen. She curled her fingers around it and pressed.

"Harder," he said. "As hard as you can. Put your weight into it."

Scowling at him, she leaned in, gritting her teeth, pushing downward as hard as she could.

Nothing happened.

After a moment of nothing happening, she lifted her hand and looked at Gideon.

"Okay, you know, as demonstrations go, that one wasn't the best," she said.

But he was nodding in a thoughtful way. "Right," he said. "Now try one more thing."

"Are you sure? I don't know if I can stand the excitement." He lifted his eyebrows at her in an are-you-done kind of way, so she rolled her eyes. "Fine," she said. "What?"

"Hit it," he said.

"The bench?"

"The bench. Same place as before, with the heel of your hand. Just bring it down quickly and firmly."

Staring at him with the look she normally reserved for people who refused cake at office birthday parties, she jutted out the heel of her hand and smacked the bench lightly. The wood stung her hand for a second and Gideon sighed.

"A little harder than that," he said.

"I don't want to hurt myself," she said, breaking off

to clutch at her stomach, where a stabbing pain was developing. She really wished she'd eaten a second bowl of cereal that morning.

"You won't hurt yourself."

"Uh, I think I will. That's heavy wood, and this is a breakable hand."

"It's not as fragile as you think. Hit it hard."

"I don't—"

"Violet, just do it."

"But—"

"*Do* it," he barked at her, so she huffed out a breath and clenched her fingers tight and held her breath and slammed her hand into the bench slat as hard as she could, wincing at the astonishing crack of sound.

She'd expected it to hurt. It did.

She hadn't expected to see her hand pass through the bench when the slat cracked in two.

Her eyes widened and her head began to spin a little. "I think I broke it," she said, staring down at the fractured wood.

"Damn," Gideon muttered, and he reached into his pocket for something and spoke into it. "Jackson, we need a little help here."

"How did I break it?" The edges of the wood were jagged, as if they'd torn like paper. "I couldn't...it doesn't..."

A man was jogging into her field of vision, and she pulled her eyes away from the bench to see Jackson running toward them. He frowned as he neared her, and she followed his gaze to the side of her arm.

And felt a swoony wave ripple over her.

The outside of her forearm was lacerated and

bloody—she must've scraped it on the way through the broken part of the bench. Without a word, Jackson stepped up to her and grasped her hand, his touch surprisingly gentle.

Her vision was going a little blurry, and it irritated her. She could handle the sight of blood, for heaven's sake. It had never bothered her before. Why was everything getting dim and gray? Her stomach stabbed at her again, and she began to hear a strange sort of buzzing in her ears. Gideon and Jackson were talking, and she struggled to hear them over the noise in her head.

"...do a better field dressing than me," Gideon was saying.

"She needs stitches."

Dimly she saw Gideon nod. "I think Severin—"

"I think I need to eat," she heard herself say, and both men turned to look at her again.

Jackson's eyes were very green, she thought. And then she thought about how woozy she felt, and then she stopped thinking altogether.

Chapter 4

The first thing Vi saw when she opened her eyes was a bad oil painting of a dolphin leaping from the sea.

She closed her eyes and opened them again, but the dolphin was still there. What the hell?

A voice, to her right and slightly above her, spoke. "She's awake." Gruff, low—it sounded familiar. With effort, she turned her head and saw him. Scary mercenary. Jackson.

Memory came flooding back. She struggled to sit up as Gideon appeared next to Jackson, his face concerned.

"Violet, are you all right?"

"Where am I? What's going on?" Something tugged at her left arm as she moved, and she looked down to see a needle taped to the inside of her elbow. A supple line of plastic led from the needle to a bag of clear fluid hanging from a metal stand.

An IV. A bad painting. A hard bed with the head raised, propping her in a sitting position. Hospital? Maybe, but the room was awfully small.

"You passed out," Gideon said. "I'll get Severin."

He opened a door at the end of the room and disappeared. Vi turned to Jackson, who looked slightly uncomfortable.

"Where am I?" she asked again.

"Doctor's office," he answered. "Severin's a friend of Gideon's. Didn't want to risk taking you to the hospital."

She didn't have the energy to decide how she felt about that. Letting her head fall back against the bed, she looked around the room, noting shabby wallpaper, utilitarian cabinets, bare countertops. It was a doctor's office, all right, but the doctor wasn't doing very well.

Gideon reappeared in the doorway followed by an older man, considerably shorter, with thin gray hair and small, sharp eyes. Without a word, the man—Severin, she supposed—came toward her, flicking on a penlight and shining it in her eyes. She squinted and tried not to squirm. He made a small "humph" sound and dropped the penlight in the pocket of his lab coat, then plugged his stethoscope into his ears and pressed the end of it to her chest.

"Extraordinary," he said, removing the stethoscope from his ears. He turned and pulled a clipboard from a bracket on the wall and began making notes.

Vi looked around. "So, anyone want to fill me in? What exactly happened?"

Severin didn't look up from his clipboard, so Gideon, standing at the foot of the bed with his hands in his pockets, spoke up.

"You fainted. Crumpled up and keeled over sideways. We tried to wake you, but patting your cheeks didn't seem to be getting the job done. So we brought you here."

"And where is here, exactly?"

Gideon motioned toward Severin. "Dr. Andrew Severin is an old friend. He can be trusted."

Vi rolled her eyes. "You guys never stop with the cloak-and-dagger, do you?"

"We're concerned about your safety," Gideon answered, lifting an eyebrow. "Which is lucky for you, since you don't seem to be."

"Well, I'm not the one who believes evil scientists are out to get me, so…"

Gideon's jaw clenched, and he didn't speak for a moment. "Regardless of what you believe," he began at last, "there are certain undeniable facts here. And one of them is that your body is giving off signs that would blow the mind of a two-day nursing student, let alone a doctor. So unless you want to be tomorrow's front-page news, I think keeping things low-key is essential."

She blinked, struck. "What…what signs? What signs am I giving off?"

Gideon looked at the doctor. "Severin, do you want to field that?"

Looking up from his notes at last, Severin regarded her coolly. "First of all, it's exceedingly rare to lose consciousness due to hunger only hours after having eaten—if that is indeed what happened. Second, and perhaps more significantly, your resting heart rate is… astonishing. Highly accelerated."

Vi pressed a hand to her chest, trying to feel her heartbeat, not sure what to make of the information.

He wasn't finished. "Furthermore, you had significant lacerations on your arm when you were brought here, and they now seem to have…repaired themselves."

She lifted her right arm, and her head jerked back involuntarily, as if to distance itself from the sight. The blood had been cleaned off, and the skin was no longer torn.

"Holy shit," she said, forcing herself to examine the pinkish welts on her forearm. She'd seen the blood, the ripped flesh…how could it…

"You should consider yourself fortunate that we just had time to disinfect the wounds before they closed," Severin was saying, but she didn't want to hear him anymore.

She pressed the heels of her hands against her eyes, ignoring the tug of the IV on her left elbow. The need to cry hit her with undeniable force, and she struggled to hold herself together. This wasn't real, couldn't be. This couldn't be her life.

She thought about Gideon's words. *Certain processes in your body have been improved,* he'd said. Like…healing? She shook her head, felt like moaning. It was crazy. It couldn't be true. Opening her eyes, she looked desperately to the doctor. He was a scientist, right? He wouldn't be buying in to this fairy tale.

"I don't understand what's happening," she said to him. She jerked a thumb at Gideon. "He said something about…genetic enhancement. That's not even possible, right?"

"It's not impossible," he said, and she felt herself deflating. Great. It figured that Gideon's personal doctor would be just as crazy as the rest of them. Or else he was playing along with whatever game they'd set up.

"Every cell in the human body has a set of instructions," Severin said. "Genetic instructions. Those instructions can be altered, that's been proven. In your case, perhaps they've just been…speeded up."

She felt so tired. "Huh?"

"Complete conjecture, of course, nothing scientific about it. Extensive testing would be needed to prove any such theory."

"But you could see it being true?" Gideon asked, his gaze intent.

"Certainly," Severin said with a curt nod. "Many things could be true."

"The pieces add up, don't they?" Gideon asked. "Her heartbeat's faster. Her metabolism's got to be faster if she passed out—you said yourself that's rare. Her arm healed much too quickly to be normal—it's speed, it's all speed. It makes sense."

Without warning he reached for her hand and held it up, peering at it.

"I'd bet your fingernails are growing fast. Your hair, too."

Startled, Vi stared at her fingernails. The ones she'd bitten to the quick the day before. They extended to the tips of her fingers now.

Jerking her hand out of his grasp, she shook her swimming head. "Wait a minute, wait. It doesn't all add up." *It couldn't, it couldn't.* "What about the bench? I broke it—that would make me stronger, not faster." She felt a small thrill of triumph—she'd found a hole in their story.

But Gideon was shaking his head. "No, I don't think you are stronger. Remember, when you pressed on the bench as hard as you could, nothing happened. But when you hit it fast, with speed, it broke. It's not strength, it's *force*. Velocity—movement, coming together at impact, making that impact harder, stronger."

No. No no no. "That doesn't make sense."

He squeezed his hands together, and for the first time since she'd set eyes on him, he seemed slightly agitated. "Think about…the wind in a hurricane," he said. "Wind by itself isn't strong—it's just air. But at high speeds it can tear off roofs, knock over entire structures. That's you. You're no stronger, but your speed is so great that it gives you more power. You're a human hurricane."

He looked at her intently for a moment, then shook his head. "And for all we know, you *are* stronger. You seem to be regenerating," he said, gesturing toward her healed arm. "Maybe your bones and muscles are building themselves up, reinforcing from within. And who knows what else, Violet? You may be able to do more, more than we can imagine."

"Stop selling it," Jackson burst out. All eyes turned to him as he pushed away from the wall. "What's the down side?" He looked at Severin.

Severin looked thoughtful. "Yes, well. That's difficult to say."

"Off the top of your head," Jackson said.

"It would be pure speculation."

Jackson's jaw clenched, and he looked darkly at Gideon, who raised an appeasing hand. To Severin,

Gideon said, "Humor us, please. Speculate. What's the worst that could happen?"

"Many things could happen. I suppose the most obvious is that the heart could fail. The organ is not designed to operate at that speed. Not for long, in any case."

In the silence that followed, his quiet, clinically cold words echoed in Vi's head as if he'd shouted them. Nausea, anger, and mostly fear all came surging up, and she fought them back down, gripping the mattress of the bed on either side of her hips.

"You're saying it's going to kill me," she said.

Severin looked at her, his small, gray eyes like shiny beads.

"It's impossible to say with any certainty," he said. "But yes, it could kill you."

She took a few deep breaths, clutching the mattress, clinging to one thought: he's lying.

Still, she couldn't stop herself from asking.

"Could you…fix it? Put me back the way I was?"

He actually laughed, a tinny-sounding chuckle. "Oh, my. As I have only the slightest inkling of what might be taking place within your physical processes, it's very doubtful that I could find a remedy. If this was indeed done to you, it was done by someone with greater expertise than anyone in the traditional medical community."

She stared at him. "That's a really wordy way of saying no, right?"

He gave a curt nod, and Vi pressed her lips together, concentrating on the anger that had boiled up when he laughed, nursing it, using it to push back all the other emotions threatening to break the surface.

"I want a second opinion," she said, sitting up and swinging her legs down off the bed.

Gideon stepped around to the side of the bed. "I don't think that's a very good idea."

She glared at him. "Well, I don't think you're a very good liar, so I guess we're even."

Pushing herself down from the bed, she felt the tug at her arm again and remembered the IV. She ripped off the tape and grabbed the needle to pull it out.

"Careful, you heal quickly," Severin warned, but she ignored him.

"Violet, calm down," Gideon said.

She ignored him, too, gritted her teeth and yanked on the needle. It resisted, and she grimaced at the pain and tugged harder. It finally came free, breaking the healed-over skin, and a small gush of blood welled out of her arm.

She dropped the needle and cupped a hand over her inner elbow to soothe the pain. She moved toward the door, but Gideon stood between her and it, his hands held out in a pacifying way.

"Just wait a minute," he said. "Don't go rushing off like this. You're weak, and you still haven't eaten, and the glucose from that IV isn't going to last long."

"I'll be fine." She stepped to the side, but he went with her.

"Violet, you could be in danger. We don't know why SynCor did this, or why they let you go—they could come for you again. They could be watching you."

"This is bullshit! You're a liar and a con man, and you've got all your friends playing along with you, but I'm not buying it. You understand?" She tried to side-step him again.

His face darkened with anger. "I'm trying to help you."

"I'll help myself," she said, and darted around him to the door. "You stay away from me." She slipped out of the room and found herself in a hallway.

"Violet, wait," Gideon said from the door, but she'd had enough. Spotting the exit door at the end of the hall, she began to run for it. It zoomed up fast, so fast she stumbled into it before she knew she was there. Flustered, she yanked the door open and stepped outside. She would run to a safe distance, then call Melissa to pick her up and take her home. Panicked, she slapped her leg for her cell phone and was relieved to find it still in her pocket.

She glanced back over her shoulder and slowed to a jog.

No one had followed her out.

Hours later Vi hurried down another hallway, and this time someone was following her.

"Ms. Marsh, please wait!" The doctor who'd just listened to her heart was jogging up the hall behind her.

Ignoring him, she walked faster and hit the swinging door to the waiting room, making a beeline for Melissa while digging in her purse for her wallet.

"You have any cash?" Vi asked, her voice breaking as she concentrated on pulling out all the bills she had.

Melissa stood, her eyebrows shooting up. "Why? What's the matter?"

"I've got to get out of here." As she said it, the swinging door banged open and the doctor appeared.

"Ms. Marsh, I don't think you understand," he said,

slightly breathless as he pulled to a stop in front of her. "You need to go to the hospital. Right now."

His voice echoed in the clinic's stark waiting room, and she could feel the eyes of all the other patients on her. *Can't handle this...*

"I heard you the first time," she said, grabbing the twenty Melissa was holding and stepping around the doctor. She slapped all the cash on top of the check-in desk, in front of the wide-eyed receptionist.

"Here. Here's my payment. Keep the change."

The doctor reached out for her arm. "You have to listen. You're approaching cardiac arrest. That's a heart attack, Ms. Marsh."

Jerking her arm away, Vi bit down on her lip to keep from shouting at him. She didn't want to hear it again, damn it.

"I have to go," she said, heading for the door.

"Let us call you an ambulance," he called after her.

"No!" she shouted, and she hit the glass exit door with the heel of her hand. The shock of the impact vibrated up her arm, and the door flew open. Too late, she yanked her hand back, while the door hit the end of its reach and made a loud snapping sound.

Then the glass shattered.

The door rebounded and slammed to a close. Vi stood in front of it, frozen with misery for a moment.

Oh, God. What in hell was wrong with her?

"I'm sorry," she whispered without turning, then stepped through the metal frame of the now-empty door.

She waited by the passenger door of Melissa's car, trying not to think, trying not to cry, while Melissa hurried to the driver's side, digging for her keys. When the doors were unlocked, Vi slid into her seat and covered her eyes with her hand. Melissa shut her own door and put the key in the ignition, then hesitated.

"Vi," she said. "Are you sure you want to leave? Maybe you should let them call that ambulance."

Vi shook her head, her hand still over her eyes. "I can't, I can't deal with it. Please, let's just go."

As soon as she felt the car backing up, she let go of her tears. While Melissa drove and occasionally reached over to pat her on the shoulder, Violet cried.

She hated crying, hated the feelings it made her remember, but she couldn't stop it from happening. And she hated that, too—her self-control slipping out of her grasp until she was reduced to this, huddled over in her seat, elbows tucked in, forehead resting on her fists, ripped with the painful, racking sobs that had been threatening for hours, since Gideon had shown her the video.

The video... She couldn't think about it and what it might mean. Enough that she was messed up, wrong. Enough that her heart was going to explode and there was no one to help her. Enough. Too much.

After a while her sobs quieted. Then she felt that increasingly familiar stab of pain in her gut, and the reminder brought on a fresh wave of tears, but it was mercifully brief. Sitting up, she sniffed and wiped her eyes.

"I need to eat," she said.

Melissa nodded. "Sure, okay. What do you want?"

"Doesn't matter, anything. I just don't want to pass out again."

Looking relieved to have something to do, Melissa

pulled into the nearest burger joint. Vi sat silently while Melissa swung through the drive-through and ordered.

Minutes later they were parked in the empty lot near the restaurant, quietly eating cheeseburgers and fries.

"Are you okay?" Melissa asked after a while.

Vi chewed thoughtfully for a moment, then swallowed. "Well, let's see. I don't know what's happening to me. I might die. And I don't know what the hell to do. So, no, I would say I am not okay."

Melissa sighed. "We need to go to the hospital, Vi. We should've gone to the hospital in the first place. This problem was never going to get fixed at a clinic like that."

"I didn't think they could fix it," Vi said, staring at her burger with watery eyes. "I just thought…if that Severin guy was lying, they could tell me. I…wanted to think he was lying." She took a deep breath. "Don't know who I was kidding. Clearly, I've been a freak for a while. Now I'm just a confirmed freak."

"You're not a freak."

"Oh, yes, I am. I'm like the freaking Incredible Hulk. Careful, don't make me angry—I'm already demolishing everything in my path, and I'm not even irritated yet."

"You're not the Hulk. You're just…sick or something. It's a medical problem, and there are people who can help you, I'm sure of it. They can get you back to normal."

Back to normal. Back to her regular, quiet life—the one she'd worked so hard to build. *Look at me now, Mom. This is more chaos than even you could cook up.* She sighed. Maybe normal just wasn't meant to be, not for her.

But for Melissa… Vi looked over at her friend, who was collecting every last scrap of fast-food trash in the car and crumpling it all into tight, neat wads. Melissa wasn't prepared to deal with all of this madness—already her face was drawn with tension. It was past time to cut her loose from whatever mess was up ahead.

Melissa rolled all the trash together into one master lump and squeezed it tight. "Do you care which hospital we go to?" she asked.

Uh-oh. Mel was shifting into action mode, and if Vi didn't stop her now, she'd be in the hospital before she could blink, and Melissa would be stubbornly staked out at her side.

"Oh, let's not go now," she said. If she could deflect long enough to get home, she'd turn around and go to the hospital by herself, leave Melissa out of it altogether. Probably she should've done that in the first place, but the habit of leaning on other people was creeping up on her more than she'd realized.

"What do you mean?" Melissa asked, eyes wide. "You heard the doctor back there—he said it was urgent."

Vi sighed. "I know. It's just…after all that's happened today, I just don't think I can handle it. Not yet."

"But—"

"I know it's serious, but I'm so tired, and the hospital—it's going to be crazy. I don't think I can face it without a little sleep, at least." Boy, that was weak. Her only hope was that Melissa would think she was completely overwhelmed and take pity on her.

"Vi, I don't think you should put this off."

"I'll go tomorrow, I promise."

"But tomorrow could be…" Melissa didn't finish it, but the unspoken words came through clearly. *Too late.*

"It's the best I can do," Vi said. "Besides, I feel fine. If my heart were right on the verge of giving out, don't you think I'd at least feel weak or something?"

Looking exasperated, Melissa tucked her master trash wad neatly under the seat. "Fine. But it's tomorrow first thing. I'm coming to pick you up early."

Vi looked away so Melissa wouldn't see her guilty grimace. She'd have to leave a note explaining everything so Mel wouldn't freak out. Notes—the ultimate one-sided conversation—were the best way to deal with Melissa when she got her mind bent on something.

Melissa said it again when she pulled to a stop in front of Vi's house.

"First thing tomorrow. Go right to sleep, because I'm going to be here early. Unless you want me to come in now? I can spend the night, if you want."

Vi shook her head, and in spite of herself, she felt a little teary again. "Thanks, but I'll be all right. I just want to be oblivious for a few hours." She reached over and hugged Melissa, then pushed herself out of the car and hurried away.

She took a deep breath as she headed up her front walk in the deepening twilight. End of the day for most people. Her day—already so long, and so bad—was apparently just beginning. She felt a little hollow inside, a little scared, as she unlocked her front door, but she forced herself to smile as she turned to wave Melissa off. Closing the door behind her, she reached for the hallway light switch and flicked on the light.

A barely perceptible blur of movement caught the

corner of her eye, and before she knew exactly why she was doing it, she ducked and reached up with both arms to cradle her head.

A fist slammed into the wall where her head had just been.

Chapter 5

Time seemed to stop for a moment, and Vi stayed absolutely still, her hands locked in place and her knees frozen in their bent position.

Then everything happened in a rush. The fist was coming at her again, and now she could see the man swinging it—a bulky, beefy guy in black clothes and a ski mask.

A wave of icy fear flooded her, and she jumped out of the way and backed toward the door, scrabbling at the knob. The man advanced on her, his big, gloved hands swinging out. Vi ducked again and turned the doorknob, yanking on the door, but it opened inward, and she wasn't going to get anywhere with the man backing her against it.

Close to panic, she gritted her teeth and bolted forward, ducking under the man's arm as he tried to grab her. *Think, think, you've got to think. Don't lose it now.* She'd never get the back door open before he caught her—stupid sliding glass door always got jammed in its track. But if she could lead him away from the front door, maybe she could get back to it and get out that way.

The man spun around to face her, moving fast for his size. He reached out and snagged her shoulder, pulling her toward him, but she jerked her whole body and stepped back out of his reach. *That's it, keep going back, lead him away...*

But he was good, and before she knew it, he had her shoulder again, and then his fist was coming at her. She tried to dodge, but he seemed to anticipate the move, and his punch caught the edge of her cheekbone with an unbelievable explosion of pain.

Shocked, she clutched her cheek and sank down to her knees. Only once before had she been hit in the face. The terror of it, the pain and the helpless fury, and the memory that never completely faded, all came rushing through time at her. Nine years old, what could she do?

She felt his fist smash into her jaw, and her head snapped back, her mind screaming with black pain, but it brought her back to now. This wasn't then, and she wasn't little, and damn it, she was going to do something.

The man in front of her was drawing back for another blow, and she began to struggle, tried to squirm out of his grasp and get back on her feet. But he was strong, his hand clamped on her shoulder, and she could only throw up her hands and brace herself as he swung again.

"Hey!"

Vi heard a high-pitched shout and then an "oof" sound, and then the man let go of her shoulder and turned away from her. Confused, she staggered to her feet and saw Natalie on the other side of the man, knees bent and fists clenched in a fighting stance.

Natalie…how? She must have been tailing her again. For the first time, Vi was swooningly glad she was being spied on.

The man rushed at Natalie, but she sidestepped and caught him with a glancing blow to the midsection as he passed. He recovered quickly and came back at her, and she kicked out, aiming for his knee. Vi winced as Natalie hit her mark, but the man staggered forward and grabbed Natalie by both shoulders, slamming her against the wall. Natalie's head banged back with a sharp crack, and Vi felt panic swelling up again.

Natalie was doing her best, but she wasn't going to be able to take this guy down—he was too big, and he was too good. Vi realized her rescue had only been temporary.

She could run away now—the door was clear. But she couldn't leave Natalie to get beaten to a pulp. She couldn't. Desperate, she cast about for something to defend herself with, and her eyes settled on Nana Martha's ugly wooden wall hanging in the shape of an owl.

The man was banging Natalie against the wall over and over, and her body was going limp as her head struck the drywall repeatedly. Vi snatched the owl off the wall and ran at the man before she lost her nerve, holding the owl high over her head. She heard herself screeching involuntarily, and just before she reached him, the man whipped around and saw her. Natalie crumpled to the floor as he let her go, and the man held up both arms to protect his head from the owl.

Vi brought it down as hard as she could, but the force of the blow was deflected by his arms. He shouted in pain, anyway, and reached out to grab the owl. She snatched it back and moved fast, swinging it sideways to catch him across the face.

There was a cracking sound that she found strangely satisfying as the wood contacted his head. He screamed and staggered sideways, and she came after him again, caught in a fury of fear and determination.

Whack! She hit him on the shoulder. *Wham!* The other shoulder. He cried out and grabbed wherever she hit, his eyes wide with surprise and growing fear.

That's right. Now you *can be scared of* me. Lifting the owl high, she prepared to swing it down onto his head. His eyes bulged behind the mask, and he scrambled backward toward the door. Before she could follow him, he jerked the door open and ran.

Vi stood there for a moment, breathing fast, the owl still held over her head. Then she dropped it, numbly hearing it clatter against the entryway's wood floor, and she hurried to the door, shut it and threw the dead bolt.

She started to shake and she felt tears threatening again—this wasn't possible, her life turned so upside down—but it wasn't really over. Natalie was still crumpled on the floor, and the man could come back. She couldn't collapse yet.

Pinching her lips together to hold everything in, she dashed across the room for her cordless phone and dialed 911, then hurried to Natalie and squatted down next to her. She was breathing; that was good. Vi didn't know whether she should move her or not.

The dispatcher came on the line, and Vi haltingly, breathlessly got the words out, got the police and an ambulance on the way, got help. Then she sat down next to Natalie to wait.

Natalie began to stir just as Vi heard the sirens getting close.

"Don't try to move," Vi said, watching Natalie's eyelids flutter. "It's okay, an ambulance is coming."

But Natalie did move, sitting up and clutching her head. "What happened?" Her voice was slow and slurry.

"You got knocked out," Vi said. "Look, just sit still, the ambulance is almost here. Just wait there." Standing up, Vi backed toward the door. "I'm going to make sure they spot the house. I'll be right back."

With a last worried glance at Natalie, Vi pulled the door open and stepped outside to wave to the approaching police car and ambulance. As they screeched to a stop, the flashing lights dazzling her, she poked her head back in the door to reassure Natalie.

But the room was empty.

Vi looked around to see the glass door sliding to a close as Natalie disappeared.

It was a long time before the police left, but for all the time they'd spent, they hadn't done much.

Vi supposed there wasn't much they could do. Huddled on Nana Martha's couch, she thought about the way she must have sounded to them. Holding her wooden owl and describing how she'd bested the intruder. Talking about Natalie—the absent, invisible Natalie—spying on her for days, then helping her fight off the attacker. Explaining about Gideon, and the taco she'd eaten, and the hospital she hadn't been in and the video…

The more she'd said, the crazier she'd sounded. In her frantic state, it had taken her too long to notice their shifting stances, the looks they shot each other, the careful way they spoke to her. It had finally dawned on her: of course, they didn't believe her now any more than they had the first time, when she'd gone to the police station. And why would they? Once again, she didn't have any evidence—the dent in her wall from the man's beefy fist could've been caused by anything, particularly when you considered the hole she herself had knocked in her dining room wall—and the bruises on her cheek and jaw had already faded away by the time they'd arrived. She didn't have any witnesses to back her up—*thanks a lot, Natalie, for disappearing*. She didn't have any *proof*.

She wrapped her arms around her shins and let her head drop to her knees. My home, she thought mournfully. Nana and Jack's home, my one safe place, and now it isn't safe anymore.

She wasn't safe—there was no denying it now. Gideon had said she might be in danger, but she hadn't believed him, hadn't *wanted* to believe him. But he'd been right, and if he was right about that…

Could it really be true? That she wasn't just sick, that this hadn't just happened?

That someone had done it to her? Drugged her up and taken her away and made her into a freak…?

Tears welled up in her eyes, and she took a heaving breath. Wow, damn. She hadn't cried this much since... ugh, fourth grade. That horrible year. Maybe it was a new constant in her life now. Tears. Fear. Intruders with ski masks and spies with bad tidings. Violet Marsh, this is your life.

Questions swam up in her mind. *Why? Why me? What do I do? What happens next? What else is wrong with me? What if that man comes back?* The ground was shifting under her feet again, tumbling her back toward the chaos she feared most. She wasn't prepared for this, didn't know how to handle it. Tears squeezed out of her eyes and she began to shake. A moan slid up her throat.

A tap on the glass door had her head snapping up and her heart shooting into her throat. Eyes wide, she flung herself off the couch and stared into the darkness beyond the glass, backing away from it.

A penlight snapped on in the darkness outside, and in its glow, she saw Natalie's face. Slumping with relief, she drew a calming breath and made her way to the door, her anger growing with each step.

She unlatched the lock and yanked on the handle, nearly breaking it off in her haste. The door skidded open, and Natalie turned off the penlight and crossed her arms over her chest.

"Well, look who's back," Vi said, her voice nearly a snarl.

"Oh, no, don't you even start that shit," Natalie said. "I saved your ass back there and got myself clocked for my trouble, so I don't want to hear it. You going to let me in?"

Stepping back with a scowl, Vi watched her cross the room and ease down into Grandpa Jack's big chair.

"Why'd you leave?" Vi asked, closing the door and returning to the couch. "Besides the fact that you probably needed medical attention, I could've used your help with the police."

"I got medical attention," Natalie said, touching the back of her head and wincing a little. "And I don't do so well with cops, so you're just as lucky I wasn't here."

"They thought I was nuts. Again. They thought I made the whole thing up. Again."

Natalie nodded. "Cops don't generally like to take a lot on faith, I've found."

"You could talk to them, back up my story."

"Oh, no. Uh-uh. Sorry, honey, but another thing I've learned is that the less I talk to the cops, the better I like my life. Besides, Gideon wants the people who work for him to keep a low profile."

Vi let her eyes close for a moment. What was she going to do? It was hard to admit it, but she was in over her head, and she needed help. But from whom?

Natalie wouldn't help her. Melissa would, but what could she do? Vi thought fleetingly of Robert, but she'd barely been on two dates with the man—she'd accidentally stood him up for the third—and he was so resolutely normal that she hadn't felt comfortable telling him even the mildest version of her childhood story yet. There was no way she was going to lay this mess on him. Friends from college, Lisa and her other friends from work…no way. She knew no one who could help her with something this big and dangerous.

Then there were the police, who would and could help her, but only if she could convince them she wasn't crazy.

She heard Natalie shifting, and she opened her eyes.

"I guess I'll be going," Natalie said, getting slowly to her feet. She was moving a little stiffly, Vi noticed. "I just wanted to make sure you were okay. I'd thank you for helping me out with that thug, but you owed me for saving you, so…"

"Wait a minute," Vi said, an idea glimmering to life in her mind. She'd thought Gideon was crazy until he'd shown her the video. If she could show that to the cops…

"Natalie, how do I get in touch with Gideon?"

Natalie frowned at her, suspicious. "Why? You all of a sudden start believing him?"

"Well…I don't know," Vi said. "But I need to talk to him. Can you take me to him?"

Natalie's brows shot up. "Now? It's after midnight."

"So?"

"So, just because he's not your average businessman doesn't mean you can just drop in on him any old time you want. He's got business hours, you know."

"Well, I can't stay here tonight. I've already pissed off one psychotic ski-mask guy—who knows what's coming next? I don't even have an alarm system."

"So go stay with one of your friends."

"Oh, good idea. Because I'd like for my friends to be killed." She shook her head. "I need to stay someplace safe. If you don't want to take me to Gideon, I'm staying with you."

Natalie backed up a step, waving her hands in front

of her. "Uh-uh. Oh no, forget that. You're a nice person and all, but I don't take my work home with me. Besides, my boyfriend would have a fit."

Vi stopped, interested in spite of herself. "You have a boyfriend?"

"Don't sound so surprised. Yes, I have a boyfriend, and he doesn't like being woken up in the middle of the night by strange houseguests. And I don't like listening to him complain all night long."

"So take me to Gideon."

Natalie sighed. "All right, all right. I'll take you. But I'm not getting the blame for this—you make sure you tell him this was your idea."

"I'll tell him," Vi said. "I think Gideon and I are going to have a nice, long talk."

Now she just had to figure out what to say.

Brian hurried down the darkened hallway toward his office, where he knew Lowell was waiting. He'd been unable to determine how Lowell always managed to get past the locks on his office door, but it wasn't the first time the mercenary had pulled that trick.

It was, however, the first time he'd called in the middle of the night.

Feeling a line of perspiration bursting out on his forehead, Brian tried to decide what he was more nervous about—meeting with Lowell, or hearing whatever it was Lowell had to say. It didn't matter—he was about to do both, and his always-acidic stomach was churning as a result.

He found his office door partly open, and when he pushed his way into the room, he saw Lowell sitting behind the desk, his big, booted feet propped on the directors' report Brian had been working on all week.

Brian opened his mouth to ask him to move his feet, then decided against it.

"I'm here," he said, sounding weak and breathless to his own ears. "What's wrong?"

Lowell was smoking one of his dark, thin cigars, and Brian tried to breathe shallowly, hoping he could keep his asthma at bay.

"Had a little incident with your girl today," Lowell said, hissing out a haze of smoke. He'd turned on only the desk lamp, and his face was half-lit by the glow. His eyes were just two faint gleams. "Figured you should know."

Brian swallowed hard. He didn't like the sound of that. "Incident? What…what happened?"

Dropping his feet to the floor, Lowell leaned forward into the light and fixed Brian with a stare, then pointed at him with his cigar. "Something's wrong with that girl. She's not right. What'd you do to her?"

A chill crabwalked up Brian's spine, and he sucked in a breath. He felt a swell—he wasn't sure if it was terror or hope. Rushing toward Lowell, he reached out to grasp the edge of the desk.

"Why? Why do you say that? What happened?"

Lowell wouldn't be rushed. He sucked on the cigar and exhaled slowly. "I was tailing her today."

Brian nodded, impatient.

"I've been checking in on her now and then since Wednesday, like you said. Picked her up today when she was leaving her house with some friend, and I got a little interested when they pulled up at one of those clinic places. I was thinking," here he tapped his temple with the hand holding the cigar, "you said look out for anything unusual. I figure, anytime you go to the doctor, that's unusual."

Brian nodded again, wishing he'd hurry and get to the point, but not about to press him to skip ahead.

"So I waited until they came out. Figured maybe I'd break in there tonight, see what her record said, but it turns out there's no need. Your girl comes out of there and barely touches the exit door, and what do you think happens?"

Brian shook his head, his heart pounding in his chest. He couldn't speak.

"Broke it," Lowell said with heavy significance. "Snapped the metal hold, shattered the glass. I'm telling you, she barely touched it." Suddenly Lowell seemed to realize he was getting a touch too excited about his story. He leaned back in his chair and took a slow drag off the cigar.

"Like I said, unusual." His voice had slipped back down to deep, sinister range. Brian knew it was an act, but it still made him nervous. Lowell might not be the cool, collected Dirty Harry he wanted to be, but there was no denying he was a killer. And a fairly unhinged one, at that.

Brian switched mental gears, trying to forget about Lowell staring at him from across the desk. This information, could it possibly mean the procedure had worked? He'd theorized that the side effects could be unpredictable, but this... He shook his head, unsure, but his chest was tightening with excitement, anyway. Something had happened within her, which meant that the regeneration might also be working.

But how? How could it be working when he'd been so sure it had failed, sure enough to let her go? He must have missed something, possibly some interference from the sedative—he'd have to check his notes, but now…if it was working…

"What happened then?" he asked. "What did you do?"

"I'd seen enough," Lowell said, tapping ash onto Brian's carpet. "Figured you'd want her back, and there was no time for slipping her a drug like last time. I got into her house and waited for her to get there."

Brian frowned, but he didn't really care how Lowell had done it. He didn't have much time before Harriman's next visit, but he could get her ready if he started now. Ready to dazzle, yes, indeed. And then everything could be right again.

"Where did you put her? In the lab? I need to get started." He stood up, already thinking of the tests he'd need, the materials.

Lowell hissed out more smoke. "Hold on there, Doc. Had a little problem."

"What? What problem?"

He studied his cigar, held at arm's length. "Whatever you did to her, she's tougher than she looks. Plus, she had someone with her, someone helping her."

Cold disappointment leaked through Brian's stomach. "Are you saying you didn't get her? She got away?"

"I'm saying you're going to need more than one man to take her down."

"But—"

"Don't worry," Lowell said, waving his cigar. "I'll take Donny and T.J. with me tomorrow. We'll pick her up."

Brian leaned forward, his gut clenching. "It has to be done quietly. And you have to make sure the others won't talk."

"Relax." Lowell pushed himself out of Brian's chair and straightened the leather vest he always wore. In the light of the lamp, Brian could just make out a bruise developing on Lowell's right cheekbone, just above the line of his beard. "Those two'll do what I say, and I'll keep them on a leash…so long as you and I understand each other."

He let the words hang in the air like the threat they were. Brian nodded.

"Just be sure you bring her in," he said. "I need her here, now."

Lowell headed for the door, trailing smoke. "Don't worry so much, Doc. No matter what you did to her, she's still just a girl."

Chapter 6

Vi waited in Gideon's office, slumped in a leather wing chair. It was a nice office, with plush carpeting, new paint on the walls and a giant mahogany desk. Too bad it was too fancy for the rest of his dump of a building. She guessed he was starting with the prosperous look in one room and working his way out.

Sighing, she leaned her head back against the leather chair. She was so tired. She'd been exhausted when the police left, and she was beyond that now, in a sort of unreal, light-headed alternate awareness.

Of course, the light-headedness could have to do with hunger again. She'd made Natalie stop at a convenience store on the way to the office to buy some snacks, but those day-old doughnuts and bags of chips weren't going to last long. Somewhere in the back of her mind, she'd thought that the eat-whatever-you-want-and-still-lose-weight thing might be fun, but it was turning out to be a pain.

Where was Gideon? If he didn't drag his ass into the room soon, she was going to conk out in his chair. He was probably standing right outside the door, anyway, just making her wait on purpose. He hadn't been sleeping when Natalie called him from the car—Vi was sure of that. He'd answered right away.

As if to prove her point, Gideon came striding into the room then, looking as composed and put together as if it were two in the afternoon instead of two o'clock in the morning. He was dressed casually, compared to the suit he'd worn earlier, in slacks and an expensive-looking sweater. He flashed his charming smile when he saw her.

"Hello, Violet. So nice to see you again."

Oh, Lord. He was going to be smug about this.

He stood regarding her for a moment with his hands in his pockets. Then he moved behind the desk and sat down.

In the position of power, she noted.

"Feeling all right after your run-in this evening?" he asked.

"I'm okay," she said, then swallowed with difficulty. *Just say it.* "But I need your help."

He looked thoughtful. "That's interesting. When you left Severin's office, you said you could help yourself."

Right. He was definitely going to be a jerk. "Clearly, things have changed," she said. "Look, I was scared, okay? I was overwhelmed, and you have to admit that everything you were saying sounded crazy. I didn't want to believe all that."

"But you do now."

She hesitated. "I don't… I'm not sure what to think. Except I know you were right about the danger, and I know I need help."

He looked satisfied. "I can help you."

That's what she was afraid of. Sheesh, she'd have to tread carefully, here, to get what she wanted without offending him. "I'm sure you could," she began slowly, "but I…I think I'd rather go the more traditional route. The police can help me."

He shook his head. "No, they can't."

"Oh, I'm sure they can. It's just…they don't really believe me, and I don't have any way to convince them.…"

Something flickered in his cool blue eyes, and he nodded. "That's why you're here. You want the video."

She half smiled and shrugged. "Well, it definitely had an impact on me. I was thinking, if I could show it to the police, that would get them to take me seriously. And since you got the video from the security system of this facility, you must know where it is—what it is. With that information, plus the video, I can convince the police to go check it out."

But he was shaking his head again. "That won't help, Violet. I promise you—this is beyond your friendly, neighborhood police force. Even if they did 'go check it out,' they wouldn't know what they were heading into. They wouldn't know what to look for. They don't know about SynCor, and they wouldn't believe you if you told them. Trust me on that."

Vi was beginning to get irritated, and she struggled to keep it under control. She needed to convince him, not curse at him. "Look, maybe you're right, but give me a chance to find out for myself, okay?"

"I can't," he said.

"Can't what?" She heard the sharpness in her voice.

"I can't give you the video, and I can't give you the information."

"I'm not asking for a favor," she said. "If it's about money, I'll pay you. I have money in my savings—oh, wait. I'm sure you already know that."

"It's not about money. I have my own objective at that facility, and I can't afford to put it at risk. Then there's the fact that the video was obtained somewhat… illegally. Not exactly the kind of thing I'm anxious to inform the authorities about."

Vi chewed on her lip, thinking. What would it take to convince him? What did he want? A faint, pitiful thought of seducing the video out of him sparked in her brain, but it died when she remembered her grubby cargo pants and the T-shirt she'd been wearing for hours. Principles aside, she'd never felt less like a se-ductress in her life.

"Come on, Gideon. There must be something I can do to get you to give me that video."

"There isn't." He leaned back in his chair and re-garded her coolly.

"But you said you were willing to help me."

"I am. On my own terms."

She had the distinct feeling she wasn't going to like his terms. Still, she supposed there was no harm in hearing him out. It wasn't like she had a lot of other op-tions.

"Fine. What are your terms?"

Instead of answering, he crossed his arms and studied her. "You know, ever since I found out about you, I've been thinking you could be useful, somehow. But it wasn't until you left Severin's that it really hit me."

Uh-oh. She'd been right. She didn't like the sound of "useful" at all. Before she could say as much, he continued.

"There's something inside that facility that I need to get. It's going to be difficult—the security is tricky—but I'm going to do it. I believe you're the key to getting in."

Vi blinked at him, trying to translate his words into logical sentences. "What are you saying? You're going to break into that place?"

He nodded. "And you're going to help me."

Her eyes opened so wide they hurt, and she laughed a little bit. "Excuse me? Yeah, no, that's not happening."

"Hear me out."

"I don't need to hear you out. I'm not helping you do that. That's illegal."

He grimaced slightly. "Only in a manner of speaking."

"Yeah, in the manner of speaking about *laws,* which you will be *breaking.* Forget it."

"Violet, if you understood—" He broke off, sighed. "I can't explain this to you, it's too risky. But trust me when I say that it's…not exactly what it seems to be."

She rolled her eyes. "What, you're going to steal something and then donate it to needy orphans? I don't think so. Besides, why am I supposed to trust you when you don't even trust me enough to tell me why you're breaking in?"

Aha, she thought. Score one for me. Of course, she wasn't sure what she'd won.

"I understand it's asking a lot for you to accept this on my word. But let me spell a few things out for you. First, in our brief but memorable acquaintance, I've never lied to you. Even when you thought I was lying, it turned out that I was telling you the truth."

As far as I know, she added silently.

"Second, I'm not giving you the video or the information about the facility. I simply can't jeopardize my own objective. It's not going to happen."

Stung by the finality in his tone, she swallowed hard. "So, that's it? End of story. I won't help you pull off some heist job, so I'm out in the cold? You won't help me at all?"

He didn't answer, just watched her steadily, his eyes cool and untroubled by remorse. She let her own eyes close for a moment. How had it come to this? The only person who could help her was a stone-hearted—no, an *ice*-hearted bastard, and she had no way to melt him.

This wasn't the way things were supposed to work. It wasn't that she expected life to be fair—she knew better than that. But it was supposed to be—if you worked hard enough and set everything up the right way—sort of predictable. Or so she'd hoped.

Showed what she knew. A lesson to learn: life could swing around and toss you off your feet at any time.

"Violet, there's one other thing you should consider."

Wearily she opened her eyes and looked at him again, letting herself hate him in that moment, letting herself blame him for everything.

"What is it that I should consider, Gideon? What

proposal do you have for me? It can only get better, right? Lay it on me."

He seemed utterly unaffected by her hostility. "It's this. Even if you could convince the police to take you seriously, they can't offer you what I can. They might be able to find evidence that someone did, indeed, perform a medical procedure on you. They might even be able to bring that person to justice. It's doubtful, but anything's possible. But they can't give you your life back."

In spite of her anger, he had her attention. "What do you mean?"

"You don't just want your safety, or to see justice done. You want your life and your body back the way they were. Isn't that right?"

Damn. He was getting to her. She could feel a stillness inside as he spoke that scared her.

"You didn't ask for this," he continued. "You didn't deserve it. Are you just going to sit back now and take it? Accept that your heart could fail at any time, accept that you'll never be normal again?"

Damn, damn. She knew he was manipulating her, but…he was kind of right. "What are you saying?" she asked slowly. "You can guarantee you'll undo whatever was done to me?"

He gave a little half smile. "Guarantees are for suckers, Violet, and there aren't any here. But think about it. All the information on what was done to you, everything a medical team would need to reverse the procedure, is inside that facility. We're going in, anyway. You come with us, we'll make sure you leave with that information in hand."

Leaning forward, he fixed her with his deepest gaze. "I don't think you'd ever get that kind of offer from the police."

He was crazy, and she'd never do it…but God help her, she had to admit he was right about that.

She shook her head, shook off the thought. "Look, you're a very smooth talker," she began, but he interrupted.

"Just think it over, Violet. Sleep on it, and we'll talk in the morning."

At the mention of sleep, all her weariness came slamming back into her, pressing her down with heavy fatigue.

"I can't sleep," she said. "I've got nowhere to go to sleep."

"I can put you in a safe house," he said, "if you trust me enough to accept my protection."

Trust him. She'd be a fool to trust him completely, but she didn't think he intended to hurt her. Use her, yes. Con her, certainly. But hurt her? Hell, if he'd wanted to do that, he'd had his chance when she'd passed out cold in the park.

"No strings attached?" she asked. "This doesn't mean I agree to do anything?"

He held his hands wide, his face innocent. "No strings attached."

She took a deep breath. "Then I guess I trust you just enough."

Vi hugged her purse as Jackson turned his SUV onto a dark, working-class street lined with slightly shabby houses. They were probably almost to the safe house now, and her chest was tightening with dread as a result. Weirdly she felt the urge to stay in the car, stay in the silence that seemed to emanate from Jackson. He'd barely said a word for the entire drive. She supposed it wasn't shocking that a scary mercenary guy wouldn't be all that chatty, but she was surprised at how comforting it felt.

She'd been surprised, too, when Jackson had materialized to take her to the safe house, but then, she guessed Gideon thought himself above chauffeur duties. He probably had a separate henchman for every little job he needed done. Natalie was clearly his stalking henchman—henchperson—and Jackson was, what? Hit man henchman? Bodyguard henchman? It was too soon to tell.

Jackson slowed the SUV to a crawl, then turned into a driveway. The headlights washed over a no-frills one-story house that gave off the distinct aura of abandonment. Something about the cold, silent place made the desolate feeling in her stomach a little sharper, more intense.

Jackson jammed the gearshift into Park and killed the engine and headlights.

"Wait here," he said, then swung out of the driver's seat, locking and closing the door behind him.

She watched his silhouette in the moonlight as he climbed the three steps to the porch. He disappeared inside the house.

Immediately she felt a prickle of fear. What if he didn't come back? What would she do? Hunching down in her seat, she shot a look to her left and right. Or what if he did come back, only to lead her into a trap waiting inside the house? Just because Gideon trusted Jackson didn't mean *she* had to—hell, she barely trusted Gideon.

The beginnings of an adrenaline surge twanged through her blood, and her skin began to tingle. She might have to fight again, like with the intruder in her house. Best to be prepared for anything. Yes, that was her new lot in life—constant vigilance.

She startled when a movement on the porch caught her eye. Jackson had reappeared, and he motioned her toward him with two fingers.

So either it was safe or she was about to walk into an ambush. Taking a deep breath, she pulled on the door handle.

Nothing happened. She leaned her shoulder into the door and pushed, tugging harder on the handle, but the door didn't budge. It's stuck, she thought, and tried not to panic. She shot a look at Jackson, who was standing with his hands on his hips, frowning at her.

"It's stuck," she said out loud, but of course he couldn't hear her. He made a motion with his hands, but she didn't understand it.

She banged her shoulder against the door and yanked on the handle as hard as she could. With a crack, the handle pulled free from the door. She sat holding it, still leaning against the door, and stared at it, bewildered.

Looking up, she saw Jackson heading down the porch steps toward her with an irritated expression. He stopped next to her and tapped on the window.

"Unlock it," he said, his voice muffled but audible through the glass.

Vi winced as humiliation flooded her. Locked. Right.

Idiot. She reached over and flipped the lock, then nearly fell out when Jackson pulled the door open. Righting herself, she stepped out of the SUV and held the handle up to show him.

"Sorry," she said. "I'll pay for it."

He didn't answer, just gave her a look that seemed to be a combination of exasperation and pity. When he turned away, she tossed the door handle into the car seat and shut the door, then followed him up the driveway to the house.

She tried to get her bearings as they climbed the porch steps and went through the front door, but it was too dark to see much. She hung back just inside the doorway as Jackson moved away, into the unlit front room.

Why wasn't he turning on the lights? Her nerves started jumping again, and she stared into the dark as hard as she could, looking for movement, shapes, anything. All she could see were shadows, and all of them seemed vaguely threatening.

She reached out with one hand and groped along the wall for the light switch. Just as her fingers found it, Jackson loomed up in front of her, and his hand slapped down on top of hers.

"Don't use the lights," he said gruffly. Pulling her hand from the wall, he pressed a large, heavy flashlight into it. "This place is supposed to be abandoned."

She found herself nodding to his back as he walked away. Fumbling with the flashlight, she flicked it on and shot the beam around the room.

It was mostly empty, with a lumpy-looking couch along one wall and a cheap coffee table in front of it.

There were large windows on two walls, covered with thick drapes. Maybe it was the drapes that made the place smell so musty.

"This way," Jackson said.

She took a few hesitant steps across the creaking wood floor, directing the flashlight all around to make herself feel safer.

"Keep that thing aimed at the floor," Jackson said. "The idea is not to attract attention."

Grimacing, she pointed the beam downward and tried to let her eyes adjust to the dim light.

"This is the living room. Kitchen's in there." He pointed to her left. "It's stocked, so keep yourself from passing out. Bedroom's through that doorway, bathroom's down the hall. There's a toothbrush and a few sets of clothes. You should have everything you need."

He moved back toward the front door, and she followed hastily, her mind racing as she tried to think of questions. Before she could say anything, he spoke again.

"Keep the curtains closed at all times. Don't answer a knock at the door unless you've been notified someone's coming. Even then, be on your guard. That flashlight makes a good weapon, not that you'd need it. You have a cell phone?"

Startled to hear a question after so many instructions, she stammered. "Uh, yes, yeah. I do."

He held out his hand. "Give it to me."

"Why?" She reached into her purse and dug out her little silver phone.

Pulling it out of her hand, he pressed a button on the back and cracked the case into two pieces.

"Hey!" she said, but he didn't even look up. He shook the battery into his hand, clipped the case back together, and handed it back to her.

"Cell phone calls are too easy to intercept. Now you won't be tempted."

"What if I need to make a call?"

"There's a land-line phone in the kitchen. Use it only if you have to. And don't be calling your friends to chat. You never know who could have a tracer on their line."

He moved away toward the door. "Any questions?"

Vi stood in the center of the dark living room, which seemed to loom larger around her with every moment that passed.

"What if I can't sleep? What if I get—" at the last second, she decided she couldn't admit she was afraid "—bored?"

In the dim light of her flashlight, she saw his eyes narrow, and he didn't say anything for a moment. Then, "This isn't a hotel, Ms. Marsh. There's no vibrating bed, and we don't get HBO. You're here because it's safe. That's your only concern."

His hand was on the doorknob, and her stomach clutched. He was an ass, but he was the only other human being around.

"Wait."

He didn't turn, and the door was open a crack. "What?"

"Can you just wait a minute? Could you turn around, please?"

She heard a short, impatient sigh, but he turned around. "You have more questions?"

"No, damn it!" She clutched the flashlight and held on to her purse for dear life. "I just… I've had a fairly terrifying day, and I don't think I'm…quite ready to be alone here. Could you just…wait?"

She didn't want to meet his eyes, but in the silence that followed, she couldn't stop herself. The light was uncertain, but for a moment she thought she saw something in his expression, something almost…pained. Then his face hardened as she watched.

"I'm not your nanny, Ms. Marsh. The house is safe, I checked it myself. You'll be fine."

He turned away again, and she barely stopped herself from hurling the heavy flashlight at him.

"You're a bastard."

He turned back, and this time there was no mistaking his expression. It was fierce, raw anger. "I'm a professional," he said, almost spitting the words out. "And if you're thinking about working with us, you'd better start acting like one, too."

Shocked, she took a step back, and he advanced on her.

"No one's going to coddle you through this gig, so get that idea out of your head right now," he said. "If you take Gideon up on his offer, you'd better get ready for the consequences."

Sucking in air, she felt her jaw clench. "Okay," she managed to say at last. "I didn't realize getting treated like shit went with the package."

"Don't take it personally," he said, in a tone that clearly implied *I couldn't care less about you.* "I just don't want a civilian endangering my operation or my team."

"Oh, yeah. I wouldn't want to screw up your little burglary assignment. God forbid that should go wrong."

He moved toward her until he was in her face, too close, looming over her, but she wouldn't step back again.

"Tell Gideon no," he said, the words low and gruff.

I plan to, she thought. Why didn't she just say it? Instead she studied his eyes for a long moment, then heard herself speaking. "I'll tell him whatever I want."

For a moment he didn't move. Then he took a step back, turned to the door and opened it. "Have a nice night."

He slid through the door and closed it behind him. Feeling a new rush of fear, she hurried to the door and turned the dead bolts, then let her forehead fall against the jamb.

She guessed a few more tears couldn't hurt now.

Chapter 7

Violet's eyes snapped open a few hours later. She stared at the ceiling, wishing she hadn't woken up, wishing for one of those where-am-I moments of free-floating nothingness.

No such luck. She knew exactly where she was, and she remembered everything that had happened.

Sighing, she turned her head to look at the digital clock on the battered nightstand next to her—6:27 a.m. Not so much earlier than she usually woke up for work, but then, on a normal night she'd have gone to bed at a much more reasonable hour.

She felt a sudden, fierce pull of longing to be at home, where her white-noise machine would lull her back into a few more minutes of sleep before she dragged herself into the kitchen for cold cereal and a peek at whatever soothing patter the *Today* show had cooking. Where she could turn the classic rock station up loud while she showered and got dressed for work. Where she could look out the window at the chittery little squirrels and think about maybe getting a cat or a dog.

Instead she was here, in a safe house that felt dangerous, and she had nothing but three and a half hours of sleep to keep her going.

Well, too bad for her. She wasn't going to be able to sleep any longer now, she could tell. Her mind was too full and her stomach was too empty.

At least the darkness was gone. She sat up and pushed back the stiff, olive-colored blanket on the unforgiving bed, noting the thin line of sunlight that gleamed through a crack in the heavy window drapes. The bare, stark bedroom was still dim and unfamiliar, but somehow, just that tiny bit of sunlight eased the oppressiveness.

She made her way down the hallway to the bathroom, peeling off the T-shirt and cargo pants she felt as if she'd been living in forever. She'd wanted to take them off to sleep, but she hadn't felt comfortable stripping down when who knew what could happen in the middle of the night. She'd had a long internal debate about even taking off her *shoes*—she had definitely not been willing to face some unexpected crisis in her skivvies.

It felt like heaven to get her clothes off now, though, and a long, hot shower felt even better. Afterward, she wrapped herself in a thin, white towel, swiped the steam off the medicine chest mirror and took a long look at herself.

Her face was pale, and there were dark circles under her eyes, but considering the ordeal she'd been through, she was holding up pretty well. She narrowed her eyes, studying her slicked-back hair. It was definitely growing fast—it was almost an inch longer than her usual chin-length bob. Fantastic. She was going to look like Crystal Gayle in no time.

A stab of hunger prodded her out of the bathroom and back to the bedroom, where she dug through the dresser until she found the clothes Jackson had mentioned.

Jackson. She frowned and tried to put him out of her mind as she pulled out a pair of gray sweatpants and a plain black T-shirt. She had bigger problems. If he wanted to be a jerk, there was nothing she could do about it. Anyway, what had she expected from a scary mercenary? It wasn't like he was the kind of person she'd want to be friends with.

She froze in the act of pulling on the sweatpants. *Melissa.*

Holy hell—Melissa was coming to pick her up this morning to go to the hospital. First thing this morning, she'd said—she could be on her way to the house now, and who knew what could be waiting there.

Cursing, Vi yanked the T-shirt over her head and jogged down the hallway to the kitchen, where she spun around in a circle looking for the phone. Spotting it mounted to the wall, she lunged for it and punched in Melissa's number with shaking hands.

It rang once, then again and again, while Vi bounced on the balls of her feet and wrapped her free hand around her waist. *Come on, Melissa, you're still there, you're still there…*

"Hello?" Melissa's voice had the husky but overly perky tone of someone trying to pretend she hadn't been asleep.

Vi let out the breath she'd been holding. "Melissa, you're still there."

There was a pause, and then Melissa spoke again, dropping the pretense of alertness.

"Vi? What time is it?"

"It's early. Sorry I woke you."

"How early? What…" There was another pause, then Melissa inhaled sharply. "Oh, God, are you okay? Is something happening?" Her voice was genuinely alert now, and filled with worry.

"I'm okay. But, yeah, something's happening." She paused, sighed, felt her stomach begin to rumble again as it slowly unclenched. Deciding she'd better get something to eat while she talked, she pulled the phone across the kitchen and started poking through cabinets.

Faintly, she heard the rustling of sheets as Melissa presumably sat up in bed. "What's happening? And where are you? You're not at home—your number didn't show up on my caller ID. In fact, nothing showed up. Weird."

"No, I'm not at home. I can't go home, and listen, Mel—you can't go over there, either. It's not safe."

"What do you mean?"

Vi pulled a can of soup from a cabinet and began opening drawers, busying herself looking for a can opener. How to explain this without sending Melissa into flat-out hysteria? She'd aim for matter-of-fact and hope it had a soothing effect.

"Well, I sort of…got attacked last night. At my house, after you dropped me off."

"What?" Melissa shrieked.

Vi winced. "I'm okay, Mel. Please, try to be calm. It's all right."

"What do you mean, 'attacked'?"

"I mean, there was some guy in my house, waiting for me. He tried to grab me, but I got that wooden owl thing off the wall and hit him with it, and he ran off." She figured the short, capsule version of events was best. Locating the can opener, she concentrated on fitting it to the can, turning the handle.

"Oh my God. Did he hurt you?"

Vi thought about the explosions of pain when he'd hit her face, about the bruises that were already just memories. "No, I'm fine."

"Oh my God," Melissa said again. "I can't believe this. What did the police say? Please tell me you called the police about this."

"I called the police. For all the good it did."

"What do you mean? They still didn't do anything?"

"There's not much they can do, Mel. The guy didn't leave behind any evidence, all they've got to go on is my crazy story, and frankly, they just didn't believe me." She got the soup open and realized she didn't have a saucepan to heat it in. She opened a lower cabinet and rummaged inside.

"What are you going to do?"

Vi pulled out the saucepan she'd found. "I think the best thing I can do is just stay away from my house."

"For how long? Where are you, Vi?"

Vi opened her mouth to answer, then stopped, clutching the saucepan. A shiver tickled up her spine. *For how long?*

The reality she hadn't acknowledged fell on her like a weight. She couldn't go home. Not today or the next day or any day in the indefinite future. She couldn't check herself into the hospital—she'd be a sitting duck for anyone who came after her. She didn't need one night in a safe house from Gideon. She needed a plan, something beyond breakfast this morning—a plan for her safety and a plan of action.

"Are you there? What's the matter?"

And she couldn't tell Melissa about any of it.

"I'm here," she said slowly. "But I think I have to let you go now."

"Why? What's wrong?"

"Somebody's looking for me," she said, thinking as she talked. "If they look hard enough, they might find you, and then...oh, God."

"Vi?" Melissa's voice was high and tense. "I don't understand what you're talking about."

Vi dropped the saucepan on the counter, knocking over the soup can she'd opened. She ignored the spreading mess and gripped the phone with both hands. "Look, you have to be careful, okay? Listen to me. I can't explain everything. In fact, you'll probably be safer the less you know about this. There's just two things you need to know. One—I'm safe, I'm fine. So don't worry about me. And two—the most important. Don't go near my house. Don't call my house, or my cell phone. Don't mail me anything. Don't try to find me. Just...pretend you don't even know me."

"Vi, what are you saying?"

"And you need to be careful in general. Try not to

go places alone. Keep your eyes open. *Damn it,* I've got to talk to Gideon about this."

"What? Wait…did you go back to see Gideon?"

Squeezing her eyes shut, Vi cursed silently and stomped her foot. *Stupid, stupid.*

"No, no. I didn't. Mel, I have to go. I'll call you again, okay? Just remember what I said, and please, be careful."

"Wait a minute—Vi!"

Grimacing, Vi hung up the phone. She shook her head and slowly turned back to the counter. It was early, but so far today, she'd managed to put her best friend in danger and botch her breakfast.

She definitely needed a plan.

On the ride back to Gideon's that morning, Jackson made Vi squish down into the foot well so that she was out of sight. He said it was for security reasons, but she suspected it was at least partly to make her uncomfortable and irritated.

Once they arrived and she'd stiffly unfolded herself out of the car, he silently led the way across the black-top parking lot to the back entrance of Gideon's run-down building. She followed him silently inside and into a storeroom, where he pulled back a metal door and hung up the keys to the SUV—apparently it was some sort of company car, rather than his own personal vehicle. Then she followed him silently down a dim, beige hallway that stretched the length of the building. Silence was a big thing for Jackson.

In spite of her determination not to let him get to her today, she could feel her nerves starting to jangle as their footsteps echoed through the hallway. She had to say something, just to break the tension.

"So, Jackson," she said, going for calm and breezy. "That your first name or your last name?"

He glanced back at her over his shoulder, but he didn't answer.

"Oh, it is a one-name thing, like Cher? Madonna? Beyonce?"

This time he didn't look back. She didn't know if that meant she'd irritated him, but she dearly hoped it did.

"So how long have you been working for Gideon?" she asked, speeding her steps a little to keep up with his long stride. "Is he a good boss? How're the benefits?"

He stopped suddenly and turned around, too quickly for her to catch herself, and she stumbled to a stop right in front of him, too close for comfort. He didn't pull back, so she refused to let herself move.

"You always ask this many questions?" His voice was gruff, faintly aggressive.

"Sometimes," she heard herself say. Why wasn't she more afraid of this guy? He was certifiably scary; he could probably break her in two with one hand. "Why? Does it bother you when I ask questions?"

His jaw tightened, and his eyes narrowed just a bit. Then he turned away and started walking again, and Vi smiled to herself. Score one for me, she thought.

Reaching the end of the hallway, he turned to a set of battered metal double doors and pushed them open. She stepped around the corner and stopped just inside the doorway.

Three men and a woman stood in a large, open room with dingy windows and an exposed-pipe ceiling. The room, which had a few pieces of exercise equipment strewn about, looked like a cross between a gym and a warehouse. The people looked unequivocally tough.

Jackson took a look around. "Where's Gideon?"

The biggest man in the room, a tall, beefy guy with a white-blond crewcut, stepped forward, his arms folded across his broad chest. "Said he was coming. This the girl?"

Jackson gave a curt nod and turned back to motion her forward. "This is Charlie Anders," he said, indicating the beefy one. "Former Green Beret."

Charlie, eyeing her suspiciously, jerked his chin up in a quick acknowledgment. She nodded back, sure her eyes were wide with apprehension.

Jackson pointed to a wiry man with dark hair and black-framed glasses. "That's Aaron Higgins. Navy."

Aaron glanced sideways at her and barely moved his head, keeping his fingers jammed in the pockets of his camouflage pants. Vi gave him a half smile and made a quick mental note—he might be just shy, but she was getting a vaguely disturbing lone-gunman vibe from him.

Jackson motioned to the only other woman in the room. "Sandra Camacho. Former police officer."

Sandra, her dark hair pulled into a tight ponytail and her jaw set belligerently, didn't even nod. Instead, she fixed Vi with a steely stare. Okay, gotcha, Vi thought, forgoing her own nod. No girl-power bonding possibilities there.

"And that's Todd Johannson," Jackson said, indicating the last man in the room, a stocky guy with thinning tufts of blond hair. "Private security."

Vi studied Todd's bland, kind face as he gave her a

friendly nod and smile and she returned the favor. He looked too wholesome and all-American to be a mercenary. Probably worked to his advantage.

Jackson jerked a thumb in her direction. "This is Violet Marsh. Accountant."

Vi shot Jackson a look, while Charlie gave an aggravated huff.

"She ain't really joining the team, is she?" he asked.

Jackson shrugged. "She hasn't said no."

Vi felt her eyebrows lifting. "She is in the room, you know."

"Gideon can't be serious," Sandra said, as if Vi hadn't spoken at all.

"Oh, but I am," Gideon said from the door. Everyone turned to face him as he walked into the room, completely at ease, hand tucked into the pockets of his suit pants. He stopped in front of her. "Morning, all. Violet. I trust you slept well?"

She smiled at him with fake sweetness. "It was delightful. Mind telling me what this is all about?"

"I thought you should meet the team you'll be working with. And everyone needs to hear the plan before any decisions are made. But before we get to that…"

He looked around the room for a moment, then beckoned the big blond guy forward. "Charlie, would you stand here, please?"

Frowning, Charlie moved to where Gideon pointed and stood with his arms still crossed.

"Right," Gideon said. "And now Sandra, you here."

Sandra's scowl was even more intense than Charlie's. "What's this about?" she asked, stepping forward with obvious reluctance.

"A quick demonstration," Gideon said. "Would you please stand in front of Charlie, and with one hand, push him backward as hard as you can?"

Sandra looked at Gideon as if he'd lost his mind. Everyone in the room looked at Gideon as if he'd lost his mind.

"What're you talking about?" she asked, her face wrinkled in suspicion.

"You'll see in moment. Please just do as I ask. As hard as you can."

Her eyebrows drawn down, Sandra shrugged and gave in. She walked to Charlie and put her hand on his chest. She bent her knees and seemed to coil herself up, then she released, pushing Charlie back with all her unleashed force.

But Charlie, who'd been braced for it, merely took a single step back and then regained his footing.

"Thank you," Gideon said. "Now let's try it again with Violet instead of Sandra."

Everyone stared at him again, and then Vi understood. He wanted a little superpower show and tell.

It didn't seem right for her to be jumping through hoops for him, when he was supposed to be the one trying to convince her, but she wasn't sure she should refuse. If she did, he might ask her to leave, and she hadn't figured out where she was going to go.

So she slouched over to Charlie and stopped in front of him. "So I just push him?"

Gideon nodded. "One hand only."

Shrugging, she stretched out her arm and pushed against Charlie's chest. He barely swayed, and she heard Sandra snickering behind her. Vi felt her cheeks heat a little, although she couldn't imagine why she cared.

"Try it again," Gideon said. "Put your weight into it this time, and remember—speed."

Fine. He wanted a demonstration, he'd get one. Bracing her feet wide apart, she flattened her palm against Charlie's meaty chest and bent her knees the way Sandra had done. Then she took a deep breath, locked her arm straight, and shoved back as fast as she could.

She gasped as her elbow sang with pain, and Charlie's smug face went surprised as he stumbled back, arms pinwheeling, then fell hard on his rear.

"What the hell?" Charlie asked as he scrambled back to his feet, his face flushed.

Vi clutched her elbow, and Jackson materialized at her side. He took her arm as if it were a stick of wood and looked it over, bending the elbow a few times. "Don't lock it like that," he said, frowning, then let her go.

"Very good," Gideon said, and Vi scowled at him, rubbing her arm.

"How come every time you want me to demonstrate I get hurt?"

With a smooth smile of apology, Gideon turned away from her and began to address the team. "As you can see, Violet has some…special abilities. We believe she's been genetically altered…"

She consciously tuned him out as he continued on—she didn't want to hear his song and dance again. Not when she still couldn't fully believe it. Flexing her arm a few times to work out the lingering pain from the impact, she kept her eyes on the floor until she felt a prickle of self-consciousness.

Looking up, she saw Jackson a few feet away, standing with his arms crossed. He was staring at her, his expression focused, assessing. She gave him her rudest look, hoping he'd turn away. To her surprise, he did, slowly shifting his gaze to Gideon. And while she knew it couldn't be true, she could've sworn she saw the faintest hint of a rueful smile tugging at the corner of his mouth.

Chapter 8

A few minutes later everyone shuffled down the hall to Gideon's plush office, where a surly-looking teenager with a shaved head slouched in front of a computer near Gideon's desk. Natalie was there, too, lounging on a leather couch against the wall.

Gideon motioned Vi toward the wing chair she'd sat in the night before as Charlie, Aaron, Todd and Sandra filed in and found seats, and Jackson leaned against the wall by the door.

"Violet, this is David Brooks," Gideon said, indicating the teenager.

David rolled his eyes. "I told you, it's 'Razor.'"

"It's David," Gideon said mildly.

The boy folded his arms and looked disgusted, but he didn't press further. Vi knew it was none of her business, and she had bigger things to worry about, but she couldn't help asking the question that came to mind.

"Um, shouldn't, uh, 'Razor' be in school?"

The boy turned to her, lip curling. "What are you, my nanny? Bite me, Mary Poppins."

Vi blinked, drawing back, and Gideon sighed. "Watch the mouth, David." He turned to Vi. "David doesn't go to school, for a variety of reasons."

Leaving it at that, Gideon moved past his desk and positioned himself next to a screen that had been set up against the far wall. Tucking his hands in his pockets, he cleared his throat once and had everyone's attention.

"We all know the objective we're discussing today," he said. "With David's help, I'm going to lay out the facility's security setup for Violet and the operation parameters as they currently stand. David, if you would."

David leaned across Gideon's desk and flipped on a projector, and a magnified replica of the desktop of his computer popped onto the screen. Someone—Jackson, she thought—hit the lights, and Vi tensed automatically at the sudden darkness. Then her attention was captured by the image David brought up on the screen.

It was the same exterior door she'd seen in the video Gideon had shown her. This was a still shot, but it was unmistakably the same. She strained her eyes staring at it, trying to find a clue about what it was, where it was. If she could find this mysterious "facility," she'd have something, even without the video.

Gideon indicated the screen. "This is the facility's only entrance. There are exits, but they're inaccessible from the outside. So this is our one and only point of entry." The image on the screen shifted, showing the door—a heavy, steel, fortresslike affair—from a different angle.

"The outer security setup is fairly standard—a card reader and keypad combo, plus a video monitor." The image shifted again, this time zooming in on a complicated-looking box next to the door. "That we can handle—Natalie can procure a passcard, David can decrypt the keypad, and as for the camera, that's a particularly simple matter, given that we've already tapped into the facility's video feed."

Vi took a breath and tore her eyes from the screen long enough to glance around the room. It amazed her how calmly they all took this; the idea of an illegal break-in was apparently old hat for these people. She wondered how they'd even gotten all this information about the facility's security system, but then decided she probably didn't want to know.

"So, getting through the door isn't a problem. However…" Here Gideon nodded to David, and the still photograph of the door disappeared from the screen, replaced by a 3-D computer line drawing of a long, narrow corridor. As they watched, a door at one end of the corridor opened.

"On the other side of the entrance door is a steel-lined corridor that leads directly to the security station, where one guard is typically posted." Gideon tapped the screen where a semicircle sat at the end of the hallway. "The guard is there to make visual confirmation that whoever's entered is authorized." A line-drawn human form appeared on the screen, coming through the open entrance door and beginning to move down the corridor.

"If he doesn't like what he sees," Gideon continued, "he initiates a security sequence that triggers an internal alarm and causes a gate to lower here." He tapped the end of the corridor near the security station, and on the screen a barred gate crashed down, blocking the human in the picture. Then a few pinpoints that clearly represented bullets crossed the screen, and the human figure fell to the ground, huge spurts of blood gushing out of it.

Gideon shot David a look. "As David has so...graphically illustrated, the outcome would be unfortunate."

Vi shook her head. If there were a prize for understatement, Gideon would definitely win it. A feeling of unreality settled around her. Was it possible this was all a dream? Maybe she'd been pulling an all-nighter at the office and was right now facedown on her keyboard, snoozing away.

"That's been the sticking point," Gideon was saying. "We've got to get someone down that corridor fast enough to get under that gate, then take out the guard and access the security panel to let the rest of us in."

The room was silent for a moment, and Vi looked around to see everyone staring at her. Her eyes went wide.

"What? Oh, no—me? You've got to be kidding."

"Violet, you've got speed," Gideon said. "Consider it your new gift. Temporary, we hope, but still useful."

"But I can't run, I've never been able to run fast..." Her words trailed off as she remembered running out of Severin's office, the surprising way the door had loomed up so suddenly she'd crashed into it. She'd been so upset at the time that it hadn't really registered, but looking back...

Then she remembered what Gideon had said the night before. *It wasn't until you left Severin's that it really hit me…* He'd seen her running down a hallway and this insane plan had clicked in his head.

"Oh. Oh. All right, maybe I can run fast, but this is nuts. I can't do…that." She gestured toward the screen, where the figure was still gushing blood.

"You can," Gideon said. "You'd need training, but we can provide that."

"I'd need a lobotomy," she retorted. "There's no way that—" she pointed to the screen again "—is ever going to happen."

From across the room, Charlie cleared his throat noisily. "I got to say, Gideon, it does seem like we'd be putting all our eggs in one basket, so to speak, and a pretty flimsy basket at that. We're supposed to trust the entire success of the operation to…her?"

Even though she agreed with him in principle, Vi still felt vaguely insulted by the sneering way he said the word *her.*

Sandra spoke up. "Yeah, Gideon, it's a bad idea."

"Agreed," Jackson said from his position by the wall.

"It's the best one we've got," Gideon said, lifting both hands, palms up.

"I thought David was going to do something to jam the signal," Todd said. "Make it so the gate can't be triggered."

All eyes turned to David.

David shrugged with one shoulder. "It might work. It's just kind of iffy, since I can't test it, and there's a chance—"

"A fifty percent chance," Gideon put in.

"Yeah," David acknowledged with a nod. "A fifty percent chance that it could cause the system's defaults to set in and bring the gate down, anyway."

Deflation swept across the room, and Vi looked around. Were they just going to give up and accept this?

"Well, think of something else," she said. "Can't you just, I don't know, send someone up to the door dressed like a pizza delivery guy? Wouldn't they let him in and down the hallway?"

Gideon and Jackson were shaking their heads before she even finished, and she noted with irritation that several of the team members were rolling their eyes.

"It's not that kind of facility, Violet," Gideon said. "The security personnel are a little too seasoned to be taken in by delivery guys."

She scowled at him, thinking hard. "What about... some kind of smoke screen? If the guard couldn't see who was coming in—"

"He'd trigger the gate immediately, on principle," Jackson finished for her. "Smoke screens don't exactly say 'authorized personnel.'"

Damn it. She jiggled her legs nervously, trying to jar an inspiration loose. "Well...hell, you guys probably don't mind killing people—why don't you just go in guns blazing and shoot the guard before he can hit the button?"

"Guard station's in a booth," Natalie put in from the couch. "Bulletproof glass."

"This is ridiculous," Vi said. "There's got to be some way to do this that doesn't involve me. What about— ooh, hey, what if you blocked the gate with something, like a big...block thing? You could slide it down the hallway to keep the gate from closing."

Gideon folded his arms over his chest. "It'd have to be some pretty precise sliding to make it stop exactly where the gate falls."

"I could build a robot," David piped up, and Vi looked at him with new affection. "With a remote control—"

"In a matter of days?" Gideon asked. "You know we don't have that kind of time." He looked at Vi. "You can keep trying, but we've all been going over this for days, and so far our only plan that doesn't involve you gives us a fifty-fifty shot. That's not acceptable."

He opened his arms, turning to the other team members. "I know this isn't a conventional plan, but I think it'll work. Even with the inherent risks, I think it's our best shot—possibly our only viable shot. She's a gift, don't you see? An opportunity, the piece of the puzzle we've been looking for—and provided by the very people we're working against. I say we use that to our advantage."

Everyone paused to digest that, and then a voice, high and nasal, came from the corner. It was Aaron, who hadn't yet spoken.

"Remind me again why we're doing this at all?"

Charlie huffed. "We need the money."

"We need the word-of-mouth," Sandra corrected.

"No," Todd said, looking irritated. "It's because we've got to get—" he broke off, and Vi looked around to see Gideon and Jackson shooting him matching icy stares "—the jewel," he finished weakly.

The jewel? Vi studied him, turning that over in her mind. Was that what this was about, what they were going after? Some jewel? Was this some kind of museum heist that had nothing to do with what had happened to her? She turned narrowed eyes to Gideon, who was shaking his head and rubbing his temple.

It occurred to her that this could be Gideon's con. Maybe he was telling her the truth about what had been done to her, about the genetic enhancement and the human experimentation, even about SynCor. Maybe he just didn't intend to help her do anything about it, but just wanted to use her instead for his own purposes.

"Violet," he said, looking at her intently, "this can work. We can train you, set your speed, do runthroughs, teach you some very basic hand-to-hand skills and get you in the door. And then you're done. It's easy, it's cake. And you get everything you want. Protection. A place to stay. You know you can't go home now. Your house is being watched around the clock. And a solution to your problems."

Oh, he was definitely playing her. She started to fume a little, her fingers itching to push her out of the chair so she could storm out of the room, except… where would she storm off to? He was doubtless right about her house, and she had to keep herself safe, make sure Melissa was safe, figure out a way to get the cops to believe her.…

She caught her breath as an idea occurred to her. Staring back at Gideon, she realized he wasn't the only one who could pull a fast one. If she told him yes now, agreed to his plan, she could stay in the safe house and stick close enough to him to snoop around and look for the video she needed, maybe even find other ways to get information.

He was playing her—why shouldn't she play him?

"Okay," she heard herself say. It came out quick and blurty in the silence that weighted the room. She could feel the surprised and disappointed gazes of several pairs of eyes on her.

Even Gideon blinked once before he smoothly smiled. "You'll do it?"

Not in a million years. "I'll do it," she said, pleased that her voice was firm.

He studied her for a long moment. It began to feel a bit too long, and she started to sweat a little. *He knows I'm lying. Or at least he suspects.*

"Good," he said with such satisfaction that she changed her mind. He couldn't know—he wouldn't be so pleased with himself. "You can start training now," he added.

"Now?" Somehow she hadn't thought about the fact that she'd actually have to do things to keep this charade going. Her stomach jittered nervously as she wondered what was coming next.

"Now," Gideon repeated. "We don't have a lot of time to get you up to speed. So to speak. Jackson will start you on hand-to-hand."

She flicked a glance over at Jackson, who was looking particularly unfriendly, and realized that knowing what was coming next wasn't always reassuring.

"Owwww…" Vi dragged the word out to help cope with the pain as she hopped around on the concrete floor of Gideon's gym and shook her right hand. She winced and stopped hopping, took a look at the scrapes on her knuckles that were fading before her eyes.

Jackson was impassive, standing beside a tethered

punching bag with his arms folded. "If you're hurting yourself..." he began.

"I'm hitting too hard, I know," she finished for him. "You've already said that like eight million times. You have a thing about repetition?"

"I'm hoping it'll get through your head at some point. You have more power than you think you do. But until you get it under control, it's useless. Hit it again."

Vi gritted her teeth and thought about hitting him instead, but she tamped down the urge. This wasn't fun, but it was part of her plan, and she'd get through it. Once this was all over, maybe she'd get the chance to hit him. For now she concentrated her anger on the bag.

She drew back her fist and shot it forward into the heavy bag.

"Owwww..." she said again, shaking her hand. Maybe it was the anger that was making her hit so hard. But she couldn't seem to get the level right—she either hurt herself or she barely made a dent.

"Again," he said, and she closed her eyes and took a breath and tried again. And again and again and again. Jackson didn't seem to notice that she was getting tired, that her hand was aching, that her breakfast had burned off and she was weakening. Either that, or he just didn't care. With each passing moment her frustration grew, which made her punches more energetic, until finally she felt a jolt of pain up her arm that shocked her into fury.

With a little shout, she cradled her injured hand, lifted her right foot and kicked out at the stupid bag as hard as she could. The cord tethering it to the gym floor snapped, and the bag swung away. She just had the presence of mind to step aside before it could swing back and knock into her.

Jackson stopped the bag and looked at her, his expression neutral. Breathing hard, she stared back at him, daring him to chew her out for her outburst. Instead he sighed.

"Take a break and cool off," he said.

"Fine," she snapped back, and she turned away and stalked to the opposite end of the gym. The pain in her hand was fading, and her temper was already waning, but it bugged her that she was losing it while he was as cool and quiet as ever. Didn't anything get to him?

Ah, something did. This morning, when she'd been pestering him, he'd gotten annoyed, she was sure of it. What could she bother him about now?

"Wow, I'm feeling weak all of a sudden," she said, keeping her back to him so he wouldn't see her little smile. "I think I have to stop and get something to eat. I don't want to pass out again."

He didn't respond, and she looked back to see him slipping out the door. Well, hell. So much for that idea. Hard to annoy someone who wasn't even listening.

She shook the last of the pain out of her hand and rubbed her temples. In the quiet of the empty gym, her mind stilled, and she didn't like it. Too much space to consider what she'd gotten herself into. It was unreal to think that her life—her hard-won, ordinary life—had swirled into this bizarre situation without warning. And here she was, on her own again, not a drop of kindness to be found.

"Here," Jackson said from behind her, and she spun around in time to see him lob something at her. Instinctively she reached out for it and caught it one-handed.

Unfolding her fingers, she saw that it was a granola bar. Well, well. She looked up at him, surprised by a little clutch in her throat. No need to get emotional, she told herself. He's not being nice, just practical. Still, he had at least been listening.

"You going to eat that or just look at it?" he asked.

Vi smiled. Aaaand we're back to our normal selves.

She unwrapped the package with painstaking neatness, pulling it apart at the seam and folding the loose ends over carefully. He watched her, completely immobile, but she could swear he was this close to tapping his foot on the floor.

"How much longer am I supposed to do this?" she asked, her mouth full of granola.

"As long as I say." His tone was flat, but she thought she heard just a hint of irritation.

"Well, I think I'm done for the day. I really do feel weak. I don't have any energy left."

"Yes, you do." He crossed his arms over his chest.

"How do you know? You don't know what I'm feeling."

"Because I know," he said. His teeth were clenched. Oh, boy, it was really working. "Now hurry up and finish that. We don't have all day."

Vi looked down at the granola bar. "This isn't easy to eat fast. It's very chalky. You should get those chewy kind. Ooh, with chocolate chips."

He glared at her. Hmm...possibly she was laying it on a little thick. If he caught on that she was goading him on purpose, he might stop reacting, and then where would her fun go? It was a perverse kind of fun, sure, but it was the only kind she was likely to get in her current circumstances.

She chewed and swallowed each bite carefully, but the bar was gone much too quickly.

"All right," she said at last, with great, obvious reluctance. "What now? More punching bag? Because I've got to say, I'm really starting to hate that thing. At this point, I'd rather fight a real person. Even an angry person." She thought about the man who'd been in her house, and suppressed a shiver. Maybe not.

"Not going to happen," Jackson said. "You're not ready."

She frowned at him. She'd just changed her mind about what she'd said, but still, it was kind of insulting, the way he said it. "Why not?"

Sighing, he unfolded his arms and braced his hands on his hips. Her eyes followed the movement. She had to admit he had really good hands. And hips. Nice, lean, sexy hips. Yes, yes, he was a very attractive man. Too bad he was a great big jackass.

"Because, Ms. Marsh, you only have two levels right now—shut down, or all-out. You're going to have to learn to rein yourself in, to use degrees of your power, before it'll be safe for anyone to spar with you. That's why I'm trying to teach you control."

"Uh-huh." Just to irritate him, she settled on the least important part of what he'd said. "You can call me Violet, you know. Or Vi. Everyone does."

He shot her a disgusted look. "Let's go." He turned away and walked over to a thick, cushioned mat on the concrete floor.

She followed him. "Why's this thing so squishy?"

"For your protection," he said.

She made a face. "I don't like the sound of that."

"What a surprise. Now, your basic fighting stance is centered in stability, so—"

"What?" she broke in. "Fighting stance—you just said we weren't going to fight."

"And we're not," he said testily. "You're learning fighting stances and basic forms of attack and defense."

She took that in for a beat, then wrinkled her nose.

"Gotta tell you, that sounds kind of dull."

A little muscle twitched in his jaw. "Then it's a good thing we're not here for your entertainment," he said, giving her a look so menacing that her feeling of satisfaction was tempered a little with nervousness.

Probably she'd pushed him far enough for the time being.

"The basic fighting stance," he began again, "is about stability. You want your weight centered and your balance steady. Show me what you think that looks like."

Taken aback, she shrugged. "I don't know. I guess— this?" She moved her feet as far apart as her shoulders and stood firmly, hands on her hips.

He sighed. "No. You're stiff as a board, you're not ready to move, and if I took a shot at your knee, it'd break like a twig."

Frowning, she looked down at her knee. "So…what? I should bend it?"

"Bend both knees."

She did, and he sighed again. "Not like you're doing a squat," he said. "Just bend them a little, and lift up onto the balls of your feet."

Awkwardly she tried to bend her knees the right amount and raise herself up on her tiptoes. He looked disgusted.

"Haven't you ever seen a boxer? Did you see *Rocky*? *The Karate Kid*? Anything?"

"Yeah, I've seen them," she said, scowling. "But I didn't run around pretending to *be* them afterward."

"Just try to be light on your feet, and don't lock your knees. And don't face toward me like that. You want whoever you're fighting to have the smallest target possible, so turn to the side."

She turned to face the left, and he closed his eyes in frustration.

"Not all the way to the side. You still need to be able to see your opponent. Just angle your body. Lead with your right side, and draw your left foot back."

"While I'm standing on tiptoe and bending my knees," she said.

"Are you going to let your arms just rest like that?"

She looked down at her hands, still on her hips. "Oh, I guess I'm supposed to put up my dukes or whatever." She raised both fists and pointed them in his direction.

"You're trying to fight me," he said, his voice low and gritty. "Not show me your engagement ring. Keep your arms close to your body."

She pulled her arms in close, trying to remember to keep her knees bent.

"Not like that," he said, his voice rising. "Elbows in. Damn it, are you listening to me at all?"

Pushed to her limit, she dropped her arms. "What do you think? I think I've done nothing *but* listen to you all damn morning."

"It doesn't show," he said, folding his arms and glaring at her.

"Hey, I'm trying," she said. "I'm sorry if I'm not quick enough for you, but this is all new to me, and you standing there barking out orders isn't doing me any good. 'Turn your body, bend your knees, keep your arms up, balls of your feet,'" she mimicked. "I don't understand what you mean. Do you get that?"

He was silent for a moment, then he rubbed the back of his neck and let out a long breath. Without warning, he stepped onto the mat and came to stand behind her.

"Hey, what are you doing?" she asked.

He didn't answer, just grabbed her hips in both hands. She sucked in a breath as a wave of shocked sensation radiated from his hands to all points of her body, and she was too stunned to resist as he turned her pelvis, angling it to a diagonal, making her chest and shoulders follow.

"Smallest possible target," he said, his voice low and tight. "Still facing your opponent, but turning the broad side of your body away, where he can't strike at it."

Unnerved as she was by his body close to hers and his hands on her, something about his words and the position of her body made sense. He bent and slid one hand down her right leg to her knee, and her eyes went wide. *Hello.*

"Don't think of it as bending. Just think of it as not being stiff." Nudging the back of her knee, he loosened it just slightly, and she positioned her left knee in the same way.

He continued down, dropping to one knee and reaching down to the heel of her foot.

"It's not about raising your body up on your toes. Just lift your heel, so your weight is centered on the ball of your foot." He pressed up on her heel until it hovered just above the ground.

Taking a few much-needed deep breaths, she tried to let her body get used to the position. It still felt weird, as if she were holding a pose, but at least it made sense.

Jackson wasn't finished. He stood behind her again and placed his hands on her shoulders, then ran them down her upper arms, squeezing her elbows in. She tried not to notice the way her skin prickled and tingled where he touched her.

"You use your arms to protect yourself as much as you use them to strike out. Keep them close." He lifted her fists, positioning them. "Power and protection. Attack and defense. It's all connected."

He stepped back at last, and she let out a slow, relieved breath. He walked around her so that he was facing her again, but he didn't meet her eyes, and she could only glance at him. For a moment they were caught in a weird, silent moment flush with something unspoken.

And then he spoke. "From this position, you have several options for attack."

His voice was even, and she forced herself to put the moment behind her, to concentrate on his words. But before she did, she had to squelch the fleeting thought that it was either a very lucky thing or too damn bad that he was the biggest jerk she'd ever met.

Chapter 9

She was almost there.

Holding her breath, Vi slid down another few feet in the hallway, torn between the need to move fast—Jackson would be coming back to the gym with her second granola bar any minute, finding her gone—and the need to move quietly.

Gideon's office door was tantalizingly close, and maybe the video was in there. Of course, maybe Gideon was in there, too, but if she opened the door and saw him, she'd just say she'd gotten lost looking for a bathroom. If he wasn't in there...

The idea of snooping through his desk, terrified of the door opening, made her stomach clench with distress, but she didn't have a choice. She had to take some action.

She slid the last few feet and reached for the doorknob, wincing as she slowly gave it a twist.

Locked. Crap. That meant Gideon was probably not in, and this would be a perfect time to get inside. If only she knew how to pick a lock. The funny thing was there were probably several people in the building who could teach her how.

She heard a noise from around the corner, and she panicked, not wanting to be found lurking in front of Gideon's door. Scuttling away down the hall, she turned a corner and tried the first door she found. It was unlocked, so she ducked inside and pressed herself against the door, listening for sounds in the hallway.

After a moment she looked around and realized she was in the storeroom where Jackson had stashed the keys to the SUV that morning. It wouldn't take him long to find her here—Gideon's building wasn't big enough for anyone to stay hidden for long. She should slip back into the hall and pretend to be lost, so at least he wouldn't catch her skulking here and get suspicious.

Damn it, this wasn't working out the way she'd hoped. It looked as though someone was going to be with her every minute, so when would she ever have a chance to search for the video? Maybe she'd been wrong to go along with Gideon's plan, to pin all her hopes on finding the video. But what else could she try?

Her eyes fell on the keys Jackson had hung up on the rack. She had access to a vehicle, then, not that she knew where to go. Her own house was being watched, and besides, the damn video—the only thing she really needed—was inside this building.

Although… She pushed away from the door and stared at the rack of keys, thinking hard. Maybe there was something else she could do. If her house was being watched, it was being watched by the people who'd abducted her in the first place. They were waiting for her, but they'd have to leave sometime, at least take shifts, and when they left, wouldn't they go back to wherever this mysterious facility was? If she could manage to follow them, wouldn't they lead her right to it?

The thought of going directly to the very people who wanted to find her—and do God knows what to her—made her feel a little dizzy and clammy. She'd be crazy to walk into their waiting arms. They were professionals. She'd be caught. She was totally out of her league.

She heard footsteps from the hallway around the corner, and her crazy-fast heartbeat skittered higher. Now or never. If she left now, she'd be alone—no Jackson taking the wheel, no Natalie on her tail, no one trying to stop her from getting information she needed. And no one to suspect she wasn't fully on board with the break-in plan.

Footsteps coming closer. Crap, no time to think about it anymore—it was either go or miss the chance. *Go, go!* something in her urged, and she felt herself moving, grabbing the keys and squeezing them into her palm so they wouldn't jingle. Grimacing, she pulled the door open silently and slipped into the hallway.

Steady, steady, she told herself as she tiptoed hurriedly down the hall to the parking lot door. *Just get to the car and get out of the lot. That's all. You don't have to make any bigger decision than that right now. Just don't...get...caught.*

She pushed open the outside door, and it squealed, high-pitched and loud. So much for slipping out unnoticed. Adrenaline propelled her forward, and she abandoned caution, sliding through the door, hitting the blacktop at a run, barely giving herself time to aim at the SUV Jackson had used that morning. She heard a shout from behind her, and then the SUV was looming up fast—too fast—she didn't have time to slow down.

She slammed hard into the driver's door, grunting with the impact and leaving a noticeable dent. *Damn.* If she was going to use this fast-running thing, she was really going to have to learn to stop without crashing. She yanked on the door handle and found it locked.

Another shout from the doorway, and with a glance to her left, she saw Jackson heading in her direction, looking pissed as hell. Frantically pushing buttons on the remote control key fob, she finally heard the chunky click that meant the doors were unlocked. Grabbing the handle, she pulled the door open and swung herself inside.

She jammed the key into the ignition with shaking hands—*steady, damn it!*—and revved the engine, then popped it into gear and hit the gas. The heavy vehicle lurched forward just as Jackson drew up to the window. His angry face was a blur as she whipped past him and out of the lot. Oh, she'd really done it now.

The SUV's tires squealed as she skidded onto the little industrial street Gideon's building fronted, but she didn't slow down. Jackson would try to follow her, she knew—he'd probably send out Natalie and some of the others, too. But if she could put enough distance between them now, she could make it. Surely they'd never think to look for her at her own house.

She sped around a corner, then another, then pulled onto a broad three-lane street and put the pedal down.

She was breathing hard, could feel a flush in her cheeks. It was scary, oh, yes—she was probably crazy to be trying to outspy these spies. And so rash—so unlike her usual careful, thoughtful self. But she had to admit it was exhilarating, too, in a strange way. Almost…a fun way.

She was definitely crazy.

Okay, time to think. She turned onto a side street and slowed the SUV to cruising speed. She'd made her getaway, she'd had her "fun." Now, the consequences. Was she really going to go through with her insane plan?

Sucking in a breath, she thought it over. It was certainly risky, but if she could be careful and stealthy, maybe it'd be worth it. Besides, she'd already gotten herself into trouble with Gideon and his pals—she should at least make it worthwhile.

But how was she going to pull it off?

It wouldn't be simple—first she'd have to locate whoever was watching the house without giving herself away, then she'd have to set herself up so that she could watch them without being seen, and all the while be ready to follow them when they moved.

She caught herself biting her nails and whipped her hand away, although…she supposed it didn't matter now, since they grew back so fast. Shaking her head, she refocused her thoughts. It'd be nice if she could take a drive down the street and look around, see if any suspicious cars were parked by the house or if any shifty characters were lurking about. But if they were watching the house, they'd probably be checking out every car that went by, too, and the big black SUV wasn't exactly inconspicuous.

The alley...she could park at the end of the street and sneak up the alley behind her house on foot, peek through the fence and see if she could spot anyone. It might work, but...

Oh, God, she was nuts to even be considering this. She should turn around and head back to Gideon's and hide herself away like a smart person. Like a normal person.

And do what? Nothing? That old feeling of helpless fear swept over her, and she deliberately whacked it back.

No. She wasn't, damn it, *was not* going to just lie back and let things happen to her. She might be stupid or reckless or nutty or all three at once, but she'd be damned if she'd be passive.

Setting her jaw with grim determination, she made the turn for home.

Gideon was full of it.

Shifting to adjust her weight off her aching knees, Vi crouched beside her house and faced the facts. There was no one watching her house. Gideon was a liar. Surprise, surprise.

And, damn it, she'd just wasted a lot of time creeping carefully up the alley behind her house, slipping silently through the back gate and peering through eight million knotholes in the fence before working up the courage to leave her backyard and move toward the front of the house.

From here she could see her entire front yard, plus the street to either side for two houses each way, and she hadn't spotted a single suspicious car or shifty, lurking character. The neighborhood street was as placid as ever on a Sunday afternoon, with a few lawnmowers buzzing in the distance and the occasional kid on a bike.

So there was no one trying to track her down. Gideon was the only one who'd ever had her watched and followed—hell, he was probably the one who'd sent that thug to hide in her house. The fact that Natalie had helped her fight him was probably just a decoy move, designed to gain her trust. Of course, it had seemed as though Natalie was hurt pretty badly, but who knew? Maybe the whole thing had been staged for her benefit.

Vi shook her head. At least she'd managed to give old Gideon the slip and pull a move he wasn't expecting. If he'd ever thought she'd sneak back here, he'd have planted some goons for sure.

Bracing her hands on her thighs, Vi straightened slowly and took a step forward into her yard. What did it mean, exactly? If Gideon was lying about SynCor, about the danger, was he lying about everything else, too? No, it couldn't mean she was home free. She still had the freaky mutant thing going on, and there was that video....

She wandered down her front lawn, staring at the street in front of her. But was it safe for her to go to the hospital? Did she still need to try to get the police to help her?

Movement caught the edge of her vision, and she glanced to the right to see a man shifting behind the wheel of a sedan parked three houses down. For a moment she just looked at him, almost puzzled by the sight, and then his eyes locked on hers and widened.

Vi froze. *Oh, no.* It couldn't be. It could not be.

Before she could think anything more, the man was leaning on the door and pushing himself hurriedly out of the car. He was a burly guy with Lorenzo Lamas coiffed blond hair and a thick blond beard, and he wore jeans and a leather vest with a tank-style undershirt beneath. He looked menacing, and he was heading her way.

A shock of adrenaline speared through her body, and she didn't care if he was actually harmless and well intentioned, and she didn't care if she was overreacting and would look like a fool. She spun on her heel and began to run, aiming for the backyard and the alley.

She heard a grunt behind her, then heavy, thudding footsteps breaking into a run. Damn it, he was going to chase her. Dread pooled in her stomach as the relief of moments ago slipped away. Gideon hadn't been lying, she wasn't safe, and the only piece of good news she had was that she'd surely be able to beat this guy in a footrace.

Bursting through the back fence gate, she hurtled across the backyard, trying to align herself with the gate at the opposite end. If she could hit it at the right angle and not get tripped up, she could zip into the alley and be gone, gone, before he could—

A sharp sting in her right shoulder broke her thoughts, made her stumble. She gasped and clutched at her shoulder, saw a yellow plastic tube with some sort of fuzzy thing sticking out of it. She'd just had time to recognize it as a tranquilizer dart before another one zinged by her left arm and plunged into the ground in front of her.

Damn it. Her brain fogged with panic. How much time did she have? How far could she get? How long until the drug...

The earth shifted and tilted, and everything went dark.

Vi awoke to the feeling of grass prickling against her face. For a moment that was the only thing she was aware of, and then her other senses began to trickle back. She heard the sound of her own breathing, smelled the soil under her nose, felt a twitch in the muscles of her arms behind her back.

Tied behind her back, she realized. She opened her eyes and saw blurred colors. Blinking, she concentrated on focusing, and gradually things became clear.

She was facedown in the grass with her hands tied behind her back, and the tranquilizer she'd been shot with was quickly wearing off.

She jolted as the memory of panic and the need to run came back, and she was on the point of struggling up to her knees when she heard a voice. Stiffening back to stillness, she listened hard.

"Take it easy, Doc. We'll have her back safe and sound in no time. T.J.'s getting the car in place now."

The voice got louder, and she assumed the speaker— it had to be leather vest guy, right?—was getting closer. She tried to look tranquilized as she listened to his footsteps approaching.

"Nah, she's out," he said, nudging her shoulder with the toe of his boot. *Asshole.* Vi felt fury boil up, and she fought the urge to bite him on the ankle.

"Only took one dart," he said. "It barely touched her and she hit the ground. Must be getting weak."

Untie my hands, and I'll show you weak.

Vi pushed aside her anger and struggled to get her thoughts in order. She had to make a plan, and fast. This guy was probably *not* going to untie her hands, so she was going to have to do that herself, and then… She swallowed hard. She wasn't sure how she was going to get away from leather vest guy and whoever was getting the car, but she'd just have to improvise. There was no way she was letting them take her anywhere.

"Not a problem. I told you, you worry too much." Leather Vest's voice had faded a bit, so he must be turned away. She should make a move now, while he was off guard, and before the other guy got back and she had to deal with two of them.

She sucked in a quiet breath and couldn't stop herself from wishing for Natalie, Jackson—hell, even Gideon—anyone who could help her. But she was on her own.

Well, she was used to that.

Steeling herself, she moved fast, rolling to her side and tucking her legs underneath her, then lifting herself up on her knees. As soon as she was upright, she clenched her jaw and jerked her wrists apart as hard and as fast as should could. With a snapping sound and a painful scrape against her skin, the cord broke and her hands were free.

"Get her to the—" Leather Vest turned toward her and stared, his mouth open but no sound coming out. She used the time to scramble to her feet, gearing herself up to try hitting him, but he dropped his cell phone and lifted the pistol-style tranq gun that was clutched in his right hand.

Shit, not another dart. She could not go down again. Moving on instinct, she reached out fast and swept her arm down, crashing into his wrist. He shouted and dropped the gun, and Vi dove for it, hitting the ground and grabbing it as she rolled away from him.

Then she heard a sound to her left, and she whipped her head around to see a man there, this one beefy and dark-haired, coming at her with a puckered brow and a mean, beady gaze.

Before he could reach her, she lifted the tranq gun and pulled the trigger. She wasn't much of a shot, but he was close, and—thank God—the dart plunged into his leg. He grimaced and clutched at his thigh, but he kept coming.

Rolling back onto her feet, Vi leaped backward to avoid his outstretched arms—why wasn't he going down? The tranq had worked on her in seconds—and found herself entangled with Leather Vest, who wrapped his meaty arms around her, pinning her arms to her sides.

Beady Eyes stumbled forward a few steps, stopped to yank the dart out of his leg, then went down on one knee.

"I'll take that," Leather Vest grunted in her ear, and she realized that he was grabbing for the tranq gun. She tried to maneuver it away from his hand, tried to get it into position to shoot him, but she could barely move her hand. Before he could wrench it away from her, she opened her hand and dropped the gun by her feet, then stepped out and smashed down hard with her booted foot, breaking the plastic casing into bits.

"Bitch!" Leather Vest said, just as Beady Eyes fell

face-forward on the grass. *Finally.* That was one down; now she had to get away before the third guy got back. Jerking wildly in Leather Vest's grasp, she fought to get free, swinging her shoulders and kicking backward with her legs. He squeezed her hard enough to knock the air out of her lungs, lifting her up so that her feet swung free, hitting air and nothing else, but she didn't stop. If anything, she felt more frenzied by the minute. Had to get away, had to, had to…

Her heel connected with his shin at last, and he yelped, his arms loosening as he flinched. Vi pressed her advantage and swung her arms up, pushing off his crushing embrace and untangling herself from his grasp. She ran hard for the gate and the alley, and she heard him following, his steps unsteady.

Good, she'd hurt him. *How's that for weak?*

She scrambled through the fence gate, slammed it behind her to slow him down, and ran down the last of the driveway just as a gray sedan pulled into view up the alley.

"T.J., watch it," she heard Leather Vest yell from behind her, and the man in the car saw her and yanked the wheel, turning the car so that it slanted across the alley, blocking her path.

She couldn't stop. Slamming hard into the side of the car, she groaned at the pain but managed to pull her legs up and roll herself onto the car's hood, scrambling across as the driver opened his door. She'd just reached the other side when the driver got around the door and grabbed her by the arm, pulling her down. She lost her grip and slid where he dragged her, hitting the concrete ground hard on her side.

The man loomed over her, large and fierce, blotting out the sunlight overhead, and she froze for an instant—*insanity, this isn't me, this isn't real*—and then she pushed herself up and got her feet beneath her as the driver reached for her again.

Furious and scared and loaded with adrenaline, she moved without letting herself think, kicking out with her right leg as hard as she could and landing a solid blow to his midsection. He doubled over and stumbled back, reaching out to grab her foot. She snatched it back and hopped once to get her balance, then jerked her left knee up to smack it into his forehead.

He groaned and fell over backward, curling into a ball and clutching his stomach and his head. Vi took a breath, shaken by the power running through her. She could hear Leather Vest sliding across the hood behind her, but she felt almost ready for him. She could take him down, she could—

"Don't move," he said, and his hand whipped around her and pressed something cold to her throat.

A knife. He had a knife.

The courage draining out of her, Vi stilled.

"I'll slit your throat," he said, his voice a rasp of menace. "Don't think I won't. I'd enjoy it. Never thought you'd fight this hard. Doing you now would be a pleasure."

Vi gulped, conscious of the razor's edge at her throat as the muscles there worked. Her breath came fast and shallow, and her mind was a blank of fear.

"I could—" he began, but a noise from the alley in front of him cut him off. An engine, a car horn...

Leather Vest jerked his head to the side, and his arm

went with it—just a fraction, but she felt it and knew it was her only chance. She grabbed his wrist with both hands and pushed down and out, forcing the knife away from her throat. He recovered quickly and tried to yank her back in, but she was squeezing through the space she'd made, slipping away, struggling...

A line of fire burned her arm, and she realized she'd run against the knife, but she didn't stop, pulled herself backward, pushing him off. She broke free just as the car squealed to a stop in front of her, and she glanced over and saw Natalie behind the wheel and nearly went limp with relief.

No time, no time. He slashed at her with the knife, and she leaped back, scrambled for the car, narrowly avoiding his lunges, and then she grabbed the door handle, putting the door between them, and she was in.

"Shut the damn door," Natalie shouted, and Vi slammed it closed just as he grabbed for it, while Natalie popped the gear into reverse, swiveled in her seat and hit the gas.

Leather Vest receded as the car sped backward down the alley, and then they were on the street and gone.

Natalie looked at the blood oozing out of Vi's arm and shook her head.

"Girl, you are more trouble than you're worth, you know that? And you're lucky I can read your damn mind and knew just where you'd go." She pulled her cell phone out of her pocket and began to dial.

Limp with exhaustion and drained of emotion, Vi couldn't even summon the strength for a comeback.

Chapter 10

By the time Natalie pulled into the parking lot of Severin's office, Vi's arm had stopped bleeding and she was dragging her feet. The last thing she wanted now was an encounter with Dr. Bad News, and she knew she'd have to face Gideon, too, who was sure to be pissed as hell. But since Natalie had just rescued her—again—she didn't think she should press her luck by protesting.

Natalie didn't say a word as she led the way across the lot and pushed open the office door. Vi followed her in and then stopped, hugging her arm to her chest, when she saw Jackson standing in the waiting area.

Natalie took one look at his expression, which Vi was trying not to notice, and held up both hands.

"Okay, I'll let you take it from here. Bye." Just like that she pivoted and headed back out the door. Vi stared after her for a moment, bereft, then slowly dropped her arms, squared her shoulders and turned to face Jackson.

He was glowering, hands planted on his hips. "Nice trick," he said, his lips barely moving.

She shrugged halfheartedly. "I figured you'd be impressed."

His green eyes flared, and she knew her joking tone was only provoking him, but what was she supposed to do? Fall on her knees and beg his forgiveness? Maybe she'd made a bad decision, but she'd been backed in a corner, and she'd be damned if she'd apologize for trying to get herself out.

"I am impressed," he said. "I'm impressed you've lived this long, if that's the kind of stupid stunt you'll pull." He took a step toward her, and his ferocious gaze was so intense that she had to fight to keep from backing up. "Don't try it again."

She felt her eyes narrowing as he stirred some well of pure defiance in her. "I'll do what I want."

"You won't have the chance. I'll make sure of that." He turned away and jerked his thumb toward the hallway. "They're waiting for you."

Clearly dismissed, she bit back the words crowding on her tongue. There was no point in making him any more of an enemy now. She had enough of those.

The fight went out of her as she made her way down the hallway, and she felt numb exhaustion creeping back in.

She stopped at an open door and saw Severin and Gideon inside the small room she'd been in before, with the bad dolphin painting and the hospital bed.

They both looked at her intently, Severin with cold curiosity, Gideon with cool rebuke.

Sighing, she stepped into the room. "All right, get it over with," she said to Gideon. "Go ahead and yell all you want."

At a gesture from Severin, she sat on the edge of the bed and let him take her injured arm.

"I don't want to yell, Violet," Gideon said. She wasn't really surprised. He didn't seem like the yelling type. He was too unruffled for that.

"I would tell you that you took a very big risk," he continued, "but I believe that point has already been made." He looked at her arm, which Severin began to swab with an alcohol-soaked pad. Vi hissed at the sting.

"Is it all right?" Gideon asked Severin.

Severin was shaking his head in a tsk-tsk way. "Half-healed already. There will be scarring."

Vi frowned at him. "Why scarring? If I've got super-healing…"

He kept his concentration on her arm. "Your skin knits together too quickly," he murmured. "The cells that do the repairing work carelessly. They don't stop to match the existing pattern of the skin. Thus, scars."

Vi shook her head. "Great. I'm going to be a human hash mark pretty soon."

"You could avoid that by being more careful," Gideon pointed out. "For instance, you could refrain from running away from the people trying to help you and toward the people trying to hurt you."

"I did what I had to do," she said, watching Severin press a bandage to her arm. "You won't give me any information about them, so I went to get it."

"And nearly got yourself captured or killed. That's not the way to help yourself, Violet. You're going to have to trust me to help you."

"Why should I trust you? You don't want to help me. You don't want me to be careful. You want me to take a much bigger risk than the one I took today."

He lifted an eyebrow. "True. In a manner of speaking. But you won't be alone, you won't be unprepared, and you won't be doing it for nothing." He stopped, looked at Severin and seemed to shift course. "Severin, would you update Violet on your findings?"

Vi looked at the doctor warily. "You found something? About me?"

"I conducted an examination of the blood sample drawn at your last visit," Severin said, his back to her as he tidily stowed the bandages and alcohol he'd used.

Shaking her head in puzzlement, Vi looked at Gideon, then the answer dawned. They must've drawn blood while she was unconscious. "God, don't you need my permission to test my blood?" She rolled her eyes. "Then again, why am I expecting ethics at this late date?"

Severin turned to face her, blinking. "I could destroy the results, if you wish."

She sighed. "Oh, just tell me what you found."

"You have a virus," he said. "Or rather, you have what appears to be a virus."

"Jenkins' disease," Gideon said, as if confirming it, and Severin nodded.

Vi looked at each man in turn, not understanding the significant glance that passed between them. "Yeah, I know. I've had it since I was a kid."

Her mind flashed to that horrible time in the hospital, six years old and sick as hell and alone too much of the time because her mother couldn't handle it.

"This is somewhat different," Severin said. "As you may recall, Jenkins' disease invades human cells and causes a violent initial reaction that typically lasts two to three months. After that time, although the virus remains in the body's systems, its effects are stabilized."

"Right," Vi said, a little impatient. "You can live with it, no problem. Living, breathing example, right here," she added, gesturing to herself.

"Exactly," Severin said. "But there is something new. When your blood was tested, a new marker appeared. Not just the childhood strain, which of course still remains, but a recent infection. Further analysis points to an artificially modified form of the virus. It would be valid to hypothesize that this is a carrier strain—not an attacker, but a medium. Do you see?

Vi stared at him. "Not at all."

He squeezed his eyes shut, and she figured he was going through the painful mental process of dumbing down his science talk to her level.

"Jenkins' disease—like all viruses—reproduces, spreads, indeed exists, by taking over other cells. Hijacking them, if you will. It invades a cell and replaces that cell's programmed instructions with its own set of commands. In this regard, it would make an ideal delivery method for a genetic-mutation code."

She blinked a few times, trying to grasp it. "Wait. You're saying that the genetic, whatever—enhancements that I have...they got in me through a virus? A fake Jenkins'?"

"It's a plausible theory," he answered, "made more compelling by the fact that, as you know, of course, you have no natural immunity to Jenkins' disease."

"So? So what?"

He lifted his eyebrows. "Ninety-eight percent of the population of this country is naturally immune to Jenkins'. You're very rare."

She'd forgotten that. Some faint memory came back to her now of all the different doctors who'd examined her during the worst of the sickness. They must have come from all across the country to study her because the condition was so unusual.

Gideon spoke up. "This could be why they targeted you, Violet."

Vi pressed her hands to the sides of her head and squeezed. "So, what do I have now? Double Jenkins'?"

"No," Severin said. "Your immune system recognized this recent infection as Jenkins' disease, something it wasn't equipped to fight. But it wasn't Jenkins'. Hidden under the viral markers was an entirely different genetic instruction code that has apparently resulted in...well, what has changed about you."

Closing her eyes, Vi rubbed her forehead with her fist and tried to absorb it all. She supposed it might explain how she'd gotten all mutated, and maybe that would come in handy later, but she wasn't sure what she was supposed to do with it now. Why was Gideon giving her this information now?

"Violet," he said, and she wearily lifted her head and looked at him. "Severin has uncovered all this information from one blood sample, with limited resources. Imagine what he could do—or what any doctor could do, anyone you want—with the information that's inside that facility."

Ah, now she understood. This was just another weapon in Gideon's arsenal of persuasion.

"I get it, Gideon, but why the hard sell? I already agreed to do what you want."

"Yes, you did," he said, eyeing her with just enough cynicism that she feared he could see right through the charade she was trying to pull. Uh-oh. "But I also want you to agree to trust me. Completely. I am working in your best interest, as this information should demonstrate. Any attempts to undermine what I'm doing will actually hurt your cause."

"In other words, you don't want me running off again." She thought about Jackson saying she wouldn't have the chance, anyway. They were going to be tracking her pretty closely now. Might as well get some goodwill out of it.

She nodded. "All right, deal. I put myself in your capable hands."

Until I can find a way out of them.

Brian's eyes felt as if they'd bulge right out of their sockets, push out far enough to touch the lenses of his glasses.

"What do you mean, you don't have her? You told me you had her." He stared at Lowell, forgetting his fear of the man in his nauseated agitation.

"We did have her when I called you," Lowell said, his tone low with menace. "Then shit happened."

"*Why* did you tell me you had her?" Brian said. He pulled off his glasses, rubbed his eyes. Why had he gotten so cocky, so overconfident? Why, oh God, why had he taken the initiative to call Harriman, to tell him he would definitely see something dazzling on his visit?

"This is a disaster," he said to Lowell. "Do you realize what position you've put me in? Do you understand how much I need her here?"

"She's special," Lowell said, almost to himself.

"Exactly," Brian said, nodding for good measure. "I need her—specifically her, no one else." He thought of the handful of viable candidates he'd identified on the list of Jenkins'-diagnosed patients that SynCor had somehow produced for him. There were others, but there wasn't time now to pursue those options. He had to have *her*—the list was useless now.

The cursed thing had caused enough trouble, anyway. Harriman, who'd been so grand about presenting it—another roadblock he'd removed from the path of science—had used it for his own foul purposes, had used it to find…

Brian shook his head, pulled himself back to the present and looked across his desk at Lowell, who was standing with his arms crossed over his thick chest, staring into space.

"I need you to get her for me," Brian said, aware that his tone was almost pleading.

Lowell turned his head slowly to stare straight ahead. "She's special to me, too. Can't let her get away now."

"Right," Brian said, ignoring the chill that raced up his spine. "You've just had a setback, that's all. She's no match for you."

Lowell finally met his eyes at that. "Of course she's not," he said gravely. "She's just getting help from someone. Gotta find out who, gotta find out where she's staying." He stroked his beard for a moment, then nodded. "Gotta talk to her little friend."

Brian had the distinct feeling he was hearing more than he wanted to know. "Fine, fine," he said. "Just… make sure you keep it quiet. I've already got enough publicity to worry about with…the other."

His gaze far away again, Lowell continued to nod to himself. "Leave it to me, Doc. One way or another, I'm going to get her."

Vi spent Monday morning making phone calls, even though Jackson had told her not to. Whatever, she was already on his bad side, and since she fully planned to return to her normal life as soon as possible, she had to do a little maintenance on it in the meantime.

The first call had been to her boss, who unfortunately hadn't become any more sympathetic to her "illness" over the weekend. *You're my go-to girl, Vi-let,* he'd said in his particular nasal way, then he'd reminded her again about the Payton quarterlies and started pressing for a doctor's note. Vi hadn't taken that very seriously until his tone had changed just before she'd hung up. A hint of a threat had crept into his voice, and a nervous clench had started in her stomach.

Maybe she'd better ask Gideon if Severin could fake up a note for her. Steve would be a fool to fire her—she was the hardest-working accountant he had, and up until this unfortunate incident, she hadn't taken a sick day in more than two years.

Of course, Steve had been known to be a fool.

Guilt and worry churned around in her gut at the

thought of losing her job. Trying to do something to reassert her control, she'd called her closest office friend to ask for a favor, and Lisa had promised to sniff around and see if Steve was really on the warpath.

Now she had just one more call to make, and she didn't have much time before Jackson picked her up for another glorious day of training. And she really didn't want to be on this call when Mr. Scowl showed up.

She frowned as she dialed and felt annoyed by the thought of Jackson. She'd had a dream about him the night before. So irking. It wasn't enough that she had to be around him all day—now she had to have him in her head at night?

And it hadn't even been a fun sex dream, damn it. Instead, he'd just looked at her in that way he did sometimes, all intent, as if he were seeing all the way down to her toes, and then he'd reached out and brushed her cheek with the back of his hand....

She closed her eyes and breathed for a moment, remembering. All right, maybe it had sort of been a sex dream. Whatever. It was still...annoying.

"Hello?" Robert said on the other end of the line, and Vi jerked, her eyes snapping open.

"Hi, Robert. It's Violet. Violet Marsh. Sorry to call so early."

There was a long beat of silence on the line, and Vi started chewing on a fingernail.

"You're calling me?" he said at last. "I don't really see how that fits into your plan to blow me off."

She winced. "I'm so sorry, Robert. I swear I haven't been trying to blow you off. My life has just...gone crazy, and I haven't had a chance to call."

It wasn't exactly true—she could've called him immediately. But she hadn't felt up to talking to him until she had some kind of grip on her emotions.

"Are you all right?" he asked, his voice still gruff but with a hint of grudging concern. "I was pretty worried when you didn't show up at Figaro's the other night. Didn't seem like you."

"And it's not, I promise you. I can't apologize enough. And I am…all right, but things are going to be a little nuts for me for a while. I've got this…family thing." She closed her eyes and silently apologized to him again for lying, but there was no way he could handle the truth.

Well, maybe he could handle it, but she couldn't handle telling it to him.

"Can I see you?" he asked, and she melted. Oh, he was so nice.

"I wish," she said fervently. "And, yes. I just don't know exactly when. Can I call you when things calm down a little?"

There was a knock at the door then, and all of Vi's nerve endings went into high alert. "I have to go," she blurted before Robert could even answer her question. "I'll call you, okay? Sorry, thanks. Bye."

She hung the phone back up in its cradle as quietly as she could and went to open the door.

Jackson was frowning at her. As usual.

"You just open that door for whoever knocks?" he asked.

She rolled her eyes. "What do you want, a secret password? I knew it was you."

"No, you assumed it was me."

"If you're thinking of giving me that speech about making an ass of you and me, please spare me." Man, the things that came out of her mouth with him. Why did she always have to antagonize him? Fun was fun, but it couldn't be a good idea to continually poke at the scary mercenary.

He glared at her, but he didn't rise to the bait. Luckily. Instead he reached into the pocket of his jeans and pulled out a silver bracelet. "Put this on," he said.

Vi looked from it to him and batted her eyes. "For me? I'm afraid it wouldn't be proper to accept jewelry from a gentleman I hardly know."

"It's not jewelry, it's a tracking device." Impatient, he grabbed her hand and draped the bracelet over her wrist, and she instantly saw her mistake. She should've stopped screwing around and put the damn thing on herself. Then he wouldn't be…touching her.

"It's got a locator chip inside it," he explained, his fingertips brushing the sensitive inside of her wrist as he worked the clasp. The metal was warm against her skin, warm from his pocket…warm from his body. Vi swallowed and tried to listen. "So if you pull a stunt like yesterday, we won't have to get lucky and guess where you've gone."

He took her hand and rotated it, then pointed to a guarded button on the bracelet's side. "This is a panic button. Lift the guard and press it if you get into trouble. And don't take this bracelet off, at all. It's waterproof, so you can wear it—"

He stopped, and she looked up, and their eyes locked together as the words *in the shower* rang clearly in the air. He was too close, and her dream was fresh in her mind, and she did not need to be thinking about nudity at this moment.

"Fine," she said, pulling her hand out of his grasp and averting her eyes. Damn it, she was not going to get a crush on this guy. It would be stupid, it would be inconvenient, it would be *hopeless,* and it might even be dangerous.

Besides, he wasn't even nice. Nothing like Robert. Jackson was a jerk ninety-nine percent of the time.

"Let's move," he said, turning for the door. "We don't have all day."

Her point illustrated. Shaking her head, Vi followed him out.

Chapter 11

Vi took a deep breath and looked down the long section of Gideon's gym floor that had been taped off in the dimensions of the facility's entrance corridor. Behind her Gideon was directing traffic, getting team members into position, but for the moment Vi was ignoring him. Instead she was trying to imagine how terrified she'd feel if she actually had any intention of going through with what they were about to practice.

She crossed her arms over her chest and squeezed. It was crazy to even think about. But she had to act as if she were fully onboard with the plan. No one was very happy with her after her disappearing act yesterday; she needed to do a convincing job today if she wanted to stick around long enough to find the video. And that meant not screwing up.

It hadn't taken much perception to figure out that the

entire team—except Gideon—thought she'd never be able to do it, that she couldn't get the job done, that she was going to blow "the op," as they called it. In spite of her better judgment, that rankled a little. She wouldn't mind showing them all that she *could* do it, if she wanted to.

"You have two seconds," Gideon said, and Vi shook herself out of her thoughts and back into the moment.

"What?" She turned to face him, and he held up a stopwatch.

"According to David's study of the security system, you'll have two seconds from the time you enter the corridor to the time the gate is fully closed. That's how long you'll have to get down the hallway and to the security station."

"To fight the guard," she said, inwardly shuddering at the thought. She'd had enough fighting in the past two days to last her a long, long time.

"To disable him, yes," Gideon said. He turned and waved Natalie and Todd over. "You two will handle the door. Todd, you'll hook up the transmitter so David can complete the pass code decryption. Natalie—how's the keycard coming?"

"Already got my target lined up," she said, examining her fingernails. "They're standard models, so I can swap it out, and he'll just think his malfunctioned next time he keys in."

"Good. Now, Violet, you'll have to do the initial run alone, of course, but once you access the security system and deactivate the alarm and the gate, the rest of us will enter. You'll find a terminal to access your data— it shouldn't be hard—while the rest of us complete our objective. We'll be going in at night, so on-site person-nel should be limited. Still, we'll need to move quickly in case the initial alarm summons reinforcements. And that's it. It's really fairly simple."

Yep, simple. Simply suicidal. "How will I know how to deactivate the system?" Ah, that was a good question. Made it seem like she was really invested in how this all worked out.

"David will be training you beforehand, and you'll be in radio contact with him during the operation so that he can direct you in anything unexpected. Understood?"

She nodded, and Gideon smiled in that charming way of his that usually only served to annoy her.

"Then let's give it a try."

The team members all stood back from the taped-off corridor and folded their arms. All eyes on her. She swallowed and got into position in front of the "door."

"Don't hold back, Violet," Gideon said. "The faster you can go, the better."

Jackson cleared his throat, and Vi looked over at his typically scowling face. "But keep it under control," he said.

She rolled her eyes. "Thanks for the conflicting ad-vice, fellas. Can I just try it?"

"Whenever you're ready," Gideon answered, hold-ing the stopwatch in start position.

She stared down the fake corridor again. The weird thing was, she wasn't sure how she was able to run fast. It didn't feel any faster to her—it felt like one foot in front of the other, just like running had always felt. It was just that everything around her zoomed by so quickly, somehow. The idea that the whole thing was basically out of her hands was a little scary.

No more stalling. Leaning back so she could push forward with a little momentum, she clenched her hands into fists and jumped forward. *Stomp, stomp, stomp*— her first footfalls were jarring and awkward, then she slid into a smoother rhythm, gunning forward hard. She saw the line of tape that represented the gate flash by under her feet, and then the gym wall was looming. Easing up, she tried to slow herself, dug in her heels with each step, but momentum carried her stumbling forward until she smashed hard into the wall with her left shoulder.

Damn it. She crumpled down to her knees and clutched her upper arm, feeling the ache from the jarring impact spreading to her chest. She heard murmurs and movement from across the gym, and then someone touched her elbow. She opened her eyes.

Jackson.

"You all right?" he asked, his voice neutral.

Grimacing, she nodded and let him help her stand up. "Guess I didn't do so well on that control part. How about the speed?" She looked at Gideon, who shook his head.

"It was two point six seconds when you hit the gate line," he said.

Her shoulders slumped. So much for proving anything. And so much for her plans. If she couldn't do it, if it wasn't possible…what would Gideon do? Toss her out to fend for herself?

She watched him nervously while Jackson crossed his arms over his chest. "Are you satisfied now?" he asked Gideon. "It's not going to work."

Gideon didn't even blink. "Not going to work? She hit less than a second away from the target time on her first try. I'm nothing if not encouraged."

Vi saw a muscle twitch in Jackson's jaw, but Gideon just turned away, his eyes focused on the taped-out corridor. "I think the cold start might be part of the problem." He turned to look at her. "Violet, if you had time to run up to speed before you hit the door, do you think you'd go faster down the hallway?"

She shrugged. "I'm not sure. I barely know how I'm doing this. But how would I get extra time, anyway? We can't exactly hold the door open while I get a running start."

"No, but if we time it correctly, we can have you start running from a position several yards back, and Natalie and Todd can open the door just as you reach it."

Jackson shook his head. "Oh, good. Let's make this more complicated."

"This is bullshit," Sandra said, stepping forward with her arms crossed.

"Easy, Sandra," Gideon said. "Give her a chance."

"She's just going to screw it up," Sandra said. "Even if she can get down there fast enough, what's she gonna do about the guard—crash into him? She can't fight."

"She did all right yesterday," Natalie noted mildly. "And that was two guys."

"Three, actually," Vi couldn't stop herself from correcting.

Natalie did an impressed little eyebrow-pop, but Sandra just laughed, a harsh sound.

"Yeah, she did so good she almost got knifed," she said. Charlie guffawed a little in the background as Sandra turned to Natalie. "If you hadn't shown up to help her, she'd probably be dead now."

Vi hoped she was imagining the relish in Sandra's voice at the idea of her hypothetical death. She wasn't sure what she'd done to inspire the venom Sandra was unleashing, but she really didn't need it on top of everything else.

"I think you can do it, Violet," Todd said, and Vi turned to look at him, grateful for the unexpected show of support. Then she noticed the way the other team members turned away from him just slightly, the faintly sour expressions on their faces—even Natalie's.

Great. She'd just gotten a vote of confidence from the team outcast. Big help.

She looked at the hard faces around her, and for a horrifying second, it was fourth grade all over again, a ring of merciless kids shutting her out, marking her as different.

"Look, can we just try it again?" she said, stomping down on her feelings. She couldn't afford to get emotional, not now, not when her plan was at stake.

"That's the spirit, Violet," Gideon said, leading the way to a spot several feet from the door line. "You can start from here this time, and we'll see what difference that makes."

Nodding, Vi squared off at the point Gideon indicated and eyed the mocked-up corridor of tape. Her left shoulder throbbed a little and her thoughts jangled in her head as she tried to focus.

Settling herself, she rocked back and jumped forward again, finding the rhythm, tucking her arms against her sides to try to make herself aerodynamic.

Sights flashed by in her peripheral vision, almost blurry, but she focused on the line of tape ahead of her, willing it to be under her feet and behind her.

Then it was, and the wall was there in front of her, and she wasn't—

"Turn!"

She heard the shout and understood it at the last possible second, planting her right foot and wrenching her ankle as she pivoted hard away from the wall. With new room to run, she managed to slow herself to a limping jog before she reached the wall that was now in front of her.

Leaning against it, she sucked in air. "Thanks," she said to the room in general, as if she didn't know who'd shouted out the instruction. As if she hadn't known his voice.

There was quiet for a moment, and then Gideon spoke. "Two point three. We're getting closer."

Vi groaned inwardly at the thought of trying it again. This was a lot of work to go through for a mission she never actually intended to carry out.

"She's hurt," Jackson said, coming toward her. "I need to take a look at that ankle."

"Let's take a break," Gideon said, and Vi watched the team members head for the door as she slid down the wall to sit with her back against it. Gideon strolled over to watch as Jackson crouched down, reached gently for her right ankle and began to hike up the leg of her cargo pants. Ridiculously, she felt herself blushing as she remembered how her legs looked—she hadn't exactly been making time for shaving the past couple of days, and her damn hair grew so fast now it was impossible to keep up with it, anyway.

It didn't matter. She had bigger problems, and it was probably a sign of impending insanity that she'd even thought about it when she had so many other worries to occupy her mind.

Jackson didn't seem to care, anyway. His touch on her ankle was clinical, impersonal, as he lightly probed for swelling.

"We need Severin?" Gideon asked, and Jackson shook his head, standing up.

"Seems like just a mild sprain," he said. "On her, it'll probably heal in minutes.

Gideon nodded, looked at his watch. "In that case, I'll excuse myself. We'll pick up in half an hour and see how she's doing."

Now it was just her and Jackson again. Her nerves tightened another notch, and she tried to think clearly. She should get him to leave, that's what she should do. So she could make another stab at looking for that video, sprained ankle be damned.

"I'm a little hungry," she began, but Jackson laughed harshly and shook his head.

"Don't even think you're going to pull that one again," he said. "I'm not letting you out of my sight, so forget it."

Damn. The worst part was, she actually was a little hungry. Of course, she was always a little hungry these days, but now that she'd cried wolf once, she was going to have a hard time getting any granola out of him again.

Crossing his arms over his chest, he leaned back against the wall. "If you're going to do this," he said, his eyes on the opposite wall, his voice low and filled with disapproval, "you're going to have to get yourself under control."

Vi flushed and fought back a sudden rush of emotion—resentment, self-pity, anger and hurt all rolled into a big, ugly ball that lodged in her gut.

"Yeah, I get that," she said.

"I don't think you do. If you make it under that gate just to crash into the security station and hurt yourself, you're going to be in a world of trouble."

Never going to happen, she reminded herself, but she felt her shoulders pulling taut with tension, anyway. "I'll figure out how to do it, okay? But you barking at me isn't going to be the thing that helps."

He turned to look down at her. "I'd like to know what would, because it seems to me you're not making much progress."

Her mouth popped open in surprise. "Hey, it's been a day since we started training. One day. And, yeah, I'm having a tiny bit of trouble adjusting to my new, mutant, weirdo body, but I'm doing my best. So why don't you just get off my back?"

He was facing her fully now, his arms at his sides, his glare intense. "Why don't you leave?"

Oh, ouch. Sucking in air, she could only stare at him as the shock of his words slapped against her.

"Where the hell am I supposed to go?" she asked when she could find her voice.

"Go anywhere. Figure it out."

"There's nothing to figure out. I'm stuck here. Don't you know I'd rather be anywhere else? I don't have a choice."

"You always have a choice." He turned away again,

his expression disgusted, and Vi glared at him, anger boiling up.

"You have a choice, too, you know," she told him. "You could help me, since you're so damn inconvenienced by my presence. I've got to have something to take to the police, and you could help me get it."

He shook his head. "I can't do that. You don't understand."

"Well, explain it to me. What is this big mysterious mission about? Don't I deserve to know what I'm helping you do?"

He looked at her, his lips compressing to a thin line, and for a moment she thought he was considering it. Then he shook his head again. "All you need to know is that if you go through with this, there's a very good chance you'll end up dead. Do you get that? Dead."

Don't listen to him, she told herself. He's just trying to shake you up. You're not going to do it, anyway.

But her stomach was quivering. She pressed a hand to it and struggled to keep her tone light and acidic. "Thanks for the vote of confidence."

"Stop making jokes!" he burst out. "What do I have to say to get this through your head? I'm talking about your death. The end of your life. Don't you care? Doesn't that scare you?"

"Of course it scares me!" Oh, shit. Now she was crying. She couldn't believe it. Crying. Again. And in front of him.

Swiping at the tears she couldn't stop, she turned her head away and fought to keep her voice level.

"You don't think I'm scared? I didn't ask for this, and I don't know what the hell I'm doing. But what am I supposed to do, just lie back and let it happen? I've got to do something, and no one's going to help me, so I'm helping myself."

Her voice was going squeaky as her throat clamped shut. She stopped talking, and concentrated on not fully losing it in front of him, trying to breathe.

For a while there was no sound but her own faintly gasping breaths. She wasn't even sure he was still there, and she wasn't sure she cared.

Then she heard him curse softly, heard a rustle of movement, and looked over to see him crouching next to her. His expression was grim, but for the first time in a long time it wasn't hostile.

"I can help you." He said it quietly, his voice a little hoarse.

She blinked at him, wary and surprised. "What do you mean?"

"I can keep you safe, give you a place to stay. But you have to tell Gideon you won't do the op."

Something sounded…too good to be true. Vi studied him for signs that he was lying. "Why would you do that?"

"I don't want you on this operation, Violet. You'd be endangering all of us, but at least we know what we're getting into, whether we like it or not. You don't…you don't seem to understand the danger."

Whoa, this was getting weird. She sniffed and swiped at her wet face. "Are you saying you're worried about me? About my safety?"

"Of course I am. You think I don't care about what happens to you?"

"Um, I didn't, no." She took a breath, tried to absorb

this new information. "You've pretty much been a jerk to me since I met you, so…"

He laughed a little, not the harsh sound she'd heard earlier but a soft, rueful chuckle. "I thought I could change your mind. Scare you off. I've been fighting Gideon about this, about you being here, but he—" he stopped, shook his head "—he sees things his own way. So I figured if I made things as hard as possible for you, you'd bail out. I thought you'd be gone by now. You're tougher than I thought."

"I'm not that tough." She sighed. "I just don't have any options."

He shook his head again. "No, you're tough. You complain a lot, and you don't know what the hell you're doing, but you're tough when it matters."

It was the nicest thing he'd ever said to her, and it made her feel a little better just to hear it.

"So, do we have a deal?" His eyes were almost urgent, and for the first time, a little tinge of guilt washed over her. He was genuinely concerned about her—had gone to some lengths to try to protect her, in his own weird way. And she could relieve his mind immediately just by telling him the truth: that she had no intention of going through with the mission.

But if she did that, and if she took him up on his offer of protection, where would she be? Hidden away, running away, safe but powerless, and far removed from her only access to the evidence she needed to ever get back to her life.

"I can't," she said softly, and his eyes flared with anger. "I'm sorry," she added, searching for some version of the truth, some way to make him understand.

"Look, it's very nice of you to offer. I appreciate it," she said. "But I have to do something, you know? Something more than hiding. They—" she grimaced, trying to get to the heart of it "—they took my life away from me. I was…" She stopped short of saying she'd been happy, shook her head. "I was content, I had the life I wanted, a life I worked hard to get, and they just blew it to hell. I can't just do nothing, accept what they did to me. I want my life back, and I won't let them make me helpless."

He looked away, and she studied the line of his jaw, clenched in displeasure. She supposed he was going to revert to jerkitude now, since she hadn't done what he wanted. It was probably just as well, since his being nice to her had felt way too good for a moment, there. She remembered the way he'd smiled at her when they'd met in the park, those two days ago that seemed like months. Probably just as well she wouldn't be seeing any more of that smile.

He stood up and took a breath, blew it out. "I guess I can understand that," he said. She blinked at him as he turned toward her again. Man, he was all full of surprises today.

He held out a hand to help her to her feet, and she reached for it reflexively, then hesitated for a split second. Somehow, his strong, masculine hand looked about a hundred times sexier now that he wasn't being a jerk. Oh, boy.

For God's sake, just touch him, she told herself, and she grabbed his hand and hauled herself to her feet, then broke the contact as quickly as she could.

"How's the ankle?" he asked.

She stepped on it lightly, testing it under her weight, and felt no stab of pain. "I think it's better."

"Good," he said, lifting his eyebrows. "Because we have a lot of work to do."

Chapter 12

Hours later Vi slumped in a hard folding chair in an unfinished room off the front hallway of Gideon's building. The room wasn't much to look at—unpainted drywall, concrete floor, plastic sheeting, and dust everywhere—but that was okay with her, since she barely had the energy to move her eyeballs.

She'd lost track of the amount of punishing physical work she'd done, the number of times she'd practiced the corridor run, the multitude of hand-to-hand drills Jackson had put her through. She only knew that she'd finally learned to run the corridor in the time limit without crashing into the wall, and that she'd never been so exhausted in her life.

Glancing over at Todd, who was standing near the door with his arms folded and a nervous half smile on his face, Vi realized she should think of a way to give him the slip so she could look for the video. But the thought of sneaking around the building made her want to groan. Hell, the thought of standing up made her want to groan.

Besides, Todd would get in trouble if she got past him—he was supposed to be "keeping her company" while Jackson got some work done—and she didn't want that to happen. Todd had brought her some Twinkies from his personal snack stash, so she was feeling very warm toward him. Jackson had brought her food from time to time, but it was always granola or trail mix or fruit, never anything good.

After a moment she mustered the energy to unwrap the last Twinkie, which she'd balanced on one out-stretched leg, and took a grateful bite. She could almost feel the sugar zinging into her bloodstream.

She must've made an appreciative sound, because Todd looked up and smiled a little more than usual.

"You ever try the deep-fried kind?" he asked.

Vi struggled not to make a grossed-out face, because he was being nice. "Deep-fried Twinkies? Um, no. Are they…good?"

He nodded fervently. "You can only get them at car-nivals or the state fair, but I've been thinking about get-ting a deep-fat fryer for—"

He broke off as a crash and a shout rang out from the tiny lobby of Gideon's building. Forgetting her weari-ness, Vi scrambled to her feet, still clutching her half-eaten Twinkie, and followed Todd to the door. More shouts and sounds of commotion kicked her crazy-fast heartbeat up another notch, pounding in her ears. Was someone trying to break in Gideon's front door? Someone coming for her?

She cautiously poked her head into the hallway and then gasped when she saw Sandra and Charlie standing over a person—a woman—who was facedown on the floor. Sandra had a gun trained on the woman, and Charlie was shouting, "Who are you? Who are you?" over and over.

In the chaos, Vi could hear the woman's muffled voice, but she couldn't understand what she was saying until Charlie finally paused for a breath. Then—

"Melissa. I'm Melissa!"

"Holy shit!" Vi shouted, and she leaped forward, recognizing Melissa's dark curls. "Back off, both of you." She pushed Sandra aside with more force than she'd intended, and the woman went stumbling back, crashing into Gideon's heavy front door.

Vi winced but didn't stop. "Sorry," she threw out, and she squatted down next to Melissa and took her arm. "You okay, Mel?"

Melissa, her hair tousled and her eyes wide, sat up slowly. "What the hell?" she whispered.

"You know this person?" Charlie asked, quivering with suspicion and anger.

"Yes, she's my friend. It's fine—she's not going to hurt anyone."

Sandra stepped forward again, still clutching her gun. "She was trying to break in. I caught her myself."

"I was just looking for Vi," Melissa said. "I knocked, but nobody answered, so I just thought I'd see if the door would open if I pushed a little."

"I saw you on the security monitor—" Sandra began, but Vi cut her off.

"It doesn't matter. She's fine, it's fine. Everyone needs to chill out."

"What's going on?"

Vi looked over to see Jackson striding down the hall toward them. She helped Melissa to her feet and turned to face him, noting the typically grim set of his face.

"Everything's fine," she told him. "My friend Melissa came looking for me, and…there was a mis-understanding."

Jackson looked around slowly, taking in Charlie's red face, the gun in Sandra's hand—hell, he probably even noticed the half-Twinkie Vi had dropped on the floor—and nodded. "So I see. Charlie, Sandra, I've got this. Go cool off."

With disgruntled faces, the two shouldered past Vi and Melissa and moved off down the hallway. Vi took her first easy breath since she'd seen Sandra's gun.

"Everyone all right?" Jackson asked.

Vi nodded. "Jackson, this is my friend, Melissa Delgado. Melissa, this is Jackson, uh…" She stopped, blinked. "Wow, I guess I still don't know your last name. Or your first name, whichever one's not Jackson."

He didn't answer her implied question, just regarded Melissa expectantly. "Nice to meet you, Melissa. What are you doing here?"

Melissa gulped a little under his scrutiny, and Vi stepped in. "She came here to find me. Don't get mad—"

"How did she know where to find you?" He shook

his head. "Damn it, Violet, I told you not to give that information out. Lines can be tapped—"

"I didn't," Vi said, deciding it was best not to mention her little slip on the phone the day before, when she'd blurted Gideon's name. "She already knew I was dealing with you guys, so I'm sure it wasn't much of a stretch to guess where I was."

"That's right," Melissa said. "And I needed to talk to Vi. I wouldn't have come if it weren't important."

"I bet you also wouldn't have come if you'd known you'd be thrown to the ground as a welcome," Vi muttered, shaking her head. "Sorry."

Melissa lifted an eyebrow and wiped some dust off her silk blouse. "You might be right about that. Of course, if you'd called me, like you said you were going to, I might not have had to come down here at all."

Vi winced. "I'm sorry, Mel. I just thought it'd be safest for you if I didn't contact you."

"What, you were afraid someone might figure out we're friends and come to me looking for you?"

"Yes," Vi said. "I wanted to keep you out of it."

"Well, too late," Melissa said, her expression grim.

Jackson frowned. "Something happened?"

Melissa nodded. "Some guy came to my apartment today, right after I got home from work. He said he was from your office, but Vi, he did *not* look like an accountant."

"What did he look like?" Vi asked, a bad feeling forming in her stomach.

Melissa's face wrinkled in distaste. "Big, burly. Poofy blond hair and a beard."

"Leather Vest," Vi breathed, and Jackson and Melissa

both looked at her. "That's the guy with the knife," she told Jackson.

"Knife?" Melissa asked. "You didn't tell me about any knife—you said a guy tried to grab you, and you hit him with the wooden owl."

Vi waved a hand. "Oh, yeah. That was earlier. Possibly the same guy, different day."

Melissa gaped at her. "Vi, what is happening? What are you doing here? What's going on?" She paused, leaned forward with intent eyes. "Are you wearing a wig?"

Vi's hand went reflexively to her messy hair, which seemed to have grown another half inch overnight. "No, it just grows really fast now. I know it looks awful."

"No, it doesn't. It looks good." Melissa eyed her thoughtfully. "You look good in general, actually."

"Can we talk hair and makeup later?" Jackson broke in. He turned to Melissa. "Tell me about this guy. What did he say?"

"He said they'd tried to contact Vi at home but hadn't been able to reach her, and they were getting worried and did I know where she was," Melissa said. "I didn't tell him anything, so you can stop looking at me like I'm an idiot."

Vi shook her head. "Don't take it personally, Mel— he looks at everyone that way."

Jackson shot her an irritated glance, and Vi shrugged. "See what I mean?" she said to Melissa.

"Did he say anything else?" Jackson asked, and Melissa scrunched up her face, thinking.

"I don't think so," she said slowly. "He just kept pressing me, if I knew anything, if I'd heard anything.

He was pretty creepy. Oh, he did write his name and number on a card." She looked around for her purse and found it on the floor by the door, where she'd dropped it in the scuffle. Digging inside it, she pulled out a white business card and held it out.

Vi reached for it—surely the name of the guy who'd attacked her would be of interest to the police—but Jackson intercepted and snapped the card from Melissa's fingers. Vi gave him her most pained expression.

"Come on, Jackson. Give me something."

He just shook his head and glanced briefly at the card, then pocketed it. "Sorry. Don't take it too hard, though—I'm sure it's a fake." He looked at Melissa again. "Anything else?"

She bit her lip, thought for a moment. "I don't…I don't think so. He left, finally, and I waited until he pulled out of the parking lot, and then I came here."

Jackson went very still. "You came here. Right after he left."

Vi studied him, not sure what to make of his expression. What did he…

Realization dawned swiftly, and she felt her mouth forming an *O* of concern as his eyes met hers.

In trying to do the right thing, there was a very good chance Melissa had just led Leather Vest right to her.

Jackson didn't give them much time to talk. Vi had barely found Melissa a place to sit down—on the folding chair in the unfinished room—and a cup of coffee to steady her nerves, and Melissa had barely started firing questions at Vi—"Why aren't you at the hospital?"

"What are you doing here?" "Who's this vest guy?"—before Jackson leaned into the room.

"You ready?" He was looking at Melissa, who glanced at Vi for the answer.

"She has to leave?" Vi asked. "Why can't she stay a little longer?"

He shook his head. "Security issues. We can't have her here. I'll have Charlie follow her home and make sure her place is safe."

Melissa shot Vi another look, and this one clearly said, "Hell, no."

Vi decided to pick her battles. She knew she couldn't change Jackson's mind about Melissa leaving, but she could negotiate on the how of it. "Um…how about not Charlie? He did just have her on the floor a couple of minutes ago."

"I'm sure he's very nice," Melissa put in apologetically.

"Actually, he's an ass," Vi told her. "But I'm getting used to him. He can take me home, and Jackson can take you."

Melissa nodded approvingly at that, in a way that seemed almost too eager. Something tiny and petty and jealous clicked inside Vi, and she did her level best to ignore it.

"No," Jackson said. "I'm not leaving you to Charlie if this guy knows where you are."

Vi looked at him pointedly. "What, he's good enough for Melissa, but not for me?"

"Melissa's not the target," he answered. "He doesn't need her anymore—he already got what he wanted from her."

Melissa was looking back and forth between them, and her expression suddenly melted into horror. "Oh, my God. Do you mean he followed me here? Oh, *stupid!* I never even thought—"

"Mel, don't worry. It's just a maybe," Vi said. "We don't know if he did or not." She didn't meet Jackson's eyes, because she already knew what was in them. There wasn't any "maybe" about it in his mind.

"Will you just take her?" she asked him. "I want to make sure she's safe, and Charlie's only going to scare her."

"Fine," he said. "But you stay here. The security's better here than at the safe house, anyway. I'll take her home and then come back for you."

Vi nodded. "Works for me."

"I'll be right back," he said, and ducked out of the room again.

Looking at Melissa, Vi smiled a little. "You okay with this?"

"What? Him following me home?" Melissa shrugged. "I guess. It's a little weird, but what isn't weird about this whole thing? I guess I trust him if you do."

That was an issue still under consideration. "I trust him...to keep you safe," she said. "Beyond that, who knows?"

For the first time, Melissa grinned. "He is a little mysterious, isn't he?"

Vi laughed. "To put it mildly."

"It kind of works on him, though, doesn't it?" Melissa said. "I mean...*damn.*" She lifted her eyebrows and made a face that Vi recognized as her "hottie alert" expression.

Frowning, Vi opened her mouth to say something about appropriate times and places, then stopped when she remembered the inappropriate zing that had shot up and down her body the first time she'd seen Jackson. And the second time she'd seen him. All right, every time she'd seen him.

Apparently, he had that effect on every woman within a ten-mile radius. She wasn't sure why she found that fact depressing.

Footsteps in the hallway caught her attention before she could say anything, and she turned to see Jackson appear in the doorway with keys in his hand. Jackson, coming to take her friend—her beautiful, elegant, size-two best friend—home. To keep her safe.

With a hug and a promise to explain everything soon, she let Melissa go. But she couldn't let go of the weird flip in her stomach as she watched the two of them walk away together.

Chapter 13

Half an hour later, Vi paced the perimeter of the unfinished room for the millionth time and thought, for the millionth time, about the moment when Jackson had led Melissa into the hallway. Had he almost touched her then, when he'd gestured with his arm? Had he *wanted* to touch her? Had there been some subtle flash of attraction in his eyes? She felt vaguely nauseated every time she thought about it, but she couldn't seem to stop.

Shaking her head, she tried to refocus her thoughts. She ought to be worrying about Leather Vest. If he and his cronies knew where she was, they could be making a plan to break in at this very moment, could start busting down doors at any second. Still, nothing had happened yet, and it was hard to stay on high alert for very long.

She blew out a long sigh and stared blindly forward.

Even if Jackson was attracted to Melissa—and let's face it, what man wouldn't be?—that didn't mean anything was going to happen, just because they were currently alone together. Melissa wasn't the type of person to hook up with random strange guys, and she would never make a move in the direction of stealing a guy away from a friend.

Not that Jackson could be stolen. Because he wasn't Vi's. Which was fine. She didn't want him. Hell, Melissa could have him, for all she cared.

Grimacing, she brought both hands up to scrub her face. It was no use. She couldn't ignore it, couldn't deny it, so she might as well admit it.

She had a thing for Jackson.

It was stupid, inconvenient and not something she had time for, but, apparently, it was there anyway. She wasn't sure how deep it went—probably not very deep, considering she'd only known him a few days, and he'd been a jerk for most of that time—but it was real.

No good can come of this, she told herself, but it had no effect. Her stomach still did that uncomfortable flip when she thought of him with Melissa, and her breath still went short when she remembered her dream about him, or when she pictured his green eyes that looked all the way through her, so focused, so intent…

Pulling her mind away from the image with effort, she looked desperately around for a distraction. Todd was walking up and down the front hallway—she could talk to him. But so far, junk food was their only common interest, and she didn't think she could muster up much more to say about that. Besides, it would only make her hungry.

She stepped into the back hallway, the long one that ran the length of Gideon's building, and saw Charlie leaning against the far wall. She gave him a brief, polite nod and moved quickly to her right. No way was she going to try to talk to him.

Passing the door to Gideon's office, she gave it a longing look, but Charlie was watching her, so she didn't have a prayer. She kept moving, going by the open-plan workspace room where she saw Sandra sitting at a computer—nope, no conversation possibilities there.

The gym was on her right, but she didn't feel like even thinking about the stupid taped-off corridor and all the practice she'd been through that day. She felt tired again just remembering.

Muffled music caught her ear, and she took a few steps farther down the hallway. She'd never been past the gym, and she glanced back to see if Charlie would stop her, but he didn't budge. With a shrug, she moved to the closed door of the last room on the left.

She thought about knocking, but the music—it sounded like death metal—was blaring so loudly on the other side of the door that she doubted she'd be heard. Instead, she cracked the door open and peeked inside.

A blast of head-splitting music washed over her, and she saw David—"Razor"—sitting with his back to the door, tapping away at a computer keyboard and bobbing his shaved head to the beat.

Did she want to talk to a surly teenage computer genius? From what she'd seen, he wasn't very friendly, but maybe he'd at least be interesting. Anyway, he was the only one she hadn't tried talking to, and it was talk or sit around thinking about Jackson, so she might as well give it a shot.

"Hey," she called out, but he didn't turn or seem to hear her at all. She took a few steps into the room, noting the cheap fold-out tables that lined every wall of the long, narrow room, the scribbled-on white boards on the walls and the computers, monitors, loose electronic parts, and unidentifiable equipment littering every surface. This must be David's dedicated space.

She spotted a portable stereo on the table closest to her, so she walked to it and turned the volume down. Way down.

"Hey!" Spinning around in his wheeled chair at the far end of the room, David shot to his feet, his face furrowed with anger. Vi held up both hands in a surrendering gesture.

"Sorry," she said. "You didn't hear me come in."

"That's why I like it," he said, his lip curling in that snarl she wasn't sure was authentic. "What do you want?"

She shrugged, a little deflated by his hostility. "Nothing. I'm just bored. Is it okay if I sit down?"

He struggled with that for a moment, his eyebrows knitting, then he turned away. "Whatever."

Vi blew out a breath. Off to a great start. She threw herself down in another wheeled chair, then heard a crack as the plastic support column snapped under the force of her flop. The chair buckled beneath her, and she scrambled to her feet, her face hot.

David was looking at her with disgust. "Gah, watch what you're doing," he said.

"Sorry," she mumbled. She found another chair and

sat down slowly and carefully. David turned around again, and she watched him hunch over his keyboard. The room settled into quiet, only the echoing click of David's keystrokes filling the empty space.

She fiddled with the locator bracelet on her wrist. It seemed as if it'd been a long time since Jackson and Melissa had gone. How long did it take to see someone home, for crying out loud? If he wasn't back in, say, fifteen more minutes, did that mean—

Forcibly breaking the thought, she squeezed her eyes shut. This had to stop. She leaned forward in her chair and clasped her hands together, watching David.

"So, what are you working on?" she asked.

"I'm trying," he said, with heavy, put-upon emphasis, "to work on a mock-up of the security panel."

Interested, she scooted her chair forward a few inches. "The security panel at the facility? The one I'm supposed to—the one I'm going to disarm?"

"Yeah," he said shortly, still not looking around. She rolled her chair farther forward to get a better look at the screen, just out of curiosity. As she pulled up behind him, he turned around at last.

"It's not ready," he said irritably, positioning himself in front of the monitor so that she could only see a corner of the screen.

"I just wanted to see it," she said.

"Well, you can't, so get the hell away from it," he snarled.

She held up both hands and stood up. "Fine, sorry." Damn, what a prickly kid. She should've known better than to try to talk to someone who wanted people to call him Razor, anyway.

She was almost out the door when he spoke again.

"Hey, um…" He hesitated, and she turned to give him an expectant look.

"Is it true," he mumbled, then paused again. "Is it true you have, like, superpowers?"

She smiled a little. It figured that a computer-geek teenager would be interested in the only thing about her that was freakish. "I guess," she said. "Gideon calls it 'genetic enhancement.'"

"Cool," he breathed, then seemed to catch himself and frowned. "What can you do? I mean, I know you can supposedly run fast or whatever, but what else?"

She shrugged, took a few steps back into the room. "Well, I can break chairs. Ha." He didn't laugh, so she moved on. "I can hit things really hard if I move fast— it's something to do with velocity, Gideon says. And my hair grows fast, and my fingernails—that's not really useful, but it happens. And I'm hungry all the time, but I don't gain weight—that's pretty cool, I guess." She thought for a minute, spotted an empty soda can on the table next to David and looked at it with longing. "I'm not supposed to drink caffeine anymore—it'd make my heart rate go out of control. And…what else? Jackson says he thinks my reflexes are faster than normal."

"That's it?" he asked, and Vi felt weirdly defensive.

"That's pretty good, isn't it?" she asked.

He lifted a shoulder, started to turn back to his monitor. "Yeah, I guess so."

She frowned at him, then remembered. "Oh, I can heal. Really fast." She glanced around, found a sheet of paper on a nearby table and picked it up, brought it over to him. "Watch this."

Before she fully realized what she was doing—was she seriously performing party tricks to impress a teen-age geek?—she sliced the edge of the paper through the skin of her left index finger. Wincing at the sting, she resisted the urge to pop her finger into her mouth.

A thin line of blood welled up from the nicked skin. Brushing it away with her thumb, she pulled on one edge of the broken skin to clearly show him the cut. "See that?"

He nodded, his gaze fastened to her finger.

"Now, wait," she said. They both stared at the cut, and as the seconds passed, the skin began to draw to-gether, the tiny wound closing with unreal speed, like a time-lapse photograph series of healing.

David looked up at her, his brown eyes shining like a kid's, all traces of the surly, too-cool teenager gone. "Wow," he whispered.

She smiled, rubbed her thumb over the healed spot. She was actually still pretty blown away by it herself. She'd mostly seen it happen with bigger wounds, but they took longer so weren't quite as before-your-very-eyes impressive.

He didn't turn immediately back to his computer screen, so Vi took advantage of the moment to get a con-versation going.

"So, what's it's like working for Gideon? You get a job title?"

The wariness came back into his eyes, but he didn't dismiss her. "Technology specialist," he muttered at last.

She raised an eyebrow. "Specialist. That's pretty im-pressive for—what? Sixteen?"

"Seventeen," he corrected. "And I'll be eighteen in two months."

Nodding, she wished David were chattier. It would make this conversation thing so much easier. "So Gideon said you weren't in school for lots of reasons," she said. "What's the deal with that?"

He did his best lip curl. "What's it to you?"

"Just curious," she said with a shrug.

"I got kicked out, all right? From a lot of schools. I'm a discipline problem."

"What'd you do?"

"Lots of stuff. Last place, I hacked the school Web site and put up fake naked pictures of the principal." He said it with great nonchalance, but she could hear the hint of a bragging tone behind it.

"I guess that didn't go over too well," Vi said. He didn't respond, so she searched for another question. "What do your parents think about you working for Gideon?"

He shot her an angry look. "Jesus, what's with the twenty questions? Why don't you mind your business?"

Okay, she'd pushed too far. Conversation with David was not meant to be. It was back to Todd and junk food talk for her. She wondered how he felt about Cheetos. Bracing her hands on her thighs, she pushed herself out of the chair. "Sorry I asked," she said, and headed for the door.

He stopped her again before she got there. "My parents don't care," he mumbled.

Vi sighed but didn't turn around right away. Why was she even bothering with this kid? It was like pulling teeth, and she really didn't need the aggravation. Still,

there was something about him, some hint of pain be-
hind his bravado and bad attitude, that compelled her.
Besides, she hadn't thought about Jackson in minutes.
That was something to hang on to.

She turned around. "They don't care?"

He kept his face turned away from her, but she could
see his scowl even from profile view. "My dad's always
working, anyway, and the stepmonster…" he shrugged.
"Long as I'm out of her hair, she's aces."

Vi took a step forward, kept her voice low. "What
about your mom?"

He shook his head, reached for the soda can on the
table and took a swig. "She married some guy and
moved to Canada. Says it's too complicated for me to
live with them, and she doesn't want to uproot me.
Whatever."

Vi sat down again. Poor kid. She'd been right about
the pain, and she knew from experience that the last
thing he wanted right now was for her to be sweet and
syrupy and pitying. So she concentrated on making her
voice casual.

"Tough break."

He huffed out a breath and turned back to his computer. "Yeah, well, at least I got a cool job and I make
a shitload of money at it. Not a lot of guys my age can
say that."

She smiled, but her mind was churning, debating
whether to say the words on the tip of her tongue. She
wanted to offer it to him, to let him know he wasn't
alone, but even after all these years, it was hard to say
out loud.

She let her breath out in a rush and said the easiest

part. "I was raised by my grandparents. Mostly." It came out blunt and loud and weird, and she wondered how he'd react.

He looked up, turned his chair a little toward her. "Your mom die or something?"

She shook her head. "She just decided she couldn't handle raising a kid, when I was about nine, so she left me with her parents and kind of disappeared."

"For good?" His eyes were surprised and—probably against his will—concerned.

"No, we saw her again, from time to time. Didn't help, though. When she was there, she just seemed to find new ways to mess things up for me. She was kind of a mess, in general." Well, that was understating it. Clearing her throat, she forced herself to say the truth. "She was a drunk. She *is* a drunk."

Silence filled the room for a moment. "What about your dad?" David asked at last.

She clenched her teeth. That was the hardest, the worst, the big one. "I never knew him. Never knew who he was. My mom wouldn't—won't—tell me. I guess it doesn't matter now."

One breath in, one breath out. She nodded, feeling surprisingly calm. For so many years, she'd worked to keep it all hidden from everyone, to make herself seem normal. Maybe it was getting easier to face the fact that she wasn't.

She looked at David and saw in his awkward teen-ager's face that he was sorry and that he didn't know how to say it and still hang on to his cool façade. So she smiled at him.

"Thanks," she said, and cleared her throat, looking

around for a change of subject. "So, you want to see me hit something?"

Several minutes later, they were swatting half a dozen empty soda cans around the room when Jackson appeared in the doorway. Vi looked over and noticed him standing there, and her stomach squeezed and her breath went shallow, and all the inconvenient feelings she'd been distracting herself from came flooding back. Get a grip, she told herself, and swallowed hard.

"Melissa okay?" she asked, straightening the row of cans she'd lined up and trying not to look directly into his eyes.

"She's fine," he said. "Safe and sound. I gave her a panic button in case anything happens, but I don't think it will."

"You checked her apartment and everything? It's all okay?" She got a quick flash of Jackson in Melissa's apartment, in her bedroom, and she squashed it with all her concentration.

"It's fine," he said. "I picked up a tail on the way over there, but he didn't stick with her, followed me back here."

Vi felt her eyes widening. "So that means…he's waiting to follow you again now?"

He nodded. "Don't worry, we have a plan."

Comforting as his confidence was, she had a feeling the plan wasn't going to be a lot of fun for her. "Just tell me now," she said, sighing. "Does this mean I'm squishing down into the foot well again?"

He didn't answer, but before he turned to lead her out, she thought she saw a little half smile on his face.

* * *

Brian had squeezed his glasses too hard, and one of the earpieces was bent. He dropped them on his desk, clutched his head in his hands and closed his eyes.

"Lowell," he said, trying to keep his voice from shaking. "You can't...you just can't keep telling me you don't have her."

Lowell hissed out a long-suffering sigh. "You don't understand, Doc. This is good news. I know where she's at now. I know who's helping her out."

"You knew that last night," Brian said, lifting his head and looking across the desk at Lowell, who had his dirty boots propped up again. "But I don't see her here."

Lowell looked at him as if he were an idiot. "Last night they did a standard decoy maneuver—to be expected. They got away once, but don't you worry. I'm gonna find their weak spots. To the patient man, all things are revealed. Just takes a little time, that's all."

Brian didn't have time. Harriman would be arriving in four days. Four...short...days. He'd been so impressed by Brian's phone call that he'd moved his trip up, and now he was expecting a real show. And now, even if Brian got her back today, he wouldn't have adequate time to prepare.

But at least he'd have something. She was strong, Lowell had said, so some part of the procedure was working. He'd be able to show Harriman some kind of display. Perhaps enough to convince him to make things right—that it wasn't too late. And maybe, if she were as extraordinary as he hoped, maybe it would even be enough to save the funding, or at least forestall the directors' decision. To have everything fall into place…a happy ending for everyone.

Well, almost everyone.

"I don't think you quite understand the situation," Brian said, hearing the desperation creeping into his own voice. "I'm running out of time. I need her now, today, tonight at the latest."

Lowell looked at him appraisingly. "I'll be following her again tonight. They might lose me again, but I might get her. Or…"

He stopped, let the anticipation build, until Brian felt himself nodding encouragement, nearly agreeing in advance to anything that wasn't a "might."

"Or," Lowell said, "I could step things up a notch. Get you a little insurance, so to speak. But it'll cost you."

Brian kept nodding. "Money is not an issue. You do whatever you have to do."

Lowell winked and reached for one of his cigars. "Then we're in business."

Chapter 14

Vi leaned against a wall in Gideon's gym, watching the team prepare for practice with a frown on her face and a knot in her stomach. She was drawn and tense from a night of too much anxiety and too little sleep. Jackson had gotten her back to the safe house without incident, as promised, after sending Charlie and Sandra out in the SUV as a decoy. Still, between worrying that Leather Vest and his pals might knock down the door at any minute, and suppressing distracting thoughts about Jackson, she'd hardly slept at all.

Then, this morning, Steve had lowered the ax. She was fired.

Fired. She shook her head, hearing the word in her mind and still not quite believing it. She'd been so shocked on the phone that she'd barely been able to form words to argue with him. But it didn't really matter. He'd made up his mind, she'd let him down, and she was out.

Lisa, whom Vi had called just after hanging up with Steve, had been spitting mad, ranting about wrongful-termination lawsuits and thinking of everyone she knew who had anything to do with a lawyer. But Vi had felt only fear and swelling panic as one more thing slipped out of her grip.

She'd held herself together through a long morning of physical drills with Jackson, her emotions wearing to a frazzle as she suppressed everything she was feeling—for Jackson, about her job, about everything.

Fired. It was impossible—she'd never, never been fired from a job. Never even been written up. How could this have happened? Sure, after everything that had been done to her lately, getting canned from her over-worked and underpaid job was small potatoes, but still. It was so unfair. How dare he fire her? She was sick, damn it. Well, she wasn't really sick, but he didn't know that, and—damn it.

She sucked in a breath and felt the tightness in her chest and realized she was a little pissed off, after all.

Jackson was walking toward her, and the predictable wave of awareness that rippled through her made her flinch. She didn't need this now—one more thing to fight off. But it didn't seem to matter. Her life was falling apart, her mental health was crumbling, but still her nerve endings found time to buzz and tingle every time he so much as looked in her direction. And behind it all was a quiet little siren song, tempting her to forget her troubles and lose herself in him.

Mistake, mistake, she told herself, but every time he

looked at her, the way he looked at her made her forget why she should look away.

"You ready?" he asked, stopping in front of her.

She nodded, trying not to meet his eyes.

"Charlie's going to be standing in as the guard for your first few runs, then Sandra will step in, and we'll keep rotating through," he said. "Remember, you're just running through the hand-to-hand drills, slowly—keep it under control."

She nodded again, barely hearing him. "I'll be careful."

"You remember the three most important things?"

She sighed and rubbed a hand over her eyes. "Use my arms for protection, look for vulnerable points and don't put everything into the first punch."

"Right. They'll be ready for your first move, so use it as a distraction and make your second or third hit count."

"I know, I've got it," she said, with more snappishness than she'd intended. "It's just a practice, you know," she added, more softly.

He was frowning at her—big shock there—but for the first time, it dawned on her that maybe the look meant he was worried about her, not angry with her. "Pretty soon it'll be the real thing," he said.

Great. So now on top of everything else, she felt guilty. She wished again she could tell him the truth, that there was no way she'd ever be doing the real thing. But she didn't have that option.

"Let's go," Gideon called from across the room, and Vi looked away from Jackson, glad for a distraction, ready to do and move instead of stand and think.

"Todd's not back from lunch?" Gideon asked.

Charlie spoke up from across the room. "He called to say he was held up."

Gideon and Jackson exchanged a frown, but Gideon only turned to Aaron and waved him over. "Take over Todd's position until he gets here," he said.

Vi took her place at the starting line they'd marked off—about twenty yards back from the line that marked the doorway—and looked down the long expanse at Charlie, who was standing at the end waiting to fight her in slow motion. She closed her eyes and tried to summon her focus—she had to remember all her tricks for stopping without crashing at the end of the run, and she had to execute all the hand-to-hand drills she'd been practicing.

Squaring her shoulders, she took off down her runway and fell into her rhythm, and *zoom,* the end was there in a flash. She used the hopping, heel-digging method she'd worked out and just managed to pull herself up short at the end. Charlie stepped into her path and reached for her, and her mind clicked automatically through the drills Jackson had taught her. *First things first—don't let him get a hold on you.*

Lifting her right arm slowly and carefully, she knocked his hand off her shoulder. Not stopping the flow, she swung out slowly with her left arm, aiming for his jaw, but he dodged the blow, just as she'd expected. What he wasn't expecting was the molasseslike crash of her instep to his knee. It was a good hit, and Charlie played along, doubling over and falling down to his one "uninjured" knee. Vi mimed a slow knee to the face, and he fell backward, disabled.

"Good," Jackson said from his observation point ten feet away. "Try it again."

Charlie grumbled as he got to his feet. "Feel like a damn fool."

Vi agreed, but she wasn't going to say anything. Slo-mo fighting practice might look stupid, but it was a hell of a lot easier than working with the heavy bag and actually landing punches. This way no one had to get hurt. Particularly her.

Jackson waved her back to the starting line, and she and Charlie ran through the drill again. And again and again. After the fourth practice, Charlie stood up and held up both hands.

"That's it, I'm out," he said. "Someone else can babysit for a while."

Vi flushed and frowned at the ground. It didn't matter. She didn't care if they all hated her, because she had much bigger problems—all of them currently knotting up her stomach—and anyway, as soon as she got her hands on the evidence she needed, she'd never have to see any of them again.

Still, Charlie didn't have to be such a consistent ass to her. She'd never done anything to him.

"Sandra, you're up," Jackson said, and Vi felt like groaning. Just what she needed—a change from Mr. Cranky and Rude to Ms. Evil Eye.

Sandra was, in fact, giving her a narrow-slitted gaze as she took her place at the end of the runway. Sighing, Vi made her way back to the start. She gritted her teeth and started down the runway. Faces flashed past— Gideon with his stopwatch, Jackson with his arms folded—and then she was hop-hopping, careful not to stumble, teetering to a halt.

Sandra stepped out and reached for Vi's shoulder,

just as Charlie had done, but not slowly. Before Vi could get her slow-motion countermovement going, Sandra had her hand clamped down and was squeezing Vi's shoulder, hard.

Frowning, Vi brought her arm up carefully and banged against Sandra's forearm with the dislodging motion Jackson had taught her, but Sandra didn't budge.

"What are you doing?" Vi asked, stepping back to shake off Sandra's grip.

Sandra's eyes were cold little slits, and she held on tight. "Just what I'm supposed to do."

"You know I can't really use any force," Vi said from between her clenched teeth. "You have to play along."

From behind, Vi heard Jackson's voice. "Sandra, what's going on?"

Sandra kept her eyes on Vi. "I don't have to do anything. What? Don't you think you can handle a taste of what it'll really be like, little girl?"

Vi felt her face go hot as her temper flared.

"Let go, Sandra," she said, her voice tight and low.

"Make me," Sandra said with a small, cold smile.

Tension, fear, anger, anxiety—everything Vi was feeling merged into a single hot flood of rage, and just like that, she boiled over. She lifted both hands and planted them on Sandra's shoulders, and she pushed with all her strength, heaving into it with a primal kind of pleasure.

Sandra took several fast, stumbling steps backward, arms pinwheeling and eyes wide as she struggled not to fall. Vi saw right away that it would be better if she did fall, or she was going to—

With a thud and a sharp pop, Sandra smashed into

the cinder-block wall. Her head bounced once, her face went lax, and she crumpled to the floor.

Vi stood frozen, remorse and panic crowding out the thrumming anger she'd just been so consumed with. Sandra wasn't moving, and Vi couldn't look away, couldn't move, barely registered the clamor that broke out behind her until Gideon and Jackson stepped into her view, kneeling next to Sandra's still form.

Oh, man. What if she'd done it, really hurt someone? What if— God, she couldn't even think it. What was wrong with her? Jackson had told her and told her to be careful, to keep it under control, and now she'd lost it and...*shit*.

Her insides were cold, and she couldn't breathe right. She felt a tiny ripple of relief when Sandra stirred and groaned under Jackson's hands, but it wasn't enough to lift the nauseating guilt sweeping through her.

She had to get her hands on that evidence and get the hell out of here, out of this place and this situation and back to her regularly scheduled life, where she had never hurt anyone.

Vi slumped in the folding chair in the unfinished room, trying to keep her mind focused on finding a way to evade the watchful eye of Todd, who had shown up just as Jackson, Gideon and Charlie were leaving to take Sandra to the hospital. If she could get past Todd, she'd have a little freedom to do a search, maybe even get into Gideon's office.

But she couldn't concentrate. Her mind kept replaying the scene over and over—Sandra reeling backward, eyes wide, then crashing into the wall. The way her face had slackened...

Shuddering softly, Vi wrapped her arms around herself and tried to pull herself together. She deserved the punishment of what her mind was doing, but she also had things she needed to do with her brain, not least of all to make sure she wouldn't hurt anyone else.

She didn't like the way she'd felt when she'd done it. Chewing absently on her fingernails, she flashed back to the fight she'd had in the alley behind her house, that thrill of power that had flooded her when she'd taken down the car driver. Was that who she was? Was that what she was becoming? Some kind of bloodthirsty violence addict?

It had to stop. She had to stop it.

Snatching her fingers away from her teeth, she sucked in a breath and glanced over at Todd. He was giving her a worried look.

"Are you okay?" he asked when their eyes met.

She nodded. "Sure. Fine." Think, she had to think. How could she get past him?

He was leaning against the doorjamb, arms crossed, and he tapped his fingers against the frame. "You're still...you're going back to the safe house tonight, right?"

She nodded again. "Jackson said he'd take me when he gets back." From the hospital. Where she'd put Sandra. She swallowed. *Concentrate. Got to think.*

"Good," Todd said. "I mean, you, uh, look like you could use some rest."

She couldn't argue with that. Weariness seeped through her at the very suggestion, and she closed her

eyes for a moment. The image bloomed in her mind—
Sandra stumbling back, crashing, crumpling.

Snapping open her eyes, she shook her head. Stop
it. Think. Maybe she could tell Todd she had to pee.
Would he follow her to the bathroom or just watch the
hallway?

"How much longer do you think it's going to be?"
Todd asked.

She looked up at him. "What?"

"Jackson. Do you think he's going to be a lot
longer?"

Shrugging, she eyed him, curious. "I don't know.
Why? Are you in a hurry to leave or something?"

He straightened up, dropped his arms, folded them
again. "No, no. I just…I could take you. To the safe
house. If you don't want to wait."

She puzzled over that. She wasn't sure why he was
offering, but maybe she should play along for a moment. If she could get him to leave, to bring the car
around to the back door, maybe…

"I don't know," she said slowly. "Do you think Jackson would be mad?"

He shook his head. "Probably not. I mean, I just…"
He unfolded his arms again and let them drop to his
sides. "I don't think you should have to sit around here
waiting. You've been through a lot, and this thing today…
I bet it wasn't your fault. Sandra makes everyone crazy."

Her heart squeezed in her chest, even though she
couldn't believe him. What a nice guy. And he'd given
her Twinkies before. She hated to think of sneaking off
and getting him in trouble. Still, opportunities to be
alone at Gideon's were so rare…

She opened her mouth to speak just as she heard the front door bang open. Jackson stepped in from the hallway, and Vi pushed herself to her feet.

"Is she okay?" she asked.

Jackson nodded, his face drawn. "She will be. She's got a concussion and a couple of monster bruises, but nothing's broken. They're just going to watch her overnight."

A small stream of relief coursed through her. At least she hadn't done any permanent damage.

He studied her for a moment, his eyes taking on that intense, searching look. In spite of everything, she felt her skin begin to prickle. Why, *why* couldn't she turn this off? Even now, when she ought to be feeling nothing but guilt, all he had to do was look at her, and off she went.

"We'll go in a minute," he said.

Vi watched him disappear down the hallway, trying to sort out and clamp down all her emotions. But standing there silently, with Todd in the background drumming his fingers on the door frame, was making her even more tense.

When Jackson returned, he was holding a jacket and a bag of trail mix. He handed her the bag and draped the jacket over her shoulders.

"Let's go," he said.

Surprised and touched, she followed him silently to the parking lot. Aaron and Todd went with them, and each man chose a vehicle—Aaron and Jackson in the black SUVs, and Todd in a silver sedan. Vi climbed in with Jackson and slid down into the foot well without being told.

The three vehicles pulled out of the parking lot at the same time. With any luck, if Leather Vest was watching, he'd pick the wrong vehicle to follow. If not, Jackson knew how to shake off a tail if he had to.

After a few uneventful miles, Jackson gave her the all-clear signal, and she pushed herself up into the passenger seat.

"That was easy," she said, opening the trail mix and grabbing a handful. Her stomach, which had begun to pinch, relaxed.

He grunted, keeping his eyes trained on the rearview mirror. "Maybe too easy."

Silence fell between them, and Vi's mind returned again to the image of Sandra, stumbling backward, crumpled on the floor. Her throat tightened, and she couldn't stand the quiet anymore.

"I'm sorry," she said. It came out a little whispery, so she cleared her throat. "I know it doesn't change anything, but I feel terrible."

He glanced over at her. "She'll be fine," he said.

"I know. But that doesn't mean I'm off the hook."

He didn't answer right away. Finally he took a deep breath and let it out slowly. "She provoked you. You reacted badly. There's no need to beat yourself up about it."

"Can't seem to help myself."

"You made a mistake. It happens."

Shaking her head, she looked out the window. She didn't want to risk meeting his eyes. "It wasn't a mistake."

Silence for a moment. "You meant to hurt her?"

"No, but…it wasn't just a reaction. It wasn't instinct

or anything. I was *mad*." She paused, chuckled bitterly. "You know, when this all started, I told Melissa I felt like the Hulk. Now I really am—You don't want to see me angry."

"Stop it," he said. She glanced at him and saw him shaking his head. "She was out of line, she goaded you, and you got mad. That's natural. You wanted her off you, and you did what you needed to do. You just...did it a little too hard. You're new at this. You still don't have everything under control. We're working on it."

She looked at him, a swirl of grateful warmth mixing with the guilt and worry tumbling through her. He wasn't what she'd call eloquent, but he did have a way of saying the right things.

"Why are you being so nice to me?" she asked, studying his profile in the dim light.

"So you'll stop moping," he said, his eyes on the road as he turned onto the safe house's street.

She thought of the first time he'd driven her here, how scared and silent she'd been and how cold and harsh he'd been. That was Saturday. Today was Tuesday. It seemed like a lifetime ago, and he was like a different person. Hell, *she* felt like a different person.

He'd refused to stay with her then. She wondered what he'd do if she asked him to stay tonight.

He looked at her, and she turned away quickly, cheeks heating in the dark.

"I still want to yell at you for what happened," he said. "I can't do that when you're miserable. So cheer up so I can start in."

She smiled, even though she knew he probably wasn't kidding. She'd doubtless get an earful the next morning in training, and he'd probably do something sadistic like double her heavy-bag drills.

Pulling the SUV into the driveway, he parked and slid out from behind the wheel. He headed into the house to do a quick walk-through, just as he'd done every night, and Vi stayed in her seat, waiting for the all-clear sign he always gave her from the porch.

Her stomach fluttered as she thought again of asking him to stay. Crazy impulse. For one thing, she'd be setting herself up for a very likely rejection, and who needed that?

And even if he did agree—she swallowed hard at the thought—it was a very bad idea. What was she even thinking? She had so many things to devote her energy to—like finding the video at Gideon's, like not getting herself captured or killed—major, serious, literally life-and-death matters to attend to. Was she really going to take a side trip to Lustville just because she'd found a guy who stirred her up?

And life-and-death issues aside, she'd really only known the man for days. No matter that it felt like a lifetime—it was *days*. So…was she seriously considering taking a break from the fight for her very life to ask a near stranger to sleep with her? Because he made her nerve endings sing?

Yes.

She had to admit it. She was. She wanted to. She wanted…him. Just to touch him. Just to forget everything and focus on the feel of his hands—those strong, beautiful hands—touching her. And yes, maybe she'd be using him to distract herself from the crazy-making worry and tension, but she'd also be kissing him, touching him…

What if he pressed her up against a wall, what if she leaned into him, what if they were that close... Her body went slack and heavy at the thought, and her cheeks were hot and her scurrying heartbeat was loud in her ears.

Yes, damn it, she wanted him, and as soon as he was back...well, what if she just told him that? Threw caution to the wind and said it out loud and found out what would happen. As soon as he was back—

She sat up straight, a chill washing away some of the heat she'd felt.

Where was he?

It never took him this long to do the walk-through. Peering at the porch as if she could have missed him, she felt her hands begin to shake, and she tried to push back the fear. Maybe he was just slow tonight. Maybe he was checking everything really thoroughly. Or maybe he'd found something—not something scary, but something he wanted to study carefully, or maybe...

At that moment, he stepped out into the shadows of the porch, and she began to sigh in relief.

Until she saw the man holding a gun to Jackson's temple.

Chapter 15

Vi gasped as shock and fear slapped her in the face. A third man stepped out of the house, and even in the dim light she could see the blond hair and the beard, and her heart froze in her chest. Leather Vest, and the other one must be Beady Eyes, which meant T.J. was around somewhere, and they had Jackson, and—oh, shit.

Leather Vest raised his hand and beckoned to her, a creepy little smile on his face. She shot a look at Jackson, who shook his head and frowned at her, but she ignored him and unlatched her seat belt. She was sure he wanted her to slide into the driver's seat and haul ass out of Dodge, leaving him to take care of himself, but there was absolutely no way that was happening.

She wished she had some kind of brilliant plan, though. Her hands were shaking as she unlocked the door and pushed herself out. For a moment she stood on the pavement with the open door between her and the men on the porch, trying to think, trying to calm her frantic heartbeat, but nothing was coming to her, and at last she just slammed the door and began to walk up the driveway.

She'd barely taken two steps when she saw Leather Vest raise his arm again, this time holding a tranq pistol, and she flinched. Damn it, not again. No way. She didn't know what she was going to do, she just knew she wasn't going to let herself get tranqed again. *Never be that helpless again.*

She didn't stop walking, and he took aim and squeezed the trigger. Jackson shouted her name, but she felt anger and calm descending simultaneously, and she let her body go, didn't try to direct it, just let it react with pure, lightning instinct. Leaping sideways and twisting out of the way, she heard the hiss of the dart as it swished by her side. Another dart was coming, but she could see it—could almost feel it coming—and she ducked and weaved and dodged it and kept walking toward the porch.

Leather Vest cursed, his eyes mad and glittering, and he took a step toward her. At that moment Jackson ducked down and twisted Beady Eyes's arm to free himself, and Leather Vest was reaching for her and from around the corner T.J. came barreling and all hell broke loose in Vi's head.

Her adrenaline spiked, and she dropped automatically into the fighting stance Jackson had been drilling her on. Leather Vest grabbed her by the shoulders, and she began to move. Just like the drills, she thought, and she lifted both arms and slammed them into his, knocking his hands from her body. She followed with a punch, swinging wild with all her strength, but he dodged and she went stumbling forward. He caught her and swung her back around, and then T.J. was in her face and *bash!* His fist slammed into her jaw.

She reeled from the pain, looked frantically for Jackson, but he was still grappling with Beady Eyes on the porch, trying to wrench the gun out of his hand. T.J. was winding up to slug her in the gut, so she twisted desperately and managed to pull herself out of Leather Vest's grip.

She hopped backward and steadied herself, then swung at T.J. He dodged, but she was expecting that and followed up immediately with a quick, savage kick to the midsection. He gave a satisfying "oof" and stumbled backward, and she whirled to face Leather Vest. He grabbed for her, but she ducked and eluded him, moving fast now, her reactions so precise he seemed to be moving underwater. She swung and managed to land a glancing blow to his nose—not a good hit, but enough to make him shout and clutch his face.

T.J. was coming back, still clutching his middle, but reaching out for her with a thick hand. He was furious; she could see it in his face. And she was glad she'd hurt him. She felt her own anger boiling over again, knew it was a bad thing but didn't care. *Go ahead. Go Hulk,* she told herself.

Gritting her teeth, she started punching fast, one blow after another, short, sharp jabs to his midsection. He backed up, waving his arms to try to deflect her, and she saw a clear shot at his jaw. Her fist connected with bone, and pain shuddered up her arm, but she ignored it. He screamed and fell backward, his head bouncing on the pavement with a crack.

Leather Vest grabbed her from behind, but she was in a full-blown fury now. From behind her, she heard a gunshot and a man's shout, and she thought of Jackson with the gun to his head, and she let loose. Shaking Leather Vest off, she turned to face him and struck out before he could deflect the blow, putting all her speed into her tightly clenched hand. Her fist sank into his stomach, and he shouted and doubled over, and she jerked her knee up to meet his face, smashing into his already injured nose.

He gave a high, animal shriek as her bone connected with his, and he stumbled back. Looking past him, she saw Jackson jogging toward her.

"Get in the car," he said, and she noticed he was limping as he ran. She turned toward the SUV, but Leather Vest came after her again, his face bloody and distorted, and she sucked in a breath. Before he could reach her, Jackson ducked behind him and cracked him across the back of the head with the butt of the gun he held. Leather Vest's eyes rolled back, and he crumpled to the pavement.

Vi darted a look around—at Beady Eyes sprawled on the porch, T.J. groaning in the driveway, Leather Vest in a heap in front of her—and felt nausea rising in her gut.

"Let's go," Jackson said, and she snapped to, scrambling for the SUV's door and flinging herself inside. He jerked the car into reverse and squealed out of the driveway, and Vi kept her head down and held on as he tore at breakneck speed through the dark streets, reminding herself that he was trained to drive this way.

After several miles he yanked the wheel to the right and pulled up to the curb.

"We'll be better off on foot for this last part. You okay?"

Her knuckles were bloody, the skin broken, but she was too numb to feel any pain. She nodded, then gasped as she finally noticed the blood oozing from his right thigh. "You're hurt."

His jaw clenched. "It's not bad, and we don't have to go far. Come on." He turned off the car, pocketed the keys and slid awkwardly from behind the wheel. She climbed out and followed him as he took off at a limping run down an ally next to a rundown liquor store.

"Where are we going?" she asked, pacing her run carefully so she wouldn't leave him behind.

"My place," he said, and in spite of everything, her heart thrilled stupidly. With all she had to think about, and despite the fact that she'd just fought for her life, she was still excited about seeing the place he called home.

Whatever it was she felt for him, it was definitely burning up brain cells.

Vi followed Jackson through the dim, cramped, faintly smelly lobby of his apartment building, and she started to have second thoughts about seeing his place.

Scratch that—she'd started having second thoughts when she'd seen the homeless guy sleeping on the street in front of the bail bonds storefront next door. Now her second thoughts were compounding, but she didn't want to hurt Jackson's feelings.

He glanced back as they neared a dingy staircase. Some of her doubt must have shown in her face, because he smiled just a little as he limped forward.

"Don't worry, it gets better," he said. "But the elevator doesn't work."

She nodded, but she was still preparing for the worst, and there was definitely no way she was touching the banister on the staircase.

Three flights later Jackson grunted as he climbed the last step and reached into his pocket for his keys. He turned a dead bolt on a simple wooden door and pushed it open.

Vi didn't know what she'd expected to see, but it certainly wasn't…another door.

There was just barely room for the wooden door to open into a tiny, brightly lit vestibule with solid-looking walls to either side and an imposing steel door straight ahead. Moving quickly, Jackson slipped two different keys into two different locks, and then he flipped open a keypad on the wall and punched in a long series of numbers.

The steel door clicked, and he pushed the handle down hard and leaned on the door to open it.

Vi watched the whole process with wide eyes. Jackson's apartment looked as impenetrable as Gideon's building, and the intense security was thoroughly unexpected after that first flimsy wooden door. She supposed that was sort of the point.

He motioned her in, and she stepped through the vestibule, pulling the wooden door closed behind her.

His front door opened to a large room with muted wood floors, clean white walls and several thick, odd-looking windows along the far wall. There wasn't much furniture, but the sofa, chairs and coffee table grouped around a big TV looked comfortable. Exercise equip-

ment took up one corner of the room, a sleek desk with
two computers sat against the back wall, and a kitchenette opened from the wall to the right.

Jackson secured the doors while she gawked, then he
limped past her to an end table by the sofa and picked
up the phone. After a moment he spoke.

"It's Jackson. Violet's safe house has been breached.
We got hit."

He paused, listening, as Vi realized he must have
called Gideon.

"Three of them. No, she's fine. Did better than me,
in fact."

He glanced up at her at that, and she saw something
in his eyes she couldn't quite identify—pride? Admi-
ration? Her stomach did a little flip-flop.

"She's safe. I'll keep her that way tonight. We'll be
there in the morning."

After a few more brief comments, he signed off and
looked up at her.

"Have a seat," he said, motioning toward the couch
as he headed for the kitchenette.

"Have a seat?" she repeated. "Jackson, we have to
go to the hospital."

He looked back at her, his eyes alarmed. "Are you
hurt? I thought you said you were all right." Catching
sight of the blood staining her knuckles, he stepped forward, lifting her hand. "What's this?"

Shaking her head, she flexed her fingers a few times
and realized the broken skin had already healed. "It's
nothing, it's not *me*. You got shot. Did you forget?" She
pointed at his bloody leg.

"Oh, that." He limped away again and opened a

kitchen cabinet. "Gun went off in the struggle, just a flesh wound. No big deal."

With an effort, she managed to keep her jaw from hitting the floor. "You got *shot*," she said again. "That is a big deal. You can't just ignore it."

"Who's ignoring it?" He pulled gauze and surgical tape from the cabinet. "I can patch it up with this, and I've got antibiotics."

"But…" She knew she wasn't one to talk, given that her possibly exploding heart should've put her in the hospital, but this just seemed wrong. When there were bullets involved, you ought to get some professional medical attention.

She bit her lip, worried, and he looked up and caught her. "It's all right, Violet. The bullet just grazed me. Hurt like hell, but it's not serious. Anyway, I'm not setting foot out of this place when I'm your only protection."

He caught the look she sent him and held up an appeasing hand.

"Not that you can't protect yourself," he said. "Still, you're my responsibility. Now quit worrying. Come on, I'll show you how to do a field dressing."

Reluctantly she gave up and walked forward, looking at the scissors and alcohol and other supplies he'd assembled on the countertop.

If she'd been using her head, she'd have been prepared when he unbuttoned his jeans and slid them down. Of course, he'd need to *get* to the wound to dress it. But her mind was in a million places, so she hadn't braced herself for the sight of Jackson standing in his kitchenette with his boxer briefs exposed. His black, form-fitting boxer briefs.

Her eyes went wide and her mouth went dry and her cheeks went hot, and she was not able to hang on to her cool in even the slightest way.

"Oh, um, oh," she stammered, looking at the ceiling and the opposite wall and anywhere but at him. Her hands flew involuntarily to her hair, looking for something to busy themselves with, then fluttered back down to her sides.

"I don't, um…" Gulping, she tried to pull her thoughts together. Be an adult, she told herself. "I don't know that I can help…you with that. I don't know much about medicine. I was, uh, I was never in Girl Scouts or anything, so I don't— Well, I haven't—" God, she was babbling.

Squeezing her lips closed, she drew a deep breath in through her nose. After a moment she was able to look up at him. He was watching her with a mixture of concern and amusement, and something about the look made her thoughts settle into grim determination.

If it doesn't bother him, it doesn't bother me.

"I'm sorry," she said. "Go ahead. What do you do— clean it first?"

He looked down at his leg. "First you stop the bleeding, but this…seems to have stopped itself. Told you it wasn't major."

For the first time, she looked at the wound in his thigh. He was right—it looked as if the bullet had just nicked the side of his leg and then gone on its way, and there wasn't as much blood as she'd thought. That was lucky, but he'd still lost a slice of flesh, and the sight made her wince.

"You sure you don't want to go get that stitched up?"

A horrifying thought occurred to her, and she looked up at him, openmouthed. "Please tell me you're not about to sew that up yourself."

He frowned, shaking his head. "It'll heal without stitches."

She didn't ask what he'd do if the wound were deeper. She didn't think she wanted to know.

He propped himself against the counter behind him and reached for the alcohol and a sterile swab pad sealed in plastic.

"If we were in the field, we wouldn't stop to clean it, but since we're here…"

He unwrapped the pad and soaked it in alcohol, then pressed it to the wound. He didn't flinch or make a sound, but she glanced up and saw his jaw tighten and knew the alcohol was stinging like fire. She felt a wash of sympathy.

"Here, let me," she said, leaning down and putting her fingers on the pad. She didn't look up at him, just waited for him to pull his hand away. He did, slowly, and she lifted the pad and blew gently on the wound.

"My grandmother used to do that," she said, as she repositioned the pad and pressed down. "It helps a little. Probably spreads germs, but it's better than keeling over from the pain."

"I'm all right," he said, his voice gruff.

She smiled up at him. "Don't be such a man." Lifting the pad, she blew gently again. Silence fell between them, and she concentrated on the few significant inches of skin in front of her, reminding herself that he was injured and trying to ignore the fact that her hands were touching his bare thigh.

Professional distance, she told herself. Think like a nurse.

His leg was like a rock, though. Even a veteran nurse would have to notice that. How could you help it? He was so very…firm.

Clearing his throat, he shifted. "It's probably clean enough."

She stood up quickly, praying that her cheeks weren't as red as they felt, and looked at the counter. "What's next? Wrap it up?" She held up a roll of packaged gauze.

"I can do it," he said, but she shook her head. That would leave her with nothing to do but stand there looking at him.

"I got it," she said, crouching down again and ripping the plastic off the gauze package. She picked up a clean dressing and pressed it to the wound, then brought the tail of the gauze roll up to it and hesitated, just realizing her mistake. Now she'd have to wrap the gauze around his leg, slipping her hands between and behind…oh, *hell.*

Biting her lip, she began to work, torn between the urge to do it quickly to get it over with and the need to do it carefully to avoid hurting him. She slipped her right hand as casually as she could to the inside of his thigh, then snaked her left hand behind and passed off the roll of gauze, wrapping the wound securely.

Again and again she repeated the action, very aware of her own constricted breathing and of the heat that seemed to radiate from his skin. What was he thinking? Was he looking down at her, or looking away? She didn't dare glance up.

Something—maybe her unsteady crouched position, maybe the fact that she wasn't breathing right—made her sway a little, and she unthinkingly braced the flat of her hand on his thigh to steady herself. He tensed and sucked in air, and before she could even stand he was moving.

"I'd better finish this…in the bathroom. Light's better," he said, sliding past her and yanking his jeans up as he went. She watched him limp away, not sure if she felt more embarrassed, relieved or disappointed.

Chapter 16

Two hours later, as Vi lay stretched out in the dark on Jackson's sofa, she decided that she was almost definitely disappointed.

They'd barely spoken after he'd emerged from the bathroom with his wound dressing completed, except to argue over who was taking the bed and who'd be sleeping on the couch. She'd won that one, at least—there was no way she'd have been able to get a moment's sleep in his bed, imagining she smelled his scent even on freshly washed sheets, fighting the urge to look through his nightstand.

Not that she was getting a whole lot of rest on the couch. Her brain was tired—exhausted, even—but it refused to quiet, and her body was so awake it was twitchy. It was too much, after the mostly sleepless previous night, and she was beginning to feel a little loopy.

And Jackson…Jackson was right there, on the other side of an easily opened door. So tempting to shut her brain down and just slip through that door, slide silently into bed with him, see what happened.

Oh, ugh. Humiliation, that could happen. Or rejection—a definite possibility. The way he'd pulled away from her earlier, in the kitchen… She didn't know what to make of that. Was he fighting off attraction, too, or was he just trying to drop her a broad hint? She thought she'd caught some inadvertent signals from him, but maybe that was all in her head. Maybe he was lying awake right now wondering what he'd have to do to get her to back off, wondering if he should post some signs that said, "Just because I'm helping you doesn't mean I want you drooling on me."

Hell. Okay, bad idea. No slipping into his bed. Her life was complicated enough, anyway. And besides, he was injured. Not terribly injured, but injured just the same, and he probably just needed to sleep.

Determined to put the whole matter out of her mind, she pulled Jackson's scratchy spare blanket up to her chin and squeezed her eyes closed. Sleeping now. Blank mind, relaxed body, time to doze off.

There was that way he looked at her, though.

Against her will, her mind sent up the image of his face, his green eyes looking at her, the way he had in her dream, the way he had only hours before. So intense, so warm, so…concerned.

All right, but that meant nothing. So he was concerned about her, so what? She was, as he'd said, his responsibility. That didn't mean he had the reciprocal hots for her.

Still…there was something there. She couldn't be a hundred percent sure, but it was enough to send a shiver and a flush through her skin when she thought of it.

God, she wanted him. No denying it. It was lust and it was loneliness and it was fear and feeling and more— things she couldn't name—but it was real and freaking unignorable.

And she could find out what he felt if she just slipped through his door and slid wordlessly into bed next to him.

Feeling wild, her skin flashing hot, she pushed away the blanket and sat up, her eyes fixing on the door to his bedroom. Her breath came short and quick.

Then she squeezed her eyes shut. No. No. *No.*

She was not going to go in there and throw herself at him. It was a bad, bad idea—*so hard to remember why*—and she had to stop even thinking about it. Right now.

Desperate, she cast about for a distraction and found Jackson's TV remote. She snatched it up and searched the controls. Of course, it was one of those complicated ones with fifteen million tiny buttons, and her emotions were so out of control that she nearly hurled the thing across the room before she found the power button.

Finally the TV flicked on, bathing her in soothing blue light, and she mashed the volume button until the sound was only a murmur. Drawing a slow breath, she forced herself to calm down, and she curled up under the blanket again, eyes fixed on the screen.

A rerun of the local ten-o'clock news was on, and she felt herself being lulled by the anchorman's authoritative tones. Maybe she would finally get to sleep if she watched for a while.

She listened to stories about a homeowners' group, a street protest, and a hit-and-run accident, growing more relaxed with each segment. By the time a story about a kidnapped girl began, she was fully absorbed in the troubles of other people.

She vaguely remembered hearing something about this missing girl a few days ago. Ruby Mulligan, right, that was her name. The details of her abduction floated over Vi—*nine years old, taken from a hospital two states away, suffering from the rare Jenkins' disease...*

Vi's eyes snapped open wide, and she stared at the screen, shock searing through her. She sat up straight, scrambled for the remote to turn up the volume. The anchorman was already moving on to another story, but it didn't matter. She knew what she'd heard.

Jenkins' disease. This missing girl had Jenkins' disease, just like Vi, and according to Severin, Vi had been injected with an altered version of Jenkins' disease. There had to be a connection. It couldn't be a coincidence.

A missing girl—Gideon was looking for something, said he was going to get something SynCor had.

Then she remembered Todd's slip in Gideon's office, when he'd almost said too much and earned some glares from Gideon and Jackson. He'd mentioned a jewel. A ruby? *Ruby Mulligan.*

Shoving off the blanket, she stood up and strode across the room to Jackson's door. Without hesitating, she knocked sharply and pushed it open.

He was up instantly, rolling out of bed into a fighter's

stance, wearing only his boxer briefs and the bandage around his thigh. When he recognized her, he straightened, his hands dropping but his expression tightening with worry.

"What's the matter?" he asked.

"Are you rescuing Ruby Mulligan? Is that what the mission is?" she asked.

He blinked once, and she could just see the struggle to keep his features from showing his surprise. But she did see it—she was learning his face—and she knew she was right.

To his credit, he didn't try to lie. "How did you know?"

She shook her head, reeling inside, trying to absorb it. "I just saw something on the news about her again, just put it together. Jesus."

For a fierce, blindingly selfish instant, she wished she didn't know, wished she'd never figured it out. Because this changed everything. One missing piece of the puzzle had just dropped into place, and her world had spun and tilted to a new plane because of it.

Nine years old, she thought. It just figures that she'd be nine years old.

"Why?" It was all she could think to ask. "Why are you doing it? The police are looking for her, everyone is. If you know where she is, just—"

"We did," he said, cutting her off and folding his arms over his chest. "We told them where she was, told them about SynCor, told them everything. They thought we were a bunch of nutcases, but they went and looked. Knocked on the door and asked politely, and got the grand tour, easy as pie."

"At the…the facility?"

He nodded. "Didn't find her. Didn't know how to look for her. They've got her hidden, a secret room with a hidden entrance. It's a SynCor facility—they're full of tricks."

She squeezed her eyes shut, not sure whether she wanted to believe him or not. Why did everyone in Gideon's circle end up sounding like a delusional lunatic?

"How do you know she's there?" she asked. "If they couldn't find her."

"It's a long…" He stopped, sighed, sat down on the edge of the bed. "You deserve to know. We should've told you from the beginning, but we didn't know if we could trust you with it. The thing is, Violet, if SynCor starts to feel the pressure, they'll move her, and we won't have a chance to get to her at all. We have to be careful now—we have one shot, and we can't mess it up."

She backed up to lean against the wall, because she knew she'd need some support to hear the rest of this. It was sure to be more hard-to-swallow insanity. "Tell me," she said.

Silence, buzzing with tension, filled the room for a moment. Then he began.

"She was taken three weeks ago. We heard about it, but we didn't get personally interested until reports starting circulating that she'd been brought here—to this state, anyway. Gideon thought…" He paused, glanced over at her. "You know he's just starting this operation up. Gideon Enterprises is only about four months old."

Vi nodded, thinking of the unfinished room in Gideon's building, the plush inner office that didn't match the rest of the building. "I kind of figured."

"His credentials are legit—hell, we've all got credentials. What we don't have is clients. Gideon was looking for a big case to break us, get our name out. Plus, reward money wouldn't hurt. So, he thought, if we could do some tracking on this kid, find something that would lead to her, it would help everyone."

Nodding again, Vi watched him carefully. His voice was tense, but his expression was almost clear. Only if you looked at the lines around his eyes could you see the worry he was holding on to.

"He got his hands on the police evidence, and it turns out there was a video from the hospital's surveillance system, from the night Ruby was taken. Caught a man's face who they thought was connected, maybe even the one who pulled off the abduction, but no one could ID him. But Gideon knew him. And Gideon knew he was a SynCor operative."

Dimly, Vi remembered Gideon talking about SynCor, about his first encounter with them. *They let me see their faces,* he'd said, or something like that. *It's come in handy.*

"The guy who shot him, from before," she said.

Jackson looked up sharply, clearly surprised, and Vi shrugged.

"Hey, I'm smarter than I look," she said.

He raised both eyebrows. "Good to know, since you look pretty smart."

Trying not to feel warmed by the compliment, Vi shifted against the wall. "What did Gideon do?"

"He started looking for a SynCor connection in the state, in the city. He didn't think there were any facilities here, even outposts, but he knows a couple of names of the operating companies SynCor hides behind. You can't cover up every record, every detail of a transaction like a land purchase, tax payments—it's just not possible. There's always a trail if you know how to look, and Gideon knows. He found the facility—it's not hidden, it looks like a regular business until you notice the security. Most people don't notice."

She shook her head. "What about the security?"

"It's too much, too heavy. No reason for an everyday business to run an operation like that."

"Maybe they're just really paranoid," she said. After all, she'd recently encountered a whole group of people who seemed obsessed with security systems.

"Possible. That's why we tapped into the video surveillance system, so we could get a look at what was going on there. To be sure."

Vi held up a hand. "Wait, wait. If the security at this place is so tight, how'd you get into their cameras?"

He smiled a little. "Every system has weak points, and Natalie's a genius at finding them. In this case, the building's almost impossible to get in—you know that—but some parts of the system have to come outside, like the cables to the outdoor cameras. Natalie managed to get a transmitter on one of them, and we were in."

"That's how you saw me," Vi said, thinking of the damn video she'd been trying to get her hands on for what seemed like years.

He nodded. "Yeah, but that was later. The first thing

we saw—and I mean the very first thing—was Ruby. It was a quick shot, and she was moved out of camera view before we could get the recording activated, but it was enough to convince us. Too bad our word wasn't enough to convince the police."

Cops don't like to take a lot on faith, Natalie had said. Vi guessed she could see why most anyone would have a hard time swallowing the story. She, personally, had long since crossed over into too-weird-to-be-true land, so it almost seemed to make sense. Except…

"But why? Why would SynCor kidnap a little girl? A *sick* little girl? Are they just evil?"

Shaking his head, he pushed himself off the bed and paced across the room to the window. "They have a reason. It might not be one we'd like to hear, but to them they did what they had to do. I'm sure it's connected to whatever was done to you—there's no way the Jenkins' thing is a coincidence."

"That's what I thought," she said, nodding. A different connection occurred to her, and she looked up. "What happened to the guy on the hospital video? The SynCor guy that Gideon recognized? Is he…it's not that Leather Vest guy who attacked me and came after Melissa, is it? Because if we could turn the cops on to him, maybe…" She trailed off as Jackson shook his head.

"It's not him. The SynCor op on the video has gone underground. I'm sure he knows he got tagged. This other guy, with the vest, I don't know where he came from. Maybe a local gun for hire. I don't think he's a SynCor op—he's not good enough. Which is a very good thing for you. If he were SynCor…" He shook his head again, and Vi swallowed hard.

Her head was full and swarming. Clutching it, she moved to sit blindly on the edge of his bed. Even in her distress, she couldn't help noticing the shadow of warmth still clinging to his rumpled sheets and covers. His warmth. She remembered the heat she'd felt radiating from his skin earlier, and she suppressed a groan.

Why did it have to keep coming back to this with him? She needed to think, not give in to distracting lust. She needed to sort out all this new information and figure out what it meant, what she'd do about it.

Except...didn't she already know?

The thought made her stomach clench with fear, and then she understood that thinking about it was exactly the wrong thing to do. Thinking about it would paralyze her, and the idea was to move, and faster than she'd ever moved in her life.

The mattress dipped, tilting her, as Jackson sat beside her, a scant few inches separating his mostly bare thigh from hers. For the first time, she realized that she'd marched into his room wearing only her underwear and one of his large T-shirts. It was a testament to how upset she'd been—she'd been half-naked in a dark room with Jackson, and she hadn't even noticed.

She was noticing now.

A moment later, as if he'd hesitated, she felt the tips of his fingers on her back. She was sure he meant it to be a comforting touch. Her skin probably shouldn't have tingled to life in response.

She lifted her head from her hands and looked over to meet his eyes. His eyes, his beautiful, deep-green eyes, looking at her now in that way that undid her, as if he wanted to cup his hand around something small and tender inside her and keep it safe.

Hell, she was getting poetic, and that wasn't what she wanted. This wasn't real—it couldn't be. It was too soon and her life was too out of whack. But that didn't mean it wasn't right.

Without a word, she lifted her hand and stopped fighting the urge to touch him. She pressed her fingertips to his cheek, his jaw, his temple, and traced little paths over his stubbled skin. He closed his eyes for a moment, his jaw tightening under her hand.

"Violet," he said, his voice low and soft.

She knew she wasn't going to like the next word he'd say—it would be *don't* or *no* or *stop,* so she didn't give him a chance to say it. Instead she slid her hand behind his head, twining her fingers through his silky dark hair and leaned forward, pressing her lips softly to his.

He made a sound, a short, broken groan in his throat, and her heart thrilled with triumph. He wanted her, he did. That was not a get-off-me sound, that was definitely a get-*on*-me sound.

Proving her right, he leaned into the kiss, moved his hand from her back to her waist and pulled her just so slightly toward him, his strong fingers gentle but urgent. Then he was kissing her, really kissing her, and she felt her head going light and delirious as his tongue slid along her mouth, his lips tracing over hers. Every nerve, every cell in her body was waking up, revving up, coming into unified focused on one thing—being touched by him.

Then, when she leaned into him, he broke the kiss, pulled back, moved his hand to her shoulder and braced it there.

"Wait," he said, his eyes squeezing shut as he breathed a little roughly.

"No."

"Violet, we can't—"

"We can," she interrupted. Not a brilliant argument, but her brain was too consumed for debating. She pushed his hand off her shoulder—noticing that he didn't struggle too much to resist her—and leaned into him again, scooting closer this time and turning more fully to face him. Without giving him a chance to stop her, she kissed him again, resting her palms on his bare shoulders, so beautiful and broad—oh, he made her ache.

He gave in again, reached out to tangle his hand in her hair and kissed her fiercely. Her body began to thrum with a slow, thick heat, loosening all the tightness of fear and tension she'd been carrying for days. Wanting more of him, she broke the kiss and shifted to her knees, leaned down to press her lips to the strong column of his throat.

It was a mistake. With his mouth free, he decided to talk again.

"Violet." His voice sounded mildly strangled, and she smiled against his throat. "I'm supposed to be taking care of you."

"You will be," she said, hearing her voice go breathy. "I need this, Jackson. I need you."

She moved to his mouth again, kissed him long and deep, trying to make him forget whatever he was thinking and get lost with her. He groaned again and shifted toward her, brought both hands to her waist and stroked up.

She thrilled with an agony of expectation, moved her hands over his bare chest—she was touching him, touching him at last—waiting for him to move his hands where she ached for them to be.

Then he was there, his big, rough, gorgeous hands cupping her breasts, making her eyelids flutter and her body ripple with sighing satisfaction and tearing need. His hands tightened, squeezing, tripling her heartbeat, and then—

He pulled away with a rough hiss of air through his teeth.

She didn't stop her groan this time, let her head fall back as he pushed off the bed and moved away.

"Jackson, you're killing me," she moaned.

"I know," he said, his breathing uneven as he looked at her from across the room. "And it's killing me, too, but we can't do this."

She shook her head. She'd had some unwilling fantasies about this guy, and one memorable semi-erotic dream, but in none of those scenarios had she been forced to chase him around a room to get him to make love to her. She wasn't going to go after him now.

"Why can't we do this?" she asked, striving to sound reasonable and calm, rather than desperate and aroused.

He was beautiful, standing in the light of the street-lamps that filtered in through his windows. He was, but it was something else that made her long for him. She knew, before he said a word, that whatever was holding him back was something to do with keeping her safe. He wanted to protect her—she could read it in him, maybe always had seen it in him, from that first moment in the park—and it tugged at something in her that she couldn't quite control.

"You're not in your right mind," he said. "You're tired, you're overwrought, and your life is in total chaos. I'm not going to take advantage of that."

She almost laughed, she'd been so right. She shook her head. "You're right, you're not."

He looked surprised, and she almost laughed again— did she see just the tiniest hint of disappointment, that she'd given up so easily?

Pushing herself off the bed, she walked slowly toward him as his expression hardened into wariness. She'd wondered earlier what it would feel like to have him press her back against a wall—she hadn't pictured doing the reverse. This definitely wasn't what she'd imagined, but she would take it. Damn right, she would.

She stopped inches from him, drank in his gaze, let a buzz of tension build in the space between their bodies.

"I'm taking advantage of *you*," she said. "Jackson, I'm scared to death, and my brain's overloading, and the only thing that makes it go away for a while is…this." She reached out, tickled her fingers over his ribs and down to his waist. "Help me." She pressed closer, brought her other hand up to his neck and pulled his head just slightly down. "Take me away from this." She tilted her head back, raised up to brush her lips over his, and said the magic words, the ones she knew would work on him.

"Save me."

"Damn it," he breathed, and then he reached for her, really reached for her, pulling her roughly to him and sliding his hands under her T-shirt to cup her bottom in his big hands.

She shivered and arched against him, kissing him urgently, and he responded with hunger, holding her close while he moved her backward until she bumped against the bed and went down. They shifted blindly until he was over her, bracing himself with one arm and pulling her close with the other. *Yes, this, this*—the weight of him pressing into her, his hot mouth and reckless touch. *This* was what she wanted.

She felt him hard against her belly, and her blood began to sing with longing and joy. *Jackson*, it was Jackson, and she could have him, he was hers for this moment, and he wanted her the way she wanted him.

Squeezing a hand between their bodies, she reached for him, took the firm, thick length of him against her palm, making him shudder and groan. He shifted to the side and moved his own hand down, sliding smoothly between her thighs and moving up—*oh*. Moaning, she let her head fall back and her legs fall apart, and he was touching her where she wanted him most, his strong, sure fingers rubbing just right and then inside her, so perfectly, until she thought her body would burst into flame.

Chaos, frenzy, heat, motion—it went on and on. Each time she exploded in his hands, her body thrumming and pulsing and thrilling, each time she shuddered to stillness and reached for him, he started again, thwarting her intentions as he made her body respond, until every centimeter of nerve and skin and muscle was flooded with the pleasure of release, again, again, again.

She loved him touching her, could've spent the rest

of her life feeling his hands, his mouth against her, except she wanted even more, ached with wanting more, wanting him.

"Jackson," she managed to whisper at last, her voice strangled. "I need you—*inside* me."

His hands stilled, and she opened her eyes to see his face strained, torn. She knew instantly that he hadn't intended to take his own pleasure, only give to her, and she felt something warm and blooming unravel in her chest. How could he...he was so...

Surprised by a prickle of tears behind her eyes, she blinked hard and pushed away all thought but that she would not let him stop.

"Vi," he started to say, but she pulled his head down, kissed him roughly, and then leaned up to whisper in his ear, letting herself loose, telling him what she wanted in the plainest, dirtiest words she had.

He groaned a little and laughed a little, and she knew she'd pushed him past his limits. With a fast, hard kiss, he rolled away from her, diving for the drawer of his nightstand while she scrambled out of her clothes.

Coming back together—breathless, laughing, kissing—felt like heaven and home and every just-right word she could think of, if she could think at all. She rolled on top of him, rubbed against him, felt him hard below her, and held her breath, waiting to be alive again when he was inside her.

She felt him pause one last time. "You're sure?" he said.

She scowled down at him and rocked against him to make him gasp. "Don't even think about stopping," she said, and he nodded, eyes closed.

With a groan, he thrust into her until *she* gasped,

pleasure flooding her, drowning her. They moved together, hands clasping and then breaking apart to grasp and stroke each other. She leaned down, kissing him frantically as all the boiling pressure and need zinging through her body concentrated in one place, one feeling, the place where they met.

She shouted, gripping his shoulders, as the pressure broke and spilled over, washing through her body until she thought she would dissolve in it. Seconds later he drove into her a last time, rough and deep, and gave his own shout, pulling her hips hard to him.

They breathed together for a moment, panting and sighing and riding out the aftershocks and the unfurling tendrils of slow satisfaction. She leaned down, resting her forehead against his collarbone and feeling her muscles go limp with fulfillment. Every part of her body felt squeezed and wrung out in the most exquisite way.

Beneath her, his chest rose and fell with each breath, and his skin was slick under her fingertips. He lifted a hand and stroked it absently down her back, and she closed her eyes. Despite the glory of what they'd just done and everything he'd made her feel, this moment, now, this was sweeter than anything. For this moment he was hers and she was safe and the world was a steady place.

"You all right?" he asked.

She smiled to herself. He would never stop watching over her; she knew it in her bones.

"I'm better than all right," she said.

He grunted, satisfied, and she felt the sound rumble through his chest and into her skin. He shifted, and she let him roll her, rag-doll-style, to her side. She pulled his sheets around her and curled up next to him and smiled, eyes closed, at the heavy drowsiness she could feel seeping through her.

"Maybe now I can finally...sleep," she whispered.

He didn't respond, and she forced her eyes open for a glance up at him. His green eyes looking down at her were the last thing she saw before she drifted off at last.

Chapter 17

The chilly gray light of early morning was filtering
through the windows when Vi woke up. She'd slept
deep and sweet, and she wasn't sure she was ready to
be awake yet.

But Jackson wasn't beside her.

Sitting up, she rubbed a hand over her eyes and saw
him standing, naked, looking out the large window at
the far end of the room.

She slid out of bed and came up behind him, slipping her arms around his waist and closing her eyes in
pleasure at the feel of his skin next to hers. Her worries
were nagging at the edge of her consciousness, but she
clung to him, holding on to her moment of peace.

"Naked in front of the window, huh?" she said. "You
have an exhibitionist streak I should be aware of?"

He chuckled a little, but he'd stiffened at her touch,

and he hadn't placed his arms over hers as she'd anticipated. Instead he'd folded them across his chest. "Afraid not."

She frowned but kept her tone light. "You sure? I'm not saying you'd get any complaints from anyone looking in."

"They can't look in," he said. "It's a special coated glass, like a two-way mirror. We can see out, they can't see in. It's bulletproof, too, in case you were worried."

"Of course," she said. Why wouldn't he turn toward her? "I get the feeling that doesn't come standard in every apartment in this building."

"Just a weekend project." He pulled out of her arms and stepped away, reaching for a pair of sweatpants and putting them on, and she went a little cold inside.

It seemed her moment was over.

Letting her hands fall to her sides, she watched him. "So, what's wrong?" He was silent, looking at the floor in the dimly lit room instead of at her. She moved to the bed and found her T-shirt on the floor, suddenly feeling much too naked for the situation.

She pulled it on over her head. "We have to have one of those talks, huh?"

"We made a mistake," he said, his voice low.

She'd known it was coming, but that didn't stop the hard slap of it. Sitting down heavily at the end of the bed, she tried to ignore the sudden, vague nausea in her stomach and think reasonably. This wasn't a surprise. He'd resisted the whole way, and she'd pushed him, so it would've been stupid of her to expect him to be happy about it afterward. She *hadn't* expected that, hadn't thought far enough ahead to expect anything, but this...

"Why?" Her voice hadn't trembled. Very good. "Why was it a mistake? I feel better for it. Or, I did."

He shook his head, still not meeting her eyes. "I shouldn't have let it get so out of hand. You're not in any condition to make a decision like that."

Her temper spiked. "Why don't you let me worry about that? I know I'm not a supersoldier like you, but I am an adult, and I've been doing my own thinking for quite a while now."

"I know that," he said, his voice careful and even, as if he were holding his own temper in check. "But this is…not a normal circumstance, you're not thinking clearly."

She studied him, perplexed and pissed. For all that he always wanted to protect her, he'd never questioned her thinking before.

"That's bullshit," she said, taking a step toward him to get a better look at his face. "What's the real problem?"

He looked at her then, and his eyes were sparking. "Violet, calm down."

"I'm calm." She took another step. "I'm not going to go all psycho-rejected-one-night-stand on you, but I'd like to know what's really going on. Why can't you just tell me the truth?"

"I am telling you the truth," he said, his jaw clenched.

"Liar." She moved closer. "What is it—are you married or something?"

"No." He looked affronted at that.

"What, then? Are you afraid I want to get married? Jeez, Jackson—we don't really know each other that well."

"It's not that."

"But it is something. Am I not pretty enough? Or is it you? Are you one of those brooding, tortured souls who can't let a woman get close? Because that—"

"I want to be out of your life," he interrupted, half shouting.

She blinked, confused and stung. "Okay. I see," she said carefully. "Well, you're free to go anytime. I didn't realize a few days of being in my life was so horrifying to you."

"It's not—you don't—" He broke off, squeezed his eyes shut and rubbed the back of his neck. When he looked at her again, the heat of anger was gone. "You don't belong here, Violet."

She eyed him warily. "In your apartment?"

"Here with me," he said simply, quietly. "Your life is off course right now. It got interrupted. None of this should've happened. You never should've met me."

She couldn't exactly argue with that. "Okay, but I did, and that can't be changed, so we're going from there."

"Where are we going?" Despite the softness of his voice, there was an urgency behind his words. He stepped forward, reached out with one hand as if to touch her, and then stopped, let it drop. "See, that's the problem. You're going back to your old life. That's what we want, what we're working for. You'll get yourself unenhanced, get the bad guys off your back and go back to normal."

"Right," she said. "And what does that have to do with…this?"

"I want you to do that, go back to that. I want you to forget this ever happened to you. Do you see?"

She was beginning to see, and it made her stomach twist in a strange way. He must have seen it in her face, because he walked closer, looked at her with that intensity.

"I don't want to be what screws that up," he said. "Maybe I'm flattering myself, but I don't want to risk it. When you can, you should leave this behind, leave me behind and go back to your life, where it's safe."

Shit. She felt like she'd been sucker punched, because even though she wanted to smack him for being so damned noble, he was right. He was. It was what she wanted, what she'd been trying to get back—her normal life, the one with no drama, no anxiety, nothing to make her feel as if she didn't fit. She thought of Robert and how easily he would fit into that life. Jackson's life was chaos and danger, far outside the comfortable mainstream she'd worked hard to reach. If she kept on with him, she might get attached—hell, she was clearly already attached—and what would she do then? How would she ever make him part of the life she'd set up?

She sat down again on the edge of the bed, feeling weak and tired, his words ringing in her ears. *Go back to your life, where it's safe.* After a moment, she gave a humorless little laugh.

"I guess it wasn't very safe, though, was it?"

He looked at her, his eyes concerned. "What?"

"My old life. It wasn't safe. It was supposed to be, but this happened, and I was totally unprepared."

"But that's…a fluke. It's not the same as inviting risk into your life all the time, living with this uncertainty. You don't want that."

He was right again, surely he was. Her chest felt

tight, her stomach heavy. "Why do you do it? Why do you choose it?"

He shrugged, looked away, but she realized she already knew the answer.

"You like saving people," she said. "You're a protector, it's who you are." He shook his head, but she knew it was the truth.

She drew a deep breath. "But I don't know if you can save me on this one, Jackson. I don't know…" She stopped. It was hard to say, hard to even think it, but the feeling of things being stripped away wouldn't be denied. "I'm not sure I can go back to my old life, even if everything works out. What if this changed everything? Changed me? Maybe it'll never be the same." She supposed the idea had been hanging around in her brain for a while, but it was crystallizing now, unwelcome but real.

"Don't say that," he said, but the words lacked conviction. They looked at each other for a silent moment.

He swiveled around and sat down next to her on the bed. They both let out long sighs and sat in the quiet. Through the window, Vi could see the streaky light of dawn.

She looked at him sideways, wishing she knew whether to feel miserable or resigned or what. She only knew one thing.

"You know where I feel safe?" she asked.

He turned to look at her. "Where?"

"With you." He shook his head, and she touched his arm. "You're not the one leading me into danger. You're keeping me safe. I think I've trusted you from the beginning. I didn't always like you, but I never thought you'd hurt me. And the way you look out for me, it's like…" She dropped her hand and turned away, embarrassed. "No one's ever protected me before."

"Your grandparents?" he asked. "They raised you, didn't they?"

She looked at him, frowning. "How did you…" Understanding dawned. "Oh. Gideon gave you all my data, huh?"

He nodded. "The basics."

That bothered her a little. He knew much more about her than she knew about him. She tucked it away as she thought about his question.

"They raised me from the time I was nine. Before that, with my mom…" She blew out a breath. "Let's just say the parent-child roles were reversed a little. She was so out of it so much of the time, and she'd let anyone—*anyone*—hang around the house."

Absently she brushed her hand over her cheek, thinking again of the first time she'd been hit there. Danny Blair, Mom's meanest boyfriend.… "I guess it was good for me, in a way," she said. "I learned how to take care of myself, how to figure things out quickly. How to survive without help."

She glanced at him, found him frowning, his eyes dark. He was wishing he could go back through time and rescue her, she'd bet. The thought was oddly thrilling, but she really should stop enjoying his protectiveness. Like everything else, it could be dangerous to get used to.

"The funny thing was," she said, "as bad as it was with her, I still fell apart when she left me behind. When she picked…everything else but me."

"She probably just thought you'd be better off without her," he said, his tone grim. "She was probably right."

"I know." She cleared her throat, deliberately made her tone lighter. "And I was better off with my grandparents. Life was stable, anyway, and they loved me. I guess it was too late to undo all the damage, but they tried. And I tried. Of course, I found out—that first year in school with them…fourth grade—I found out I didn't know how to be a regular kid. I knew things I shouldn't know, and I didn't know normal stuff—how to play the games, what to say and when to shut the hell up. I feel like I've been running to catch up, working to blend in, ever since then."

Why was she saying these things? She never talked about this stuff, tried not to even think about it. She shouldn't be telling him now, but the words kept coming out.

"I thought I was doing it," she said. "I thought I'd *done* it, made myself normal, patched it all over. I guess I was kidding myself."

Her stomach felt queasy, and her throat was tight, and she had to suck in a big breath to stop herself from crying. It still had the power to make her so sad, and she had to wonder, sitting there in the near darkness with Jackson's warmth by her side, why that was. Why she let it be that way. How long was she going to regret what she hadn't had?

"So, you see," she said, trying to push away the dark mood even though her voice was quavering a little, "my life wasn't so safe."

"Sorry," he said gruffly.

She shrugged. "I guess it was what it was. I bet your childhood wasn't any picnic, either," she added, slanting a look at him.

He cleared his throat. "It was all right." She didn't say anything, just kept watching him, and he frowned. "It's no great story. Single mom, no money, this kind of neighborhood. The usual."

"Your dad run out on you?" She felt a little guilty for asking such personal questions, but she wanted to know, and it was only fair—she didn't have an information file about him.

"He died, before I was born. Some accident in the military. Or so my mother said."

She had a vision, with a flash of kindred spirit insight, of him as a boy, a little adult with a grown-up look of worry. "That's where it started, huh? Little man of the house, taking care of your mom."

He was silent for a long moment. "No, I didn't take care of her," he said at last. "She died when I was fourteen. Wasn't much I could do about that."

Vi sucked in a breath, pain and sorrow for him twisting in her chest. "I'm sorry," she breathed, understanding instinctively that this was why he took care of everyone else who needed him.

He shrugged. "These things happen. Nothing to be done."

It had the ring of a much-practiced line that he'd been reciting to other people—and maybe himself—for years.

"What did you do?" she asked. "All alone at fourteen?" Her heart ached at the thought.

He looked at her with one eyebrow lifted, and she

could tell she was getting close to pushing too far. "Mostly got into trouble, until Gideon came along."

"That's when you met—"

Without warning, he leaned in and kissed her and reached up with one hand to trace her cheek with his thumb. Heat flared up again at the feel of his lips against hers, warm and soft and completely distracting.

He pulled away slowly, almost regretfully, and she felt her eyelids fluttering for a moment.

"Hello," she managed at last. "I thought you thought that wasn't a good idea."

"Sorry," he said, his voice husky. "Bad impulse."

Studying him through half-closed eyes, she detected a faint hint of a smile. "Did you do that just to shut me up?"

His grin broke through, and it sent a thrill and a shiver through her. "Of course not."

"Yeah, yeah. Well, look what you started now." She leaned into him and returned his kiss, lingering and soft.

"We shouldn't do this," he said, a murmur against her lips.

"You're right," she said.

And then neither one of them said much of anything coherent for a while.

"So, we have a leak," Gideon said, in his usual cool and unperturbed way.

Vi looked around the office to see Jackson and Natalie nodding and Charlie and Aaron looking grim. David seemed fine, but that was probably because he wasn't listening. He appeared to be absorbed in picking at something on his elbow.

She and Jackson had just finished their report on the attack the night before, and she'd expected some kind of response from Gideon, but not this. She shook her head. "Sorry to be slow, but…what? What do you mean?"

"The men who attacked you didn't follow you to the safe house. They were waiting for you there," Gideon said. "That means someone told them where it was. And only people within this organization know the location."

She blinked. Wow. Somehow, in all the commotion, it had never occurred to her to wonder how Leather Vest and Co. had found the house. But the idea of one of Gideon's people selling her out was surprisingly painful.

Sandra, she thought suddenly. It had to be. Who else hated her enough—and, after the accident yesterday, who had better cause? Before she could say it out loud, Gideon spoke again.

"Todd call in this morning?"

Charlie shook his head slowly, his mouth a thin line. "He's AWOL."

Vi stared at him, the implication settling in slowly. "Todd? You think Todd did it?" Nice, Twinkie-sharing Todd? The same Todd who'd been so concerned about her the night before, so…

Ah, crap. Dismay twisted in her gut as she replayed the conversation she'd had with him the night before, while she'd waited for Jackson. Todd hadn't been concerned about her; he'd just wanted to make sure she got to the safe house. Because he'd known what was waiting for her.

She said as much out loud, and Gideon rubbed thumb and forefinger over his eyes.

"He has some gambling debt," Gideon said. "They must have made him an offer he couldn't turn down. He'll regret it."

Vi wasn't sure if that was a prediction or a threat, and she decided she didn't want to know.

"What're we going to do?" Charlie asked.

Natalie shook her head. "I say we forget it. If they got the safe house out of him, God knows what else he told them. They probably know our whole damn plan."

Gideon's jaw clenched. "We can't just abandon —" he shot Vi a look "—the plan."

"But now," Aaron said from the corner, "we're down Sandra *and* Todd. And Jackson's injured. Could we even do it with just us?"

"We could," Charlie said. "But if they're waiting for us, it'd be plain suicide."

"We don't know that Todd told them everything," David said, and Vi looked at him in surprise. Apparently, he had been listening.

"No," Jackson said. "We don't. But we'd be idiots not to consider it a possibility."

"So we call it off," Natalie said.

"No," Vi said, loud enough to get everyone's attention. "We go get her tonight."

Shocked silence filled the room. Vi swallowed hard, almost unable to believe she'd said it herself.

Gideon turned cold eyes on Jackson. "You told her." His voice was flat.

"He didn't spill it," Vi jumped in. "I saw it on the news and put two and two together. Then I made him tell me the rest."

"Damn it, Jackson," Gideon said.

Vi glared at him. "You should be glad. Because the truth is..." She took a deep breath. "I never intended to go through with the break-in. I was just stringing you along waiting for a better option."

She saw Jackson's eyes widen just the slightest bit, but Gideon didn't look all that surprised. He'd probably suspected all along.

"But now," she began, then stopped. Everything she'd felt when she'd realized the truth about the mission came flooding back—the fear, the tightness in her chest, the hollow feeling in her stomach. She was crazy, out of her gourd and apparently nursing a secret death wish to be signing up for this, but now...she didn't have much choice.

"It's bigger than just me," she said at last. "And I can't let some poor kid suffer when there's something I can do about it." She drew another shaky breath, trying to make her voice firm. "Now, it seems to me that if Todd told them our plan, they might be thinking of moving Ruby somewhere else, which means we've got to move fast. Which means...tonight."

The idea terrified her. She wasn't ready, not even close to ready. But then, she wouldn't be ready for this with a whole year of practice. She'd never be any more ready to risk her life.

Jackson was nodding with what looked like reluctance. "It might also give us a little bit of a jump on them. Even if they know we're coming, they don't know when, and they might not expect us to move fast. And the sooner we do it, the less time they have to prepare."

Gideon looked at Natalie. "You have the access card?"

Sighing, she reached into the back pocket of her black jeans and pulled out a gray plastic rectangle. "I still say this is one bad idea."

"Noted," Gideon said. "David, you ready with the decrypt and the wireless setup?"

David nodded. "No problem."

"Easy for you to say," Charlie grumbled. "You're staying here."

"Hey," Gideon said, looking hard at each person in the room in turn. "We're doing this. It's our only chance to get her. If you can't be a hundred percent on board with that, I need to know about it right now."

Vi wasn't sure what she was waiting for, but she found herself holding her breath. No one spoke.

"Good," Gideon said, standing up. "Then let's get to work."

Jackson was the last one out of Gideon's office, and Vi pushed herself from her leaning position against the wall when he emerged.

"Hi," she said, because she didn't know what else to say.

"Hi," he said in return.

She glanced at the floor. A little awkward, being with him here after the night before. A little weird to look at him now, look at the places she'd touched, and feel the difference between them. Still, with all the fear clutching her by the throat, she was glad to have him close by.

"I'm sorry," she said.

He frowned at her. "For what?"

"For lying to you. About doing the mission. I wasn't

trying to waste your time, I swear. I just didn't know what else to do. I wanted to tell you the truth, so you'd stop worrying, but…" She shrugged.

He shook his head. "No, it was smart. I just wish I'd had a chance to feel relieved that you weren't going to do it before you actually decided to do it."

Laughing a little, she peered up at him. "You understand why I changed my mind?" It was hardly a question. Of course he understood—he was used to heroics. She was the one who was usually too preoccupied with taking care of herself to look out for anyone else.

"Yeah." He studied her. "It's a hell of a gutsy move, Violet."

She chuckled again. "Does it matter that I'm scared half to death?"

"That's what makes it gutsy," he said.

Wrapping her arms around herself, she squeezed and sucked in air. "Well, you're never going to believe this, but…" She paused for effect, lifted both eyebrows. "I'd like to practice drills on the heavy bag now."

"So this is what it takes to get you to be serious about your training," he said, moving toward the gym and guiding her with a hand at the small of her back.

She smiled, but silently thanked him for the gentle touch. It made her feel steadier, and she was going to need all the steadiness she could get.

Chapter 18

Brian hadn't slept well in weeks. His hair was falling out at an alarming rate, his asthma was acting up, and rational thought—his stock in trade—seemed to be eluding him at times. He was drowning, drowning in this nightmare, and if he weren't in it up to his neck, he'd throw it all over and walk away.

He chuckled wearily. That was a false dream. SynCor would never let him walk away. Period. No question about that. And even if he did manage to leave, he'd be leaving everything—his research, his work, the palace of a laboratory SynCor had built him—what amounted to his whole world.

And then, too, if he walked—or rather, if he ran— he would be leaving Ruby to their mercy. He hadn't sunk so low yet.

His mind flashed to the moment when the SynCor

operative had delivered poor little Ruby to his lab. He shook his head, remembering the horror that had clutched him then as he'd put it together, recognized her name from the Jenkins' list that SynCor had given him, realized what Harriman had done. "It won't work. I'd need an active viral sample to make it work," he'd told Harriman, never imagining that wouldn't be the end of the entire Jenkins' tangent. He himself had certainly given up on it as a mutation medium...until Ruby's arrival had made him truly desperate.

Now he was at the end of his hope. Once again, Lowell had failed him, failed to get *her,* and time was almost up.

"Two days," he said to Lowell, his voice coming out as a strangled whisper. He cleared his throat. "My superior will be here in two days. Do you know what it means if he comes here and I have nothing to show him?"

Lowell slouched in a guest chair in front of Brian's desk. "Yeah. I get it. He'll be pissed."

"He'll be more than 'pissed,'" Brian said. "He'll be homicidal. And no matter what else he does, you can be sure he'll return with a recommendation to cease funding this facility, my research. It only makes sense, you see. If I can't produce results, why should they continue to give me money? A child —" he flinched "—a fool could understand the very precarious situation I am in."

"Well, I have good news, Doc."

"Unless your news is that you have her hidden in your pocket, I can't see how good it could be," Brian said. "You don't have her, I need her, and everything you've tried has failed. Forgive me for not seeing the silver lining in this situation."

"I went back to see him," Lowell said, as if Brian hadn't spoken at all.

"Who?"

"The one we paid off," Lowell said, as if it should've been obvious. "When things didn't...work out, at the safe house," he paused and touched his nose, which was swollen and purple, "I caught up with him before he left town. Somebody had to pay for that."

Brian recognized immediately how unfair it was—the man had given Lowell the information he'd been paid for, the location of the safe house—but Brian didn't care. More than that, he felt a fleeting but savage satisfaction that someone, somewhere, was in as bad a state as he was.

"He got real talkative real fast once I waved the stick and not the carrot. Man babbled like a brook. Hell, he told me more than I wanted to know about some things."

More grandiose talk from Lowell. Brian was rapidly losing faith in the man's abilities, his smug promises. He shook his head as Lowell talked on. Perhaps he should give up, admit everything to Harriman now, explain it all and ask for help. With SynCor operatives instead of these hired thugs, he would have Violet Marsh in his possession within hours.

In fact, perhaps he'd have been wisest to have involved Harriman from the start, from the moment he'd identified Violet as his optimal candidate. But after the Ruby debacle, he'd been determined to handle things in his own way. He hadn't wanted Harriman to know anything at all about Violet, and when he'd given up on her and let her go, he'd been relieved about his decision to keep it all from Harriman. God knows what Harriman would've done to an unwilling participant in a failed experiment.

No, he couldn't risk telling Harriman—the man was too unpredictable, too cruel. And besides, if Harriman knew what he'd done—and how he'd botched it by letting Violet go—he might decide the situation was too far out of hand, that Brian wasn't competent, that he'd lost control. He could lose everything by that path as surely as any.

"You listening to me, Doc?" Lowell asked, his voice going hard with irritation. "I'm telling you, your problems are solved. Minimum effort, maximum return."

"I'm listening," Brian said, tuning back in. "What are you saying?"

"I'm saying we're done chasing after her. I'm saying she's coming to us."

Vi crouched on blacktop in the dark just inside an electrified fence, watching Charlie make his way quietly over the snap-together wall-breach ladder Gideon's team had assembled to negotiate the fence. She'd gone over right after Natalie—terrified she'd let a foot slip and make contact with the fence wires. Jackson was poised to bring up the rear.

Yards ahead of her, looming up in the light of the security beams, stood the facility, and that ominous doorway she'd seen in the video was directly in front of her. After all the mystery, it turned out to be a biotech company operating under the name ReGenetics, a bland one-story building three blocks from the highway. As

Jackson had said, it was hiding in plain sight. She might have passed it on her way somewhere and never given it a second glance.

It looked a little different from behind, through the face mask of a tactical helmet, after sneaking over the security fence.

Charlie hit the ground next to her with a soft thud, and she heard Jackson start up the ladder on the other side. She tried to steady her breathing, tried to steady her hands, tried to stop her mind from repeating, "This is it this is it this is it."

Don't think about how suicidal it is, she told herself. Just think about what you have to do.

Go through the door that Natalie would open with Aaron, now that Todd was gone. Down the hall, fast, faster than she'd ever done it. Take out the guard—she wouldn't let herself dwell on that, but she'd do it. After what she'd fought through in the past few days, one guy was nothing, really. Right?

Then on to the security panel and hope it looked like the one David had mocked up. Find the override switch and type in the code David would give her over her earpiece.

Once she got the gate open and the others were inside, she'd take out the wireless network card David had given her, plug it in to the nearest computer and get the hell out of Dodge. David would initiate the system-info dump while the others went farther in to find Ruby, and they'd all meet up over the ladder on the other side of the fence.

Simple.

She closed her eyes for a moment and thought about

throwing up. Probably she shouldn't have eaten two cheeseburgers and all those French fries right before leaving Gideon's, but she'd been afraid of getting hungry and weak in the middle of the mission.

Jackson hit the ground, and Gideon snapped his fingers to get everyone's attention. She looked over at him, still shocked to see him out of his usual expensive suits and in camo pants and bulletproof vest like the rest of them. He pointed at Natalie and Aaron and received a thumbs-up sign from each of them, then he nodded and pointed to the facility's door. The two moved off toward it with quick, quiet steps.

Standing up, Vi edged closer to Jackson and caught his eye. They couldn't speak now that Gideon's silence order was in effect, but there was nothing to say anyway. The plan was in place, they were here, and it was really going to happen. She tried not to let her fear show, but he must have seen it. She could read his eyes, and they were an agony of worry.

Gideon stepped in front of her. Thumbs-up? She shot a last glance at Jackson, then turned back to Gideon and nodded, made the thumbs-up sign with a shaky hand. Gideon swirled his index finger through the air and pointed forward, then moved off, taking Charlie and Jackson with him.

She was alone.

The fence was her starting point, farther back from the doorway than she'd ever practiced, but that should give her plenty of space to get up to speed, and give Natalie and Aaron a little cushion to get the door open. By now David should already have overridden the security cameras with a looping view of innocuous nothing.

She'd tried to imagine this moment, had assumed all through the drive over that she'd be sick with fear, crippled with terror. Now that she was here, she felt instead strangely blank. She knew it was real, really happening, but it felt impossible, distant, like a dream where she was watching herself move around from outside her body.

She'd take it. It was a false kind of calm, but she needed whatever kind she could get.

Up ahead, she could see Natalie and Aaron carefully approaching the door. They were in place. Any minute Natalie would give her the sign…any minute…

Natalie's hand flashed up, and Vi's stomach lurched, but thank God, her legs had started without her conscious command. She was running now, and the steady thump of her boots on blacktop was soothing her with its rhythm. *Don't think, just move, just move, move move move—*

She was almost there, and Aaron was still punching buttons on the keypad, Natalie standing by with her fist wrapped around the door handle. It was going to be close, she was almost at the door. She fought the urge to slow down a beat or two—she had to trust them, they'd get it open, she wouldn't crash.

Still she squeezed her eyes almost closed for the last part of it. Just in time, Aaron swiped the card and gave a nod, and Natalie yanked on the door. It flew back and Vi raced through, and then she was in the corridor, bright white lights nearly blinding her after the darkness outside, cool air in her nostrils, her boot steps echoing against the white tiles. She could see the end of the hallway in front of her, the security station beyond it, but…

She couldn't see anyone there.

And the gate wasn't coming down.

With a few final, furious steps, she passed under the gateway threshold and hop-stumbled to a stop in front of the security station, ready to fight.

It was deserted. Silent. She could hear her own rough breathing in the quiet. No alarm, no guards, nothing.

They'd gone. They'd taken Ruby and gone.

Fumbling for the radio microphone in her helmet, she began to speak. But before she could get out a coherent word, her headset exploded with sound. Shouts, shots, loud voices and scuffling steps, just outside the closed door at the end of the corridor.

"Jackson! Gideon!" she shouted into the mike, her crazy-fast heartbeat tripling with terror.

Then a dozen guards in full riot gear jogged out from three adjoining hallways and surrounded her. Every one of them had a tranquilizer gun pointed squarely at her.

She froze, icy fear flooding her as her breath went short in her chest. Shit. Oh, shit.

"There's no point in calling your friends."

A voice, to her right—she could just hear it over the clamor in her earpiece. She turned to see a slight man in glasses and tan slacks coming toward her. He stopped just inside the ring of guards.

"They can't help you anymore," he said, and shook his head sadly.

Then her headset went quiet.

"What's happening?" Vi asked, almost surprised that her voice worked, her throat was so tight.

"Just relax," the man in glasses said. "It's over now."

"What did you do to them?" She couldn't breathe right, sucking in quick, jerky gasps of air.

"I'm sorry," he said, and his thin face seemed sincerely regretful. "I didn't want it to be this way, but you didn't leave me much choice. Your friends had to be eliminated."

No, no, no no no. She could feel her head shaking back and forth involuntarily. It couldn't be. Gideon, Charlie—oh, Jackson—they were good at fighting, they were professionals, they couldn't be—

"Unit two, report." It was the guard next to the man in glasses, and he was speaking into a two-way radio. Static crackled and hissed as he waited for a response. Nothing came.

The man in glasses shot a frowning look at the guard, and a flicker of hope tingled up Vi's spine.

"Unit two, report," the guard said again. In the crackling silence, Vi put it together. Gideon had half expected an ambush once she was inside, and the team must have been hit just outside the door. But they'd been prepared for that, so surely… She clenched her teeth in agony, clutching the locator bracelet around her wrist.

"Unit two reporting," came a tinny voice through the radio. It wasn't a voice she knew. "All clear." She felt horrified tears begin to start as her hope drained away.

The man in glasses nodded, satisfied, as despair began to drag at her. She panted for air, looked around wildly, concentrated on not collapsing into tears. What was she supposed to do? She couldn't think, couldn't even let herself feel or—

"Now, calm down, Ms. Marsh. You don't want to do

anything rash. As you can see, any one of these men can tranquilize you with an easy shot, and if you try to move or fight, that's what will happen. But that's not what I want to happen."

"Why?" she asked through gritted teeth. "Is it going to mess up your big experiment if I get knocked out? It didn't seem to matter when I was here before."

"Oh, you're wrong about that," the man said. "It mattered a great deal. You don't think I'd have let you go if I'd known the procedure had worked, do you? It was the sedative that blocked the indicators." He stopped, shook his head. "But you don't want all the details. The important thing for you to know is that we don't want to hurt you. We want to take good care of you."

She laughed a little, nearly hysterical. "Take care of me? Is that what you think you're doing? By messing with my body and turning me into some kind of mutant freak?"

"That's not a very positive attitude, Ms. Marsh. One could argue that I've given you a gift. Think of the power you have now. The regenerative power alone, the implications of it—of course, we'll need another delivery method, Jenkins' won't work on many, but the procedure does work. You've proven that it works, and now think what can be done—"

"Is that how you justify it in your mind?" Incredulous, she shook her head, felt a spark of anger begin to consume her pain and fear. "Is that how you justify kidnapping a little girl, a helpless, terrified nine-year-old, and holding her prisoner? Are you taking good care of her, too?"

He flinched, his eyes blinking rapidly. "You don't understand." He smashed his thin lips together and sucked in air through his nose. He turned to the nearest guard. "Take off her helmet and protective gear, and we'll all escort her to the laboratory."

Vi stepped back instinctively as the guard advanced, and she felt the barrels of several tranq guns following her movement. She froze, the truth fully sinking in.

She was trapped. Alone and trapped, no help coming, no help in sight. They'd take her to that lab and strap her down, and it would truly be over. She felt tears finally spill over as the guard pulled off her helmet, detached her vest, removed even the bracelet from her wrist.

Then—

BOOM!

The loudest noise she'd ever heard exploded behind her, tearing at her ears and sending a wave of sound rumbling through her chest. Without thinking, she fell forward to the ground as the guards around her erupted in chaos.

What the hell, what had happened? More crashing booms, smaller but still jarring, followed the first, and the guards began to flood toward the door. She saw the man in glasses turning in a circle in the middle of the room, his eyes wide and blinking fast.

And she saw a clear way to run.

She didn't know what was happening behind her. She only knew it was a distraction that gave her a moment's chance. And she was taking it.

Scrambling to her feet, she stumbled forward toward the empty hallway in front of her and began to run. She heard the man in glasses shout as she passed him, saw his gaping mouth and panicked eyes, and then she was past him, and she was running.

He was yelling at the guards to follow her, and a quick glance over her shoulder told her some of them were doing it, but at least she had a little lead.

But she was running out of hallway, coming to the end and a choice between left or right. She veered right because it was easier to turn that way, skidded around the corner, kept running. Spotting a door on her left, she beelined for it, grabbed the knob to jerk herself to a stop, and leaned on the door.

It was unlocked. Thank God, it was unlocked.

She slid through and carefully pushed it closed, then turned to look wildly around, breathing hard. The room was dark, and she could vaguely make out dim shapes of worktables. She jogged to the nearest one and tucked herself under it, scooting back until she was braced against the wall and out of sight.

She heard heavy boot steps in the hallway, held her breath and squeezed her eyes shut. *You're okay, it's okay,* she told herself silently, frantically. They didn't stop, continued down the hallway, obviously thinking she had run on.

Oh, God. Okay, she had a moment, but just a moment. They'd look in here eventually, and she had to have a plan. How the hell was she going to get out of this? Christ, how had this gone so wrong? She should've known, should've expected to have to bail herself out, should've planned for it. This is what came of depending on other people.

Her eyes were adjusting to the dark, and she noticed

a faint glow lighting the room. Inching forward, she poked her head out from under the worktable to look for the source of the glow, and then she spotted it.

A window.

It was small, and up high in the corner near the ceiling, and it had the look of the kind that only swung open halfway, for ventilation. Even if she broke it open all the way, she'd barely have room to squeeze through it. But still, it led to outside, and that made it her best way out—probably her only way out.

She looked around for chairs to stack on the table under the window so she could get up high enough to jerk the pane out of the frame, and then she saw the computer sitting across the room.

Her breath caught in her throat. Patting the thigh pocket of her camo pants, she felt the hard shape of David's wireless card. She could still get the data, David was surely still standing by, even if the others—

She grimaced at the stabbing sort of pain in her gut and pushed the thought away. *Can't think about them now. Just...don't.*

Footsteps outside the door had her shuffling back to the wall, tucking her legs back out of sight. She could hear her racing heartbeat throbbing in her ears, impossibly loud, impossibly fast. She couldn't get caught. Not now, not when she'd figured out an escape that might actually work.

The door banged open and the lights came on, shocking her with their brightness. She huddled into the smallest ball she could make as footsteps entered the room. It sounded like two—no, three people. From the door she was hidden, but if they came all the way across the room and turned around, they'd see her. It was too late to move now.

After a moment she heard a pinched, breathless voice. "She's not here, let's move on." It was the man in glasses, she knew it was. Relief trickled through her as she realized the guards with him were slowly moving back toward the door. They were going to leave, and she could make her escape, and—

Her brain screeched to a halt on one word.

Ruby.

Damn it, what about Ruby? She couldn't just leave the little girl here. That was the point, the reason she'd decided to go through with this stupid, doomed mission. Somebody had to save Ruby.

But not me.

It was the most cowardly, terrified part of her, but it was speaking up, and she couldn't ignore it. She had never been the one who was going to save Ruby. She was just going to help, in a small, auxiliary role, and then the others—the experienced professionals—were going to rescue Ruby. She wasn't qualified, she wasn't equipped, she wasn't, damn it, she wasn't brave enough.

But she was the only one left.

The thought squeezed her heart as the guards headed for the doorway. In a flash, she realized that she had a chance, right now. If she bolted out of hiding as soon as they turned off the lights and rushed them quietly from behind, she could probably take out both the guards and grab the man in glasses. She could make him take her to wherever he had Ruby hidden, and she could figure out the rest as she went. If she waited, she'd have to chase through the building, she'd never find Ruby, and she'd get caught in the process.

But…if she went after the man now, she'd have to throw away her chance to escape. And almost as important, she'd be kissing her access to the precious computer data goodbye. Even if she did manage to get out, without that data she'd never get her normal life back. She'd be stuck like this, for good.

Time seemed to grind to a halt as she agonized. Her life or Ruby's. A likely shot at everything she'd been working toward, or a near-hopeless quest to save someone else.

The lights snapped off. And she knew what she would choose.

Chapter 19

Determination flooding her, Vi pushed herself silently from under the table, her skin buzzing with electric energy, her mind focused on one purpose.

The answer was clear in that moment—saving Ruby *was* the way to get her life back. Not the old one, the sham production she'd created to convince herself and everyone else that she was normal. That empty life was gone.

And her control was gone, too. Those things she'd held so tightly and tried to hide were slipping out, and her life had damn sure spun out of her grip, and it was terrifying. But it was also the most freedom she'd ever felt. Because none of it mattered now. Nothing mattered but saving Ruby and saving herself.

And if she got really lucky, then maybe she could find her way out the other side to a life that was worth the saving.

She pounded across the floor, fixated on the man in glasses, the man who'd done this to her. He'd said it was a gift, and maybe he was right.

He was about to find out how it felt to have the gift turned against him.

She caught up with the guards as they reached the doorway. They both turned as she approached, their eyebrows drawing down under their helmets and their mouths grimacing in surprise. Vi felt as if time were running in slow motion, it was so easy to reach for them before they could react.

"Shoot her, shoot her," she heard the man in glasses say, his voice a squeak in her consciousness. She used both hands to grab the tranq guns the guards were lifting, wrapped her fingers tightly around the barrels and yanked back hard, wrenching the guns free.

Both guards stumbled forward as she pulled, and she seized the moment of their imbalance, sweeping her leg out and across to kick their feet out from under them. They went down hard, and she scrambled to turn the guns around in her shaking hands. Unsteadily, she aimed and fired, fired, fired, fired, using all the darts loaded and managing to hit each man once.

Both men groaned and struggled to get up, but she knew they wouldn't last long with the tranquilizers speeding into their blood. She dropped the empty guns and turned to the man in glasses, who was frozen in the doorway, eyes still wide with shock.

"Where's Ruby?" she asked, her voice rough with anger and adrenaline.

He turned and ran, but she took three steps and

caught up with him, grabbing his arm and wrenching it behind his back.

"You of all people should know you can't outrun me," she told him.

He gasped and went up on his toes, trying to ease her grip on his arm. She held it fast.

"I used to be a peaceable person," she said, her jaw clenched tight. She was furious now, enjoying his pain. "But I can hurt you. I'd probably take some pleasure in it, too."

He squeaked. "Please," he gasped, "be reasonable."

It was actually a good reminder. She was trying to get Ruby, not revenge. "Take me to Ruby," she said.

"Fine, fine," he said, and started moving down the hallway to the left.

Too easy, he'd given in too fast. Now he could be leading her anywhere, and they'd surely run into more guards, and how would she handle it? She could use him as a shield, but if there were too many of them, what then?

Not sure what else to do, she went with him for the moment, watching him closely, her reflexes on high alert. He took her all the way down to the end of the hall, past several unmarked doorways. She wondered if she should check each one, but then reminded herself that Ruby was hidden. If she'd been behind a door that was in plain sight, the police would've found her when they'd searched the place.

He rounded the corner, leading her back toward the front of the building, and she tensed. This couldn't be right, he was trying to pull something, she had to—

She jerked to a halt as he stopped in the middle of

the hallway and turned to the left. Puzzled and wary, she watched as he pressed his palm carefully against the wall. To her shock, a square of the wall around his hand began to glow, and then the wall shifted, and then...

Where there had only been an ordinary wall before, a door was sliding open. She stared at it, amazed in spite of her anger and tension and fear. Even now, watching it open, she could barely see where the seams had been.

He stepped forward, drawing her along, before she could figure out how it was done, and she forgot about it when she saw the little girl huddled in a corner.

"Oh, Christ," Vi whispered. Ruby was sitting with her eyes fixed on the floor. Her long brown hair was tangled, and she wore a dirty yellow nightgown, and her feet were bare. She was very still.

Vi's stomach went cold, and she rushed across the room. The girl didn't start or look up—she was so still, her face so blank—but there wasn't time to do anything but take her and run.

There were restraints at her wrists and ankles made of some kind of fabric, and Vi didn't waste time figuring out how to unfasten them, just jerked them apart hard and fast to break them off.

She leaned over into the girl's line of vision.

"Ruby, honey, I'm going to pick you up now. I'm going to take you out of here."

Ruby didn't move, didn't even blink, and, wincing, Vi gathered the girl up and lifted her as gingerly as she could.

"I'm sorry, I can't let you go anywhere."

Vi whirled around with Ruby—shit, how could she have forgotten about the man in glasses? In her rush to get Ruby, she'd let him go and turned her back on him completely—so stupid.

He was pointing another tranq gun at her now. Damn it. He must've had one stashed here—that was probably the only reason he'd actually led her to the right place.

Breathing fast, she clutched Ruby's limp body and tried to think. There had to be a way out of this. Or at least a way out for Ruby.

"Please," she said, taking a step toward him.

"Stay back," he said, brandishing the gun. "I will use this."

She stopped, swallowed. "Please, just let her go."

He was shaking his head. "It's not that simple. If you want to save her, you should be working with me, not against me."

Vi stared at him. "What are you talking about? You're the one she needs saving from."

"No. No, it wasn't me. It wasn't my idea. I've been trying to help her, but I need you to help me. You have to understand."

"I don't," she said. "Why are you keeping her locked up if you want to help her?"

"You have to understand," he said again, his voice cracking a little. "I've been under a great deal of pressure to produce results. The mutation procedure was a success, but the directors—they're not scientists. They don't understand test tubes and Petri dishes—they want to be dazzled." He laughed bitterly. His hands were shaking as they clutched the tranq gun.

Vi watched him carefully, weighing her options. He seemed unstable, maybe weak—if she could keep him talking, maybe she could distract him enough to take him down before he could shoot. But she would have to be very cautious. If she tried to dodge his shot and missed, she'd be completely helpless, and Ruby would be back in those restraints before she could blink.

"So you...you decided to dazzle them by trying the procedure on me?" she asked.

"No, no, not at first. There were plenty of volunteers, but it didn't work on them. The delivery method was weak. I needed something the body couldn't fight. When Jenkins' disease occurred to me, I thought it could be the answer—the short-term answer, of course. But enough to prove my work to the directors, ensure continued funding."

"The directors," she said, seizing on the term. "At SynCor?"

His eyes went wide. "How do you know about SynCor?"

Good, she had him off balance. If she could keep him there, she might be able to find a way to rush him before he could shoot. But she couldn't do much with Ruby in her arms. Shifting her carefully, she began to lower her slowly toward the floor.

"Oh, I know all about SynCor," she lied. "They're not nice people, you know. But then, I guess you aren't, either, if you'd do this."

She gestured to Ruby, using the movement to slide her all the way to the floor. The girl was still lifeless, staring straight ahead, but she stood when her feet touched the floor instead of crumpling into the heap Vi had expected.

"No, I didn't, I'm trying to tell you," he said, wav-

ing the gun back and forth for emphasis. "I was ready
to give up on Jenkins' long before you came into the picture. It's impossible to get samples unless you have direct access to someone recently infected. I mentioned
this to Har—to someone, just in passing, in frustration,
and the next thing I knew, SynCor operatives were de-
livering...her. To me. Can you imagine my horror? I
never meant for anything like that to happen. I tried, I
assure you, I tried to make them take her back, but I'm
afraid...they can be very stubborn."

"So you just went along with it," Vi said, edging
slightly to the left. If he waved the gun again, maybe
she could run at him from an angle, grab the gun before he could sweep it over. But she had to keep him
going so he wouldn't notice her moving. "You locked
her up, and then—what? You decided one prisoner
wasn't enough? You had to get me, too?"

"To help her," he said. "Don't you see? To save her.
I couldn't test the mutation on her—her infection is active. I needed a healthy subject. She's the donor, you're
the recipient—a perfect combination. And I knew—I
thought—that if I produced in you the results the directors wanted, they'd listen to reason, let me let her go,
return her quietly to her parents, and no one would be
the wiser. And it can still happen." He clutched the gun
with both hands now, squeezing it. Vi winced, hoping
he wouldn't pull the trigger accidentally before she
could make her move.

"If you'll only cooperate," he went on. "Stop struggling, stay here, show them what you can do. I can still
save her."

"And you'll be the hero, is that it?" Vi said.

He frowned. "I only want to help her, to undo what was done."

Vi edged a little farther to the left. "If that were really true, if all you cared about was her, you'd let me take her now. Just let us go. Tell them I overpowered you and got away—I'll be happy to rough you up a little if you think it'll sell the story."

He was silent, blinking at her, his eyes large and uncertain behind his glasses. Then he began to shake his head.

"Right," Vi said. "You want to save her, as long as you don't have to sacrifice anything to do it. You still get your funding, you still get your dazzling result—that'd be me, I guess—and you get to call yourself a hero."

His face hardened. "More of a hero than you, I imagine, considering you won't be leaving here with her."

"I'm not leaving without her," Vi said, glancing down at Ruby. She froze. Where was Ruby?

"That's the plan," the man said, his voice turning nasty.

Ruby was no longer at Vi's side. As Vi had edged to the left, Ruby must have been doing some edging of her own, unnoticed by either Vi or the man in glasses. Vi tried to keep her expression calm—if Ruby had gotten this far, she might be able to make it out of the lab entirely if Vi didn't call attention to her absence.

"If you won't agree to cooperate," the man was saying, "then we'll just have to do this the hard way."

Vi spotted Ruby. She'd made her way behind a lab table and across the room to a spot just behind the man, out of his line of sight unless he turned. The girl was getting carefully to her feet from a crawling position, and Vi tore her eyes away, her heartbeat thumping fast in her throat as she urged the girl silently to *run run run*.

"What's the hard way?" Vi asked, keeping her eyes pinned to the man so she wouldn't betray Ruby. "You shoot me with that thing? I can probably get in a couple of decent punches before I go down, you know. Are *you* ready for the hard way?"

It was a bluff. If this tranquilizer worked on her as fast as the one Leather Vest had shot her with, she'd be out in seconds. But maybe he didn't know that.

Unable to stop herself, she glanced at Ruby and found the girl looking back at her. *Go, go,* Vi thought, but the girl wasn't moving. Their eyes held for just a moment, and then Ruby began to run.

But she wasn't running away. She was running toward the man.

Vi fought back the impulse to shout and instead began waving her hands, desperately trying to keep the man's eyes on her.

"Hey, you going to shoot me or what? I'm right here." She began dancing from side to side.

The man stared at her, following her movements with the shaking gun, and then Ruby crashed into him, slammed into his knees and pushed him hard.

He shouted and stumbled sideways and squeezed the trigger, but his shot went wild, and Vi didn't hesitate. She ran to him, yanked the gun away from him, and turned it smoothly in her hand. Then she grabbed his arm and shoved the gun right against his skin, at the fleshiest part of his skinny arm.

"No!" he screamed, and she pulled the trigger.

He reached out, grabbing for her, but she knocked his hand away, dropped the empty tranq gun and bent down to pick up Ruby.

"Good job, honey," she whispered, and the girl gave a tiny nod, her brown eyes wide, and wrapped her arms around Vi's neck.

"You can't go," the man gasped, clawing for the dart in his arm and falling to his knees. "This isn't…how it's supposed…to work."

Vi pushed past him through the door, then turned to watch him fall to his side and lie there, twitching a bit, on the floor of his lab.

"Sorry. I guess we get to be the heroes today," she said. Then she turned and ran.

Ruby was heavy, and Vi was lost, and they would be running into guards at any minute, she was sure. There'd been so many of them—they should be swarming the building like ants, but the hallways seemed empty. From somewhere she could hear occasional shouts and scuffling sounds, but she couldn't pinpoint the location. God, what she'd give to have radio contact with David now. If they hadn't taken her helmet…

But all she could do was try to retrace her steps to the room she'd hidden in, then back to the main hallway she'd first run down. She moved fast, gripping Ruby and panting for air. If she could get back to the front security station, maybe she could send Ruby running for the door while she fought her way out. And if they both made it out… run? There was no one to meet up with on the other side of the fence.

She swallowed hard and tried not to think about it.

Right now, she had to concentrate on getting to safety. She'd deal with the emotional trauma after that.

Still, her throat was tight and she was near tears when she rounded the corner to the main hallway. And skidded, stumbling and sliding, to a halt.

Five guards were clustered at the security station, and they turned when they heard her footsteps. One of them had no helmet, and it was—oh, God—it was Leather Vest. When he saw her, his eyes lit with furious fire.

Vi felt every muscle clench with terror as she clutched Ruby and stumbled backward. The guards lifted their guns—from this distance, she couldn't tell if they were tranqs or real, but it hardly mattered. Either one was a death sentence for her now. She had to try to make it back around the corner to the other hallway.

She turned away to shield Ruby and ran, waiting for the sting of a dart or the pain of a bullet. And then she heard the sounds—loud popping thumps that no tranq gun would make, then several long rattles, like—what? Automatic rifles? Cursing, she hit the ground, rolling to her side so she didn't crush Ruby, and squeezed her eyes shut. Ruby screamed, high and piercing, and the rattling and heavy thudding sounds filled her ears, and then everything went still.

Opening her eyes, she scrambled to her feet, dragging Ruby along, and spun around to see all the guards on the ground, groaning and stirring feebly. Stunned, gasping for air, she began to back down the hallway. Someone must have been standing in another of the intersecting hallways, must've hit the guards from the side with…something. An enemy of her enemy might be a friend, but she wasn't sure she wanted to meet a new friend at the moment.

Before she reached the corner, someone stepped into the hallway. Helmet. Camo pants. Bulletproof vest.

She froze, her knees turning to jelly, and she sobbed involuntarily. *Jackson.*

She tried to call his name, but her voice wouldn't work. She watched as he pulled a pair of handcuffs from his back pocket and grabbed the nearest guard. Then Natalie appeared and began to do the same, then Gideon. Vi felt weak, her chest clutching. She'd had no idea how much she cared about these people until she'd thought they were all dead.

Jackson cuffed the last guard, then turned and saw her. His eyes went wide behind his face mask, and he began to run toward her.

Vi was glued to the ground, couldn't run another step, not even to run to him. She felt her legs giving way as he neared, and she grabbed his arm with her one free hand and leaned into him as he reached for her.

She couldn't resist holding him for a moment, burying her face against the hard vest on his chest, a few hoarse animal sobs tearing out of her as her tears began to flow. "I thought you were dead," she managed to say around the strangling tightness in her throat.

"Vi," he said, his voice raspy. "I thought…" He stroked her hair, her back, gave her a hard squeeze and then held her gently away by the shoulders.

"I'm sorry, we need to move," he said. "I'm not sure we've found all the guards." He looked at Ruby. "How did you get her?"

"I don't know," she said, shaking her head. "It was… crazy."

"She's heavy, I'll take her," he said, reaching for Ruby, but the girl drew back and clutched Vi tighter.

"She's too scared," Vi said. "It's okay, I can keep her. What are we going to do?"

He moved beside her and braced his hand at the small of her back, guiding her forward. "We're going to get you somewhere safe, just in case. Maybe inside the security station."

She trotted alongside him, clutching Ruby. "We can't go out?"

"There's tear gas," he said. "We used it to disable the unit that hit us outside."

Her eyes went wide. "Was it you on the radio, then?"

"Aaron. He picked up their radio after we took them down."

Aaron. No wonder she hadn't recognized the voice—Aaron barely talked, so she hadn't learned his voice.

"Is he okay? And Charlie?"

Jackson nodded. "They're still scouting the building."

They reached the group of guards on the ground who were coming back to life now and beginning to struggle against their handcuffs.

"What about them?" she asked. "What did you do?"

"Tasers," Jackson answered, steering her past them. "Trying not to seriously injure anyone. Not that they don't deserve it," he said, shooting a look back at Leather Vest. "It's just that we're going to have a hard time explaining all this. Easier if no one's dead. Did you kill anyone?"

She drew back, shocked at the question. "No. I...I tranquilized a few guys."

"Good," he said.

A new sound penetrated her consciousness then, distant but coming closer. As they met up with Gideon and Natalie at the security station, she recognized it. Sirens.

Gideon was nodding. "Now the cavalry arrives."

Natalie snorted. "Yeah, now that we already took out all the bad guys."

Gideon held a gas mask to his face, then jogged down the corridor to the blasted doorway and poked his head out. He turned back to face them.

"So, who wants to be on TV?"

Chapter 20

"It was chaos at a local biotech company as members of a private security team rescued Ruby Mulligan, the nine-year-old girl who'd been missing for three weeks."

Vi watched, morbidly fascinated, as the TV news camera panned over the wreckage of the ReGenetics entrance, wisps of smoke still curling up from the blast of explosives Gideon and Jackson had used to get through the door after they'd gassed the ambush team. Even in the safety and relative comfort of Severin's waiting room, she had to shudder at the sight. Already the mission of only hours ago was receding to the distance of an unbelievable dream.

"Several ReGenetics security guards were arrested at the scene," the TV reporter continued as the screen showed guards in handcuffs. Vi thought she recognized the two she'd tranqed in the group, and she was almost sure she caught a glimpse of Leather Vest. "As was ReGenetics president and lead researcher, Dr. Brian Bolsham. Police sources say a weeping and hysterical Dr. Bolsham unofficially confessed to the Mulligan kidnapping upon his arrest."

Dr. Brian Bolsham. Vi watched the man in glasses being led away, turning his face from the cameras, and tried to analyze the well of emotion surging up in her gut. Was it anger? Fear? Sorrow? It was going to take a while to sort it all out.

Gideon's face appeared on the screen, and a cheer went up from the group around her. She glanced around at Charlie, currently getting his arm stitched up by Severin, at Aaron, icing a swollen knee, at Natalie, sprawled in a chair in the corner, and at Jackson, sitting close beside her on a couch. Everyone was banged up, but no one seemed to mind. The mood in the room was high and nearly giddy.

"We knew she was in there," Gideon was saying on the screen, "but we didn't have the evidence to give the police. So we knew it was up to us."

She glanced over at the live Gideon, leaning against a wall, hands in his pockets and a small smile on his face. He was good, she'd give him that. He'd managed to avoid pointing a finger of blame at the police, and he looked damned fine on camera. If he didn't get clients out of this, he'd at least get a few phone numbers.

"Sam and Helen Mulligan flew out immediately, and nine-year-old Ruby was reunited with her parents just hours ago. She's now back in the care of medical experts, who report that she is expected to make a full recovery," the reporter said, as a brief shot of Ruby held tightly by both parents flashed on the screen.

Vi's heart lurched at the sight, and she wanted to cry again, but with relief this time, with gratitude and joy. She'd probably never see that little girl again, but she would never, never forget her courage when it counted most. *If she can be so brave...*

She shook her head, nearly overcome with it all. They'd done it, Ruby was safe, and it was worth it. For this result she'd do it all again.

And maybe...maybe...she was supposed to.

The door to the office banged open, and everyone tensed. Then David appeared in the doorway, arms over his head.

"Woooo!" he said, pumping his fists a few times. "We did it!"

The room relaxed with laughter as David dragged a cooler into the small, crowded room and began tossing beer cans to everyone in range.

Vi caught hers before it smacked her chest, and she turned to Jackson. "Should the teenager really be in charge of the beer?"

Jackson opened his and took a long swallow. "At the moment, I don't really care."

She smiled and looked around again, at Natalie and Charlie clinking cans, at Gideon laughing and shaking David's hand, at Severin frowning disapprovingly at everyone. She set her own beer unopened on the floor by her feet.

What a group. It would be weird not to see them every day. The past few days had felt like a lifetime, and she was amazed at how attached to them all she felt. Her teammates. They'd come through for her, and she knew she couldn't have made it out alive if not for their help. This was what came of depending on other people.

She felt Jackson's hand on her lower back, her skin tingling to life where he touched her. She closed her eyes. Oh, and what was she going to do about him?

"Sure you're all right?" he asked.

She opened her eyes and nodded slowly. The cuts and bruises she'd picked up had healed by the time they'd finished the long ordeal of questioning at the police station.

"Not a scratch on me," she said.

"And there won't be," Gideon said from her left. Surprised, she turned to face him, and he smiled. "How does it feel to be safe again?" he asked.

She laughed a little, shook her head. "Am I?"

"You did it," Gideon said, his eyes warm and…admiring? "You did more than we could have ever expected. Ruby owes her life to you."

Wow. A compliment. From Gideon. Vi wasn't sure what to do with all the warmth she was feeling.

"I got very lucky," she said, and knew it was true.

"You were smart, resourceful, brave. I don't think luck had much to do with it." He paused. "It's too bad you'll be going back to accounting. I could certainly use someone like you on my team."

"All right," Jackson cut in, a warning note in his voice. "Cut the sales pitch."

Vi swallowed, unable to process everything coming at her. She focused on one thing. "Do you really think I'm safe now? What about…the rest of SynCor? Will they come after me?"

Gideon shook his head. "If they're smart—and they

are—they won't come anywhere near this disaster. As we speak, I'm sure they're doing everything they can to cover what there is of a connection between ReGenetics and any of their operating companies. If they even know about you, they're not going to risk coming after you now."

Safe. It didn't seem real. "So, I could go home tonight."

Jackson made a disapproving noise. "I think you should stay with me for a while."

Gideon looked up, his eyes sharp, and studied them for a moment. Then he nodded, and Vi felt her face heating a little.

"Hey, Violet, catch!" David yelled, and she glanced over in time to see him tossing something small and plastic her way. She reached out and snagged it with one hand.

It was a small, shiny CD in a clear case, and she turned it over, puzzled.

"What's on it?" she asked.

"All your data, duh," David said, and rolled his eyes.

She looked up, her mouth falling open. "But I didn't…how did you…"

Jackson shifted and dug into a side pocket of his camo pants, then pulled out a wireless card just like the one she'd carried. "I brought another one, just in case. David said you never plugged yours in, so I did mine."

"Oh my God," she breathed. "So this…this is…" She couldn't finish. A weird mixture of emotion swirled in her chest. What she held in her hand was the key, the key to going back.

But what if she wanted to go forward?

* * *

A week later Vi was curled up on Nana Martha's ugly flowered couch, eating peanut butter cookies and talking to Melissa on the phone.

"Well," she said, taking a quick swallow of milk, "Severin says I could turn the data over to the top medical experts in the country, and they might be able to reverse the procedure that Bolsham did."

"But…" Melissa said, her tone expectant.

"Two things. First, if I do that, it might get SynCor's attention, and I don't want that, no matter what. But mostly…"

"You don't want to give up your superpowers, do you?" Melissa's voice was equal parts amused and disbelieving.

Vi smiled. "Well…Severin studied the data, and from what he can tell, it looks like my heart's not going to explode anytime soon. Apparently whatever strain the crazy-fast heart rate causes is canceled out by the way the cells regenerate so quickly. So if I'm not in mortal danger, I kind of think the bonus skills might come in handy, you know?"

"Sure, I get it, but…" Melissa paused, and Vi could just picture her shaking her head, her face squinched up in concern. "I thought you were trying to build your little Stepford life."

Vi felt her eyes going wide. "What?"

"Well, you're always worried about being normal, and I swear you picked the most boring job you could think of, and—"

"How did you— I never said— What do you mean?" Vi stammered out.

"Oh, please, Vi. You're about as sly as a rock. And I took psych in college, remember? It's not that hard to understand why you'd want an ordinary life."

Huh. Sitting back, Vi took another cookie off the plate and considered. Melissa knew her better than she'd thought. Which, after eight years of friendship, was kind of nice to know.

"I guess," she started, and stopped to take a breath. "I guess I finally accepted that I'm not normal. I'm weird. I always have been. Might as well embrace it."

"Good," Melissa said. "Besides, it'll be nice to have a best friend with superpowers. It'll come in handy when I need pickle jars opened and stuff."

"Ha. Don't call me for pickle jars. *Normal* people can handle pickle jars. I'm on to bigger things."

Melissa sighed. "Fine. I'll just have to keep using them to lure the hot guy in my building into my apartment."

"Yeah," Vi said, rolling her eyes. "I know what a challenge it is for you to get a guy's attention."

"Hey, it's tough out there in the dating world. Not that someone with a *steady boyfriend* would know."

Vi felt her cheeks go hot. "Will you stop? Jeez, you're one step away from singing the 'sitting in a tree' song." Lowering her voice, she added, "Anyway, he's not my steady anything. We're just dating. I think. Actually, we're both sort of trying not to bring it up."

"Uh-huh," Melissa answered, her voice thick with disbelief. "I've seen the guy, remember? You're doing a lot more than dating."

"Melissa."

"Hey, I think it's great. He's a much better match for

you than that Robert guy, or anyone else you've ever dated, for that matter."

Vi winced guiltily, realizing she still needed to call Robert and tell him she couldn't see him again. She'd forgotten all about him.

"All right," Vi said. "Time for a new subject. We can talk about this later."

"What's the matter? Oh, is he there right now?"

Vi pushed herself off the couch and tiptoed over to the hallway to peek down it. "Yes, he's here," she whispered. "He's installing my new security system."

"Ooh," Melissa said. "He's working with tools? That's so hot. Is he wearing a tool belt?"

"Stop it!" Vi said, laughing. "That's it—new subject or I'm hanging up."

Melissa sighed. "All right, I have to go, anyway. Are we still doing movies tomorrow?"

"Yep, you bring the movies, I'll supply the food."

"Uh-uh—let me bring the snacks."

"No way," Vi said. "I've already got Jackson trying to force-feed me granola and trail mix. I'm not doing movie night with fresh fruit and rice cakes. We're having cherry cheesecake and cheddar popcorn, and that's final."

"Fine, you win. But if I ever rescue a child from a secret lab facility, I'm picking the snacks."

Vi laughed. "Deal," she said, rolling her eyes as she hung up the phone.

Brushing cookie crumbs off her sweatshirt, she hauled herself off the couch and ran a hand through her hair. It was nearly to her shoulders now, and she kind of liked the undisciplined feeling of letting it grow long and free. She smiled at herself. Yep, really getting crazy now. Never mind the superpowers—she was *growing out her hair.*

She found Jackson in the back spare bedroom.

"Hey, how's it going?"

He looked up from the sensor he was installing by the window. "Not bad. Should be finished in about an hour." He turned from the window and looked around the room. "I've got to know—what's the story with this room?"

She glanced around at the framed needlepoint squares on the walls, the homemade window curtains, the mammoth sewing machine in the corner. "It was my grandmother's sewing room," she explained. "I don't ever use it, so I've never put this stuff away."

"Ah," he said. "So I don't have to worry about getting a homemade turtleneck sweater anytime soon?"

She smiled. "Not unless you have a grandma who knits. Do you have a grandma, by the way?"

"Yes," he answered, turning back to the wires he was connecting. "But she doesn't knit."

She was tempted to follow that line of questioning, but she had other things to talk about. Moving to the sewing machine, she sat down in the chair in front of it and regarded his back, wondering how to say what she wanted to say.

"Hey, remember when we had that big argument in the gym?"

He must have heard something in her voice, because he let go of the wires and turned around, his expression wary. "Yeah."

"Remember how I said that I'd rather be anywhere else than at Gideon's?"

A beat of silence. Then "Yeah."

She took a breath and looked up at him. "I changed my mind."

His eyes went wide. "What?"

"Don't freak out," she said, standing up and moving toward him. "I've thought about it a lot, and I've made my decision. I'm going to work for Gideon."

"Violet, no."

"I know, I know—you want me to be safe, but listen, Jackson. We already know my old life wasn't as safe as it seemed, and if there's going to be danger, I'd rather go into it with my eyes open, you know? Instead of bumbling around thinking I'm protected when I'm not."

He was shaking his head. "But your eyes are open now. And we can keep training—I'll teach you all the self-defense you want to know. You'd still be safer living a normal life than you'd ever be working for Gideon."

"That's probably true," she said. "But there's more to it. It's not just about what the safest choice is. It's about what *I* want."

"And you want this?" He studied her, his eyes piercing. "What, you like the hours?"

She laughed softly. "All right, then. Call it, what I… what I'm supposed to do. I don't know that all this happened to me for a reason, but it did happen, and now I have this…well, hell, it is a gift. It can be a gift, if I use it. I can help people, Jackson. I helped Ruby, and it was scary as hell, but it was worth it. It was so worth it. That means so much more to me now than being normal, or even being safe. So, yeah. It is what I want."

He didn't answer for a moment, and his face was set in a frown. Finally he sighed and rubbed the back of his neck. "Gideon's about making money, not helping people. You know that, right?"

She nodded. "But he has a good heart. You all do. I think working for Gideon will lead me to people I can do something for." She paused, tilted her head. "Besides, who else is going to take me on with no experience and no training? I've got to start somewhere."

He didn't look convinced. "But this gift thing... Look, maybe it is a gift, but maybe there are other ways to use it. Have you thought about that?"

She frowned at him, skeptical. "Like what?"

"Like...I don't know—tennis. I bet you could really send a ball flying. You could be great."

"Jackson," she said, starting to laugh.

"Or professional...eating competitions. They have those, you know."

She laughed out loud at that. "Give up," she said, moving into him and slipping her arms around his waist. "Just go ahead and accept this, and I'll let you hover over me as much as you want. Deal?"

He sighed and looked up at the ceiling. "I don't have a choice, do I?"

"Not really. But there is a condition."

"What's that?" he said, lowering his head to look at her again.

"I want to know your name. Besides Jackson," she added quickly when he started to speak.

Grinning, he shrugged. "No big secret. It's Cooper."

She stared at him. "Your name's Cooper?"

"My name's Jackson. My last name is Cooper."

Absorbing that, she ran over the name in her mind. "Jackson Cooper. Huh. Why didn't you just tell me before, if it's no big secret? I expected something like Engelbert."

"In my business—" he broke off, sighed "—our business…the less people know about you, the better."

"Hmm…I'm kind of a talker. I'd better learn to do something about my mouth," she said.

He leaned down and nipped at her bottom lip. "I like your mouth."

She felt those thrilling sparklers of sensation beginning to shoot through her body.

"Likewise," she said, reaching up to pull his head back down. His lips met hers, warm and insistent, and his hands were stroking up her back, and she felt herself melting.

"Your security system's not finished," he murmured, moving down to kiss her neck.

She tilted her head back and smiled. "Then I guess you'll have to keep me safe."

* * * * *

Can't get enough of Silhouette Bombshell?
Every month we have a thrilling variety of compelling
and unpredictable stories just for you!
Turn the page for a sneak peek
at one of next month's novels

HER BEST DEFENSE
by Jackie Merritt and Lori Myles

Available November 2005
at your favorite retail outlet

Chapter 1

It was May, pleasantly warm during the day and chilly at night. Not consistently, of course. Chicago was known for its erratic weather and at this time of year it could be hot and sunny one day and snowing the next. Lake Michigan was beautiful to the eye, a fabulous playground for water and beach enthusiasts, and essential to Chicago's commerce, but it could stir up a dilly of a storm in the blink of an eye. Lisa enjoyed the good weather when it came and endured the bad without complaint; it was, after all, Chicago, and she loved the city.

Thursday dawned sunny and bright, making Lisa Jensen feel especially good. Arriving into the law offices of Bonner, Drake, Ludlow, and Kirten around eight, as usual, she stopped at the reception desk to pick up yesterday's phone messages and mail from Madeline, who had the inside scoop on all the gossip. They chatted a few moments about last night's fun at the Pub where Lisa put herself into work mode.

"Thanks for these, Madeline." Lisa eyed her mail and messages. "Looks like a load of work here." With her briefcase in one hand and the stack of items Madeline had just given her in the other, Lisa walked down the hall to her office.

She left her door open, as was her habit, and was getting settled at her desk when the intercom line on her telephone beeped. "Lisa Jensen," she said after hitting the speaker button.

"Just checking to make sure you were there. Mr. Ludlow is on his way down to see you." The caller was John Ludlow's private secretary, Audrey Muldaney.

"I'll be here," Lisa said. It wasn't an everday occurrence for a senior partner to visit the 16th floor, but it happened often enough that Lisa wasn't at all uneasy about the meeting. She tidied her desk a bit and waited. In mere moments she saw Ludlow walking toward her office, and when he entered it, he shut the door behind him.

"Good morning, Lisa," he said.

She stood and smiled. "Good morning, Mr. Ludlow. Please, have a seat."

"Thank you, I will."

Ludlow was a tall, gaunt-looking man well past sixty. He no longer did trial work, but his reputation from former years, Lisa had learned, was that of a brilliant litigator, a real tiger in court. Given his present soft handshake and nonabrasive personality, Lisa had trouble picturing him as a tiger at anything.

But he was always polite and pleasant around the firm, and Lisa liked him. They sat down and Lisa waited for him to speak, which he did with little pause.

"I'm sure you are well aware that the firm in general and I personally appreciate your intelligent approach to the many intricacies of the law. There are a lot of good attorneys, some of them right here in this firm, but only a few of the mass rise to the very top of the heap, like cream on a container of whole milk." He smiled. "That analogy harks back to my youth, as I grew up on a farm. Lisa, I believe you've been proving all along that you're one of the chosen few. In time you'll be a full partner in this firm, but I'm sure you already know that."

Lisa's heart skipped a beat. "I've been hoping, sir."

"Of course you have. I didn't come down here to talk about your future, but I began thinking of your accomplishments in the elevator. I'll get to the point of this meeting now. Lisa, I have a bit of a problem waiting in my office. I'm sure you're familiar with the Witherington name?"

"Most people in this part of the country are, I believe." The Witheringtons were an extremely wealthy family that had, reputedly, begun amassing their fortune during the early 1900s. She'd never had reason to look into their background and find out *how* they had become so wealthy. In fact, other than seeing their name in the society pages of various newspapers, she really knew nothing of consequence about the family. "But name recognition is about the extent of my knowledge," she added.

"That's about to change," Ludlow said. "There's

been a serious mishap at the Chandler and Glory Witherington home. A young man was found dead early this morning in their driveway, obviously a victim of foul play. I'm speaking of young Chandler and his wife, with whom I'm acquainted because of my long association with his father, Chandler Sr. You may recall his passing from several days of publicity surrounding his death two years ago. I want to say first of all that young Chandler's premonition of impending doom, by way of the police coming down on Glory because she was the only one at the house all of the night, could fizzle out to nothing. I personally am leaning in that direction, but there's also a chance of this case becoming quite serious. I thought of you at once because of your enviable flexibility. I think you could deal with Glory's, uh, shall we say, little eccentricities, better than most."

Lisa waited a moment before realizing he was waiting for her to say something. "Little eccentricities? Could you give me a hint as to what that term actually covers?"

"Well…perhaps I should have used another term. Yes, I think so. Glory is lovely and can be very charming, but she can also be as scatterbrained as they come."

"Scatterbrained," Lisa repeated, wondering if that was a polite word—and abbreviated version—for a more accurate phrase, *nuttier than a fruitcake.* What Ludlow was doing was appeasing the Witheringtons, she suddenly realized. They had come in asking for legal support for some imagined threat and Ludlow had chosen her because of her "rising star" reputation in the firm, which might possibly impress them.

She could impress the hell out of them, if that was

what Ludlow wanted, she thought. Of course, at this point that idea was mere conjecture. She would play it by ear, she decided, take her cue from the Witheringtons themselves.

"I would be happy to meet with the Witheringtons," she said.

Ludlow got to his feet. "Give me about ten minutes, then come up to my office."

Lisa rose. "Yes, sir. Ten minutes."

Alone again, she wasn't quite so subservient, and it struck her that she wasn't overly thrilled with what sounded like a time-wasting, kiss-ass project. She loved really tough cases, the kind that made her work hard and think hard. The ones that she became so immersed in that she lived and breathed every segment of the legal process necessary to defend her client to the fullest.

Checking her watch, she stood, straightened her skirt and jacket, picked up a notebook and pen, and left her office to head for the elevators. In minutes she had arrived at the 17th floor, greeted Audrey and been ushered into Ludlow's office. John rose to his feet and introduced her to Chandler and Glory Witherington. The first thing that Lisa noted about Chandler was that he had remained seated when John acknowledged her presence by standing. He also wore an arrogant, condescending expression and his "Pleased to meet'cha," sounded lame as a one-legged duck. Lisa sized him up over a limp handshake and from behind the businesslike smile she gave him she could see he was starting to bald, appeared to be in late fifties and looked physically fit in an obviously expensive custom-made suit. He was also, in her estimation, a jerk.

She turned to Glory and felt struck by lightning. The woman was flamboyantly gorgeous. Flashy as all hell in a hot pink and orange outfit, with flaming red hair and eyes so blue they didn't seem real. Actually, Glory didn't seem real, Lisa thought. She looked more like a life-sized doll than a human being. She was obviously very high maintenance and well tended, and it wasn't hard for Lisa to picture Glory spending a great deal of time in Chicago's best beauty spas, which offered every procedure known to mankind to keep a woman…or a man…looking young.

And so far she hadn't moved a muscle or uttered a sound. In truth, she intrigued Lisa. Certainly Lisa knew that she had never met anyone to compare her to.

Lisa stepped over to her and held out her hand, obviously requesting a handshake. "I'm very pleased to meet you, Glory."

Glory looked at Lisa's hand for a long moment and finally touched it with hers. "Thanks," she said in a bored-sounding voice.

Lisa almost laughed. These two were something else. Questions about them began piling up in her mind, questions that she would definitely remember and get the answers for directly from their own lips or indirectly by other methods.

John Ludlow, who was still standing, said, "Lisa, I think it best if you and the Witheringtons get acquainted in the small conference room."

Lisa looked into his eyes and thought she saw a message: Get these two out of my office. Whether or not that was an accurate interpretation of the vibes she was picking up from Ludlow, she hastened to deliver on his suggestion.

"Come," she said to the Witheringtons. "The room is just down the hall."

It was tastefully decorated and offered comfortable furniture on which to sit and hopefully relax enough to converse without reservation. Lisa indicated the sofa for the Witheringtons and took a nearby chair for herself.

She opened her notebook and asked Chandler to relate the story he'd told John earlier.

Almost sullenly, obviously because he had to repeat himself, Chandler said, "A man was found shot to death in our driveway. Someone called the police and all hell broke loose."

"Who made that call, Chandler?"

He glanced at his wife. "You did, didn't you, hon?"

"I think it was me. Everything was so confusing after Maria started screaming."

Lisa was busily writing, wondering if she should perhaps be using a recorder. But she had discovered that the sight of a recorder often made people uncomfortable and cautious of what they said, so except in extreme cases she relied on her own brand of shorthand to get down nearly every word spoken between herself and whoever she was interviewing.

"Do you know who the man was?" Lisa asked, expected a fast and forceful denial.

"Mateo Ruiz," Chandler said.

Lisa was genuinely surprised, although her demeanor didn't change. "Did you actually know him, or merely overhear someone mention his name. A police officer, for instance."

"No, I knew him. Not well, but…well enough."

Chandler's answer struck Lisa as a bit strange, but

she accepted it and turned to Glory. "Did you know him, Glory?"

Glory's hot pink lips twitched in a semblance of a smile. She looked Lisa directly in the eyes and drawled with an odd little smirk on her face, "I did from the waist down."

Silhouette® BOMBSHELL™

CIA agent Miranda Cutler needs an

EXIT STRATEGY

The exciting novel

by Kate Donovan

November 2005

She'd helped colleague Ray Ortega out once
before, and had almost been fired for her
troubles. So Miranda wasn't thrilled to be
teaming up with him on her most dangerous
mission yet. She decided to go solo—
but leaving Ray behind wasn't so easy....

Available at
your favorite retail outlet.

www.SilhouetteBombshell.com   SBES

When a Chicago society wife
is accused of murder,
top-notch attorney
Lisa Caputo has to put on

HER BEST
DEFENSE

by **Jackie Merritt**
and **Lori Myles**
November 2005

The more Lisa learns about her client's
family and their ties to big-time crime,
the more she thinks that maybe a little
self-defense would be in order....

*Available at
your favorite retail outlet.*

www.SilhouetteBombshell.com   SBHBD

e**H**ARLEQUIN.com

The Ultimate Destination for Women's Fiction

For **FREE online reading,** visit
www.eHarlequin.com now and enjoy:

Online Reads
Read **Daily** and **Weekly** chapters from
our Internet-exclusive stories by your
favorite authors.

Interactive Novels
Cast your vote to help decide how these
stories unfold...then stay tuned!

Quick Reads
For shorter romantic reads, try our
collection of Poems, Toasts, & More!

Online Read Library
Miss one of our online reads?
Come here to catch up!

Reading Groups
Discuss, share and rave with other
community members!

For great reading online,
visit www.eHarlequin.com today!

INTONL04R

If you enjoyed what you just read,
then we've got an offer you can't resist!

Take 2 bestselling love stories FREE!

Plus get a FREE surprise gift!

Clip this page and mail it to Silhouette Reader Service®

IN U.S.A.
3010 Walden Ave.
P.O. Box 1867
Buffalo, N.Y. 14240-1867

IN CANADA
P.O. Box 609
Fort Erie, Ontario
L2A 5X3

YES! Please send me 2 free Silhouette Bombshell™ novels and my free surprise gift. After receiving them, if I don't wish to receive any more, I can return the shipping statement marked cancel. If I don't cancel, I will receive 4 brand-new novels every month, before they're available in stores! In the U.S.A., bill me at the bargain price of $4.69 plus 25¢ shipping & handling per book and applicable sales tax, if any*. In Canada, bill me at the bargain price of $5.24 plus 25¢ shipping & handling per book and applicable taxes**. That's the complete price and a savings of 10% off the cover prices—what a great deal! I understand that accepting the 2 free books and gift places me under no obligation ever to buy any books. I can always return a shipment and cancel at any time. Even if I never buy another book from Silhouettte, the 2 free books and gift are mine to keep forever.

200 HDN D34H
300 HDN D34J

Name	(PLEASE PRINT)
Address	Apt.#
City	State/Prov. Zip/Postal Code

Not valid to current Silhouette Bombshell™ subscribers.

Want to try another series?
Call 1-800-873-8635 or visit www.morefreebooks.com.

* Terms and prices subject to change without notice. Sales tax applicable in N.Y.
** Canadian residents will be charged applicable provincial taxes and GST.
All orders subject to approval. Offer limited to one per household.
® and ™ are registered trademarks owned and used by the trademark owner and
or its licensee.

BOMB04   ©2004 Harlequin Enterprises Limited

They were a father and daughter
who had never been close but
something about rebuilding the
lighthouse made sense.

Could a beacon of light that had
always brought people home be
able to bring understanding and
peace to two grieving hearts?

the LIGHTHOUSE
MARY SCHRAMSKI

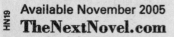

Available November 2005
TheNextNovel.com

HN19

COMING NEXT MONTH

#65 IRON DOVE by Judith Leon

They'd called her the Dove. But former agent Nova Blair never
wanted to return to the world of spying. She'd started a new
life…until her former partner came to her with a mission she
couldn't refuse. Going back to the shadowy, seductive life of
an international spy was a small price to pay to save millions of
lives—if only she could save her soul, too.

#66 LETHALLY BLONDE by Nancy Bartholomew

The It Girls

Porsche Rothschild's attempts to "find herself" had always been
halfhearted. But when the Gotham Rose spy ring tapped her to
be undercover bodyguard to a Hollywood bad boy, the spoiled
socialite suddenly had a purpose. With the self-centered actor
facing death threats, Porsche rallied his entourage, his handsome
manager—and even her own trusty ferret, Marlena!—to the
cause of keeping the cool in Hollywood.

#67 EXIT STRATEGY by Kate Donovan

Every good spy had an exit strategy. But when CIA rookie
Miranda Cutler was asked to work with Ray Ortega, the reclusive
agent who once nearly ended her career, she couldn't see a
way out. Heading out solo to infiltrate a covert paramilitary
group might prove once and for all that she could stand on her
own—but when she landed in the group's deadly trap, she soon
learned she hadn't escaped Ray after all….

#68 HER BEST DEFENSE by Jackie Merritt and Lori Myles

The accused was a Chicago society wife; the crime was
murdering the gardener who moonlighted as her lover. And
up-and-coming defense attorney Lisa Caputo was up to her
eyeballs in the case. Then her investigation revealed the unsavory
underworld ties of her client's family and a surprise connection
to her own father's mysterious death twenty years earlier. The
truth could set Lisa free—but it could also lead her into danger.

SBCNM1005